HIS *Savage* WAS HER *Weakness* 3

A NOVEL BY

TYA MARIE

Published by Royalty Publishing House

www.royaltypublishinghouse.com

Contains explicit language & adult themes suitable for ages 16+

Nubia

The homicide detective sat in his seat, staring long and hard at me as he tried to figure out his angle. I had all night because there was no way in hell they were going to charge Vincent's death as a murder. As much as he terrorized, beat, and belittled me, if they thought I would come out and say "yes I killed him" they were obviously out of their fucking minds. I planned to tell them as much.

"Mrs. Morris," the detective said after a few more minutes of silence. "On the walk out of your apartment, Francesca, a friend of the victim, said to you, and I quote, 'You killed him.' Do you recall what your response was?"

I crossed my legs. "I'm sure you're going to tell me."

"You said, 'It was kill or be killed, bitch. If I had to I would do it again.' You don't seem the least bit remorseful over the death of your husband."

"Why would I have any remorse for the man that followed me home with the intent of kidnapping my child?" I countered. "Vincent was a monster to me. It wasn't the most well-kept secret in the hood. He nearly beat me to death last year just for leaving him."

"We spoke to the detectives on that case, Mrs. Morris. They said you refused to give them any information on who your attacker might have been. Not only that, hours later, your husband's shop was shot up and he was kidnapped. The following morning, he was admitted into the hospital with a broken jaw along with several fractured ribs. You know what that looks like?"

"Once again, I'm pretty sure you're going to tell me."

"It looks like your husband wasn't the only one with a hand problem."

I sat up straight in my seat. "I know you're not saying what I think you're saying. I know you aren't sitting here trying to make Vincent the *victim.*"

"Your husband was stabbed fifteen times in the chest and abdomen. The type of anger it takes to repeatedly stab someone that many times—the blood, the crunching of bone, the look on your dead husband's face—stems from hatred. A deep hatred at that if the police didn't show up when they did, how many more times would you have stabbed him?" Silence. "That type of anger, Mrs. Morris, doesn't make you look like anyone's victim."

He opened the manila folder in front of him without taking his eyes off of mine. Pictures of Vincent's dead body littered the table, taken from close and far away angles. As I stared at each one, the only thought that ran through my head was, *he's finally gone.*

"Mrs. Morris, we spoke to Francesca and she told us exactly what happened. How you and Vincent made plans to meet up so you could discuss custody arrangements for your child since you were unable to care for her. You didn't show up to the predetermined location so your husband came to your residence. A fight ensued, the authorities were called, and they walked in on you stabbing your husband to death."

"That's a nicely put together story, except it's not the truth. None of that is the truth save for Vincent and me agreeing to meet up. The rest is bullshit."

The detective leaned in ever so slightly. "So tell me, Mrs. Morris, what's the real story?"

I was poised to give him my account of the story when the door opened and in walked an older white man. "Questioning my client without representation, Detective?"

"No, we were just having a discussion," the detective replied easily.

My lawyer glanced down at the photos sitting on the table. "Sure you were. Can I have a few minutes alone with my client?"

"Sure."

The detective picked up his pictures, and left out to give us some time alone. My lawyer waited for the door to slam shut before picking up the conversation. "You didn't say anything incriminating, did you?" he asked, occupying the now empty chair across from me.

"Incriminating how? Vincent entered my house, attacked me, and tried to take my child. I'm the victim in this entire situation," I shot back, crossing my arms.

"That's not how they're spinning this. According to Francesca, you left Vincent while on vacation with him in Miami, refused to allow him to be there for any of your doctor's appointments, and when you finally agreed to let him see your daughter, you didn't show up. He confronted you, it turned into a fight, you killed him, and here we are."

"Vincent abused me our entire marriage!" I exclaimed.

"Are there any witnesses that can corroborate this? Have any of these instances of abuse been documented? Because as of right now it's your word against Francesca's, and being that Vincent was an upstanding member of the community, her word is looking better than yours."

"She's his mistress."

"She's presenting herself as a friend of the family that recently fell on hard times and has been staying in your residence, which you abandoned, with Vincent."

I held my face in my hands, shaking it back and forth, trying to find the right words to ask this next question. I couldn't, and settled with, "What is my best move from here?"

"The prosecutor on the case is offering a plea. Fifteen years."

"Fifteen years for being the victim!" I screamed. In a lower voice, I said, "No. I will not stay in jail while my daughter is raised by her father's family. You need to tell the prosecutor that I didn't deserve any of this, and after being mentally abused by Vincent, I stood up for myself. He couldn't take it and tried to kill me. Cheyenne, her mother, daughter, and little cousin can testify to that."

"We're still collecting witness statements, but that does not take away from the fact that the police walked in on you repeatedly stabbing him. Self-defense in New York City is reliant on three factors: is the threat imminent, does the force match, and did you have the opportunity to get away. If Vincent was there to kill you as you claimed, when you had taken him down the first time that should've been it. But it wasn't, was it?"

"You're supposed to defend me!"

"I'm doing the best I can, but it's pretty hard to do with what you've given me." He shuffled the papers in front of him. "If we take this to trial and lose, you could be doing twenty-five years to life. Are you sure you don't want to take the plea?"

The door opened once again, and this time in walked someone I wouldn't have expected in a million years. I hated him, the touch of his fingers caressing my skin, his lips pressed against mine, but I knew if there was a person that could get me out of here, it was my uncle. He was dressed in a smart Brooks Brothers suit with his game face on.

"Nubia, you're free to go," Cornell said, shooting a withering look at the public defender. "If you haven't figured it out yet, your services are no longer needed. Come on."

I did as I was told, following Cornell out of the interrogation room. I didn't say a peep as he led me past uniformed officers, detectives, and people waiting to be processed. The chilly winter air smacked me in the face, but it was the press cameras flashing that caught me off guard. Reporters were hurling questions at me about the case, whether or not I was innocent, and all the usual bullshit they asked at the worst time. Cornell led me through the crowd to his car parked out front. Once I was in the privacy of his car, the tears flowed fast and hard, blurring my vision. I remembered when watching my parent's die was one of the worst living nightmares I'd had; now me being a killer replaced it.

"How'd you get me out?" I asked Cornell as he pulled off into the early Monday morning traffic. "My public defender was telling me to take a plea."

"Because he's an idiot," Cornell replied briskly. "I saw the breaking news and started investigating right away. Myrna finally gained consciousness and told the police she let Vincent in. I was also able to track down the associate from Target that sold you your phone. He was able corroborate your story by mentioning that you waited a significant amount of time in the baby section for someone. Funny enough, Vincent was inside of Target as well, watching you. The associate recalled seeing him follow you. I got the surveillance footage and it was easy sailing from there."

"Does it also help that you're one of the most infamous defense attorneys in New York City?" When he wasn't being a rapist, Cornell practiced law. He had gotten off everybody from kingpins to murderers. "If you hadn't come when you did, I would probably be on my way to Rikers to serve a bid."

"I wouldn't have let that happen to you." Cornell stole a glance in my direction. "I know the world doesn't approve of the love I have for you...but I genuinely want to see you happy. Even if it means disobeying my wife."

"Vivica knows you're here?"

"I was in bed with her when the news broke. She had it in her head that I should leave you be, but my heart wouldn't allow me."

My stomach turned at the genuine affection in his tone. If I wasn't afraid of being recognized in public, I would've jumped into oncoming traffic rather than sit another second with him. The desire to get to Rhea was what kept me quiet, aside from giving him directions to Cheyenne's place. He pulled up fifteen minutes later, killing the engine, and waiting for something unbeknownst to me.

"What?" I asked with my hand on the handle, poised to yank it open.

Cornell leaned in a few inches. "I don't get a thank you?"

"You want a thank you?" I asked with a laugh. "Okay, I have a thank you for you. After raping me for ten years, making me do all types of shit to you in exchange for trinkets, and impregnating me with your rape baby, thank you for doing something for me without asking for more than a thank you in return, you sick fucking bastard. And you know how you can provide a great you're welcome? By leaving me the fuck alone. Have a nice life."

I hopped out without a backwards glance. Cornell pulled off right after, no doubt pissed that his Captain Save-a-Hoe shtick didn't get him the brownie points he felt he deserved. I wouldn't have to worry about his bitch ass anymore because like everyone else on that bullshit, he was left in the past. I was still seething as I climbed the stairs to Cheyenne's place. She answered in a fit, hugging me close and dragging me inside. The girls were at the table eating a bowl of cereal while watching TV. They scrambled from their seats, wrapping their little arms around my legs and chanting how happy they were to see me.

"It's good to see you too, girls," I choked out, running a hand through Marlee's hair. "Enjoy your breakfast, Aunt Nubia isn't going anywhere."

"Girl, I called that number you told me to and left voicemails until the mailbox filled. No one picked up," Cheyenne said as she tugged me deeper into her apartment. I had no idea why she spent so much time at mine because hers was decorated like something out of a magazine. She led me to a guest bedroom with a private bathroom. "You take a nice shower to wash off that precinct smell. When you come out I'll have a nice meal prepared for you."

"I still need to pick up Rhea from Manhattan."

"It'll take some time for her to get to the agency. By the time you're fed and dressed, she'll be ready." Cheyenne squeezed my shoulder. "Get strong for baby girl."

The shower was a definite purification for me, washing away the nightmare of last night. After being processed, I spent the majority of my time in an interrogation room, sitting and waiting for the detectives to figure out their angle. They came in and out, each time with a tidbit of information, asking me if I wanted something to eat, and taking DNA samples. I refused to give them the satisfaction, which robbed me of a meal I desperately needed. I inhaled the eggs, bacon, and grits Cheyenne placed in front of me with a side of OJ.

"Damn," was all she could say at the sight. "They stopped offering a hot bologna sandwich with tepid water?"

"Girl, I ain't eat nothing from those people. So they could use it against me? I refused to give them the satisfaction. Thanks for the clothes," I said, admiring the pantsuit she laid out for me. "I'm sure people will be looking and waiting to talk shit about me. I haven't been by the apartment, but I know I have to in order to get the baby's clothes and my cash."

"I packed Rhea a full baby bag before we were pulled from the house. As for cash, I was able to grab your wallet. Please don't go back to the apartment, Nubia. Especially with it looking the way it looks—"

"You mean with Vincent's blood all over the place? I'll be fine," I promised her. I glanced at the time on my phone. "I've gotta get to the agency before I have to wait another day to take her home."

"You want some company?" Cheyenne offered.

I shook my head. "It's bad enough you had to deal with all of those cameras last night. I don't want you to put the girls through it again. I'll be back with Rhea in a little while."

"Call me if you need anything."

"I sure will."

I closed the front door and leaned against it, taking slow and measured breaths. Before I picked up my baby girl, I had to make sure I was mentally put together. Rhea was my world, and there was no way I could risk breaking down and leaving her in the same environment that made Vincent the monster he was.

******

"What do you mean she isn't here yet?" I said to the receptionist. "It's been well over five hours. I'm pretty sure they were alerted of my release and told to bring my daughter here."

The receptionist hit me with an apologetic nod. "Mrs. Morris, we've been trying get Mr. and Mrs. Morris on the phone since earlier. If they still don't pick up then we'll have to wait until we have a case worker available to go over to the house—"

"What if they've kidnapped her? She could be anywhere by now and you're wasting time by—"

"There they are," the receptionist said, inclining her head. "I'll call a caseworker to handle the exchange."

I was getting ready to ask her why that same worker hadn't grabbed my child hours ago when I heard Rhea cooing. Mr. and Mrs. Morris stood in the lobby looking like zombies. Harriet's eyes locked with mine and she broke down, letting Rhea's carrier fall the last two inches to the floor. Rhea groaned from the drop, and I acted before I could think, which put me right into the path of Mr. Morris, who grabbed me by the throat. The loss of air brought on an intense flashback from last night. I cried at the sight of Vincent hovering over me, choking the life out of me as he laughed.

"Sir! Let go of her!" NYPD police officers appeared out of thin air, commanding Mr. Morris to let go of me.

His hands faltered for a split second, which was all I needed to break free. With the help of an officer behind me, I was freed and pulled away from the pandemonium. I held my throat and watched as he was dragged from the building while hurling obscenities at me, calling me a murderer, she-devil, and telling me how he planned to kill me the next chance he got. Mrs. Morris shot me a withering look before following the police, screaming for them to let go of her traumatized husband.

"Would you like to press charges, ma'am?" the officer who held me asked, his eyes widening in recognition. "It'll look good for you in case they try to arrest you again."

I shook my head. “No, all I want is to take my daughter home.”

“Okay,” he said with a tip of his hat. “Stay safe, ma'am.”

Rhea’s carrier was on the floor next to an officer that rescued her from harm’s way. I got two more steps closer to my baby girl when a caseworker appeared, asking what the commotion was all about. After settling everything with the caseworker, the officer left us alone. I could tell that any reservations she might’ve had with handing Rhea over disappeared after Mr. Morris’ outburst. Not even half an hour later, I was walking out with my baby girl. I was safely tucked into a yellow cab when I felt my back pocket buzzing.

“Nubia,” Shahani groaned. “I just got finished looking at the news. Where are you? What's going on?”

Shahani started firing off questions in her usual fashion, except she didn’t sound too good. I told her as much. “Shahani, you sound like you're on drugs.”

“I am on drugs. Donovan and Nia lured me back to the old apartment so they could kill me. The only reason I’m not dead is because—hey baby. You're back so quick,” Shahani said to someone in her background. “Nubia, lemme call you back in five minutes. Sampson wants me to eat something.”

“What hospital are you at? I wanna come and make sure you're okay.”

“Nubia, please don’t worry yourself about me. I’m hideous, but doing just fine. Please head home and take care of your baby girl,” Shahani urged. “My raggedy looking ass will still be here tomorrow. I promise.”

"Are you sure?"

"I'm positive. I'll see you tomorrow, boo."

I laid back in the taxi, dreading the next stop. I thought I could put it off by stopping to see Shahani, but that wasn't the case. Instead of harping on the negativity, I focused on Rhea for the rest of the ride, leaning over and taking in her scent, listening to her coo—simply trying to find some normalcy before I had to reenter hell.

"Nubia," Donette said, hugging me tight. "Girl, I've been sitting here all day praying for you. I told my husband 'the one time we go out for a family night and this happens.' I'm just happy they let you out. Oh, you got baby girl back too..."

"Can you watch her for a few for me? I need to go inside and—"

Donette waved a hand. "I'll watch her as long as you need to me to. I still have some of her milk here as well. Do you, boo."

I approached my door, which had that infamous NYPD sticker on it. The landlord fixed the lock the best he could. The key slipped in easy enough. I opened the front door with my nose plugged and made the mistake of unplugging it. The smell of dried blood pervaded my nostrils. Last night came crashing back. Vincent walked through this door and left in a body bag. I flicked the lights on, feeling my heart plummet at the sight of his blood all over the floor. I approached it like it would bite me, scared for it to even touch the tips of my shoes. I can't do this, I thought as I barreled into my bedroom, slamming the door shut. I slid to the floor, crying as I relived my daughter's father telling me he would kill me and let her grow up never knowing who I was. The destructive thoughts tortured me for what felt like forever. I needed someone to talk to, and with Shahani in the hospital, I knew there was only one person I could call.

"Please pick up," I said under my breath as Maine's line rung. It connected and I said, "Thank God you picked up. You're the last person I'd expect to watch the news, so I need to tell you about my terrible night. Fuck, Maine, it's officially over with Vincent and me. He broke into my house, we fought, and I had to…I killed him."

The line was silent for two beats, followed by a woman saying, "Who are you, and how do you know my fiancé?"

"Excuse me?" I choked out.

"I said, who the fuck are you and how do you know Jermaine?" she spat in a thick accent. "Don't get caught up now, *puta. ¿Quién eres?*"

"Sorry, I think I dialed the wrong—"

"You didn't dial the wrong anything. Tell me! I am sick and tired of feeling like I'm living with a stranger because his heart and mind are somewhere else. Who are you?"

I hung up.

I couldn't deal with any more blows in one day. I was homeless; there was no way in hell I could live here ever again. By tomorrow the media would be on the lookout for me once again, making it hard for me to return to the club. And now, to top it all off, the one person I saw myself building with proved himself to be just like the rest of these men. My phone buzzed next to me.

Maine.

I turned the phone facedown, unable to deal with him or his

fiancée, whichever one of them was blowing up my phone. I had enough heartache to last a lifetime. I didn't need anymore.

I was done with Maine.

Shahani

I lay in my hospital bed watching as Sampson drifted off to sleep for the third time tonight. He had been by my side ever since I woke up from surgery. Donovan had done a number on me—breaking my nose into pieces, fracturing two of my ribs, and giving me two swollen black eyes—and instead of focusing on how hideous I know I looked, Sampson supported me. When he first found out where I had been he was livid, then I mentioned it was because I thought Nia needed my help, which cooled him down instantly. He told me there was no way on earth he could ever be mad at me for having a good heart. Those words alone told me that walking out of Donovan's life was the best thing I could've ever done for myself.

Until now.

"Sampson," I called out. He was knocked out snoring, and there was no way I couldn't laugh at how cute he looked. I dug in my ice bucket and threw an ice chip at him, scaring him awake. His hand instinctually went to his waist and out came his Glock. "Baby, that was just ice. Put that thing away before my nurse comes around."

Sampson, who went from knocked out to scoping out the room with his piece, sobered instantly. "What happened?"

"You need to go home and get some rest. You're going to mess your back up," I chided.

He scoffed. "You think I'm leaving you here alone? You must be out of your mind."

"You can leave one of the guys behind," I said, referring to one of the many bodyguards he kept. "They'll do just fine for the night."

"Not where they are." Sampson chuckled at the confused look on my face. "After they allowed you to shake them, you think they're still employed by me? Nope, I'm having my head of security find some new replacements as we speak. Until then, I'm here in this hospital with—agh, shit."

I shook my head at the sight of him lying back in the uncomfortable hospital chair. "Sampson, you're going to have to get realigned again if you keep it up. One night in that chair was enough; you spend another, they'll be wheeling you into the bed next to me. Get some rest at home. In our bed, where I'll be in a few more days."

"Shahani, security isn't the only reason why I don't wanna leave you…we still don't know who killed Donovan and shot Nia."

"Whoever it was is an ally more than they are an enemy," I noted, thinking it would settle Sampson when it only riled him up even more.

"No, they're a wildcard and what I don't like is wildcards running through my territory unspoken for. You're not leaving my sight until I find out who this person is." He paused thoughtfully. "You sure you didn't get a look at their face?"

Lonzo's face flashed brightly in the back of my mind as he knelt over me. "No…I didn't see anything but a flash of gunshots, then everything went black. Baby, you think if I knew who it was I'd hide it from you?"

"Of course not." Sampson dismissed the thought as if it were absurd. "Baby, just get some rest and stop worrying about me. I'll be fine."

I knew there was no swaying Sampson at this point, so I blew him a kiss and closed my eyes. The entire night I dreamed of Lonzo's face and the good times we shared, with the last one being the night he proposed to me. It was magical; dinner, slow dancing, and a performance from one of our favorite underground artists, Bose, rapping our relationship from the beginning to where we stood. I had barely wore my ring when some young niggas ran up on us and robbed us. Lonzo, who was a prominent name in the streets, couldn't take such disrespect lying down and went after them. He never came home.

His parting kiss on my lips was what woke me up. That, and the familiar tinkling laugh of the nurse.

"Look who's finally awake," the overfriendly nurse said to Sampson. "Sleeping Beauty."

"Don't flatter me," I said drily. "I asked for a mirror all day yesterday to see the damage and you still won't give me one. I know my nose is fucked up, I know Donovan knocked out a tooth or two, and my face got scratched up on the floor. There's nothing beautiful about me."

"Baby, don't say that," Sampson said, reaching for my hand. He gave it a comforting squeeze. "I fell in love with who you are—not your face. We'll get the best surgeons that money can buy and have you looking like yourself again, you hear me?"

I pressed his hand against my face. "Okay, babe."

"Surprise!" came a familiar voice from the door.

Nubia entered the room juggling flowers, a teddy bear, and balloons. Sampson stood to help her with the balloons, which kept bouncing in her face with every step she took. She smiled up at him gratefully, nervously rambling about how she bought more than she could handle. Sampson's eyes widened like he saw a ghost and returned back to normal.

"Shahani, boo!" Nubia cheered, giving me a gentle hug. "What the fuck happened?"

"How much time do you have?" I asked.

"Shahani, I'm gonna head home to take a shower and make some rounds, will you be good?" Sampson asked, pointing to the door as he studiously avoided eye contact with Nubia.

"Yeah," I said slowly. "Is everything okay?"

"Everything's good. I'll see you later."

Nubia waved at a retreating Sampson. "Bye, it was nice meeting you," she called out. "So…that's the guy you're—"

"Yup," I quipped. "That's him. He's usually much friendlier, but I don't know what's going on with him right now."

"He could be concerned with your wellbeing with everything that went down. Start from the beginning…"

I told Nubia the entire story from beginning to end, only leaving out my cooked books for obvious reasons. My heart plummeted when she told me she was the unknown number that kept popping up on my phone. I believe in my heart that Sunday night would've been much different for me had I answered her call instead of Nia's. My girl wouldn't have had to worry about the cops trying to make her out to be a murderer because I had plenty of corroborating stories concerning Vincent's abuse. Now they could be put to rest with his abusive ass. Speaking of which—

"What are you going to do about Vincent's estate? I'm sure as his wife you would get everything. The shops, apartment, car, everything," I reminded her. "My advice is to get you a lawyer to fight this out; you deserve everything and more for what you went through."

"I don't have lawyer money. As ashamed as I am to admit it…my uncle is the one that got me out of jail. He was acting like he wanted a 'reward' for all of his hard work. I cussed his ass out and kept it pushing."

"As you should have," I cheered her on. "Look at you, coming into your skin. The amount of baggage you've dropped in the last two days is nothing short of a miracle."

"Yup, it's also bittersweet because a piece of it is Maine. I called him looking for support and instead got his fiancée."

I clapped my hand to my mouth. In my haste to make up with Nubia, I completely forgot about Maine and his engagement to Estalita. Once Sampson told me it was all for show I placed it to the back of my mind. Nubia and I had come too far for me to hide something like this from her. "I completely forgot about their engagement."

"You knew?" Nubia exclaimed.

"I was at the engagement party." Nubia's jaw dropped at the revelation. "Before you cuss me out, allow me to remind you that this was when we weren't speaking. Maine works for Sampson and they're really close—like father and son close. Naturally, Sampson showed up as support. Afterwards, he mentioned it wasn't a marriage for love. Maine was helping the cartel princess get away from her father and in exchange, he was given a huge piece of territory to command."

"She wasn't talking like it was an engagement of convenience."

"That could be because she has no idea. Or at least she didn't," I rationalized. "The point I'm trying to make is that not every relationship starts off as perfect, but with time, it can certainly get there."

"Like you and Sampson?"

I felt a pang in my chest. "Just like me and Sampson. We obviously started in a really different way—I was his date for the night—and we somehow felt a connection like no other. He was the best thing to come from this entire situation."

And he truly was. Lonzo couldn't have appeared in my life at a worst time; a time where I really found someone I could see myself settling down with after losing him. He might have saved my life, but he couldn't reenter it thinking everything would go back to the way it was. I was building, building with a wonderful man, and there was no changing that. All I had to do was find him and tell him as much.

******

My visit with Nubia was enjoyable while it lasted. I didn't want her to keep coming to the hospital to visit me and possibly bringing something home to Rhea, so I told her I would let her know when I was being released so they could visit me. By then I would be able to find out where she was staying, considering the state of her apartment. It would take some discussing, but I was sure Sampson wouldn't mind her moving in with us until she found a safe place to stay. I was still practicing my pitch when an orderly entered the room. Or at least I thought it was an orderly until he yanked the mask covering his face down.

"Lonzo?" I hissed, placing my hand to my mouth. "It really was you. You're not dead?"

"No, I'm not," Lonzo replied as he steadily worked, cleaning surfaces and emptying my trash.

I grabbed his hand. "Can you please stop cleaning and have a seat?"

"Nah, I can't sit; if your man or one of his soldiers walk through the door I can't risk being caught up." He kissed my hand. "I missed you, baby."

"Missed me? Lonzo, don't come back here with none of that 'baby, I missed you' shit, because if you really loved me or even cared you wouldn't have left me thinking you were…"

"It was the only way I could move the way I needed to. Shahani, I know shit was smooth on the outside, but in reality, I was losing my grasp on the game. New niggas were coming up and sniffing out my territory. The night I proposed to you was the night some serious shit popped off. My partner flipped on me, took everything I had, and planned on killing me too. I vowed to protect you the best I could, which meant having my last loyal soldier tell him I was kidnapped and killed by the enemy."

I snatched my hand away from him. "You could've written me a letter, sent a text message, something, anything to let me know to wait for you…"

"I needed you to move on from me, Shahani. If they felt like I was still out there somewhere that would've put your life in danger. I lost my soldiers, territory, my best friend; I couldn't have you be next. I headed to the south and worked some odd jobs, saving up to buy myself a seat at the table."

"That's all you came back for? A seat at the table?" I wasn't looking to rekindle anything with him, but it hurt to hear I wasn't one of the reasons why he returned. "You leave me heartbroken and that's the only thing on your list of priorities?"

"Shahani, you aren't my priority; you're my life. You don't think I've been keeping an eye on you since I left? How else would I have known what was going on with Nia and Donovan? Or how you and Sampson were together?" Lonzo sighed. "I know there can't be an us until I sort out all of my loose ties. The niggas that set me up? They gotta go. My partner that turned on me? I'm handling him tonight. When all of this is done, I'll have my territory back and then some. Once I've secured the game, then you'll be placed right back on the throne where you deserve to be."

"And what if I don't want to be there?"

Lonzo pecked me on the lips. "You're saying that now because you're upset with me, Shahani. I understand; you went nearly ten years thinking the love of your life was dead. If I have to take us back to day one to make it work then I will because that's how much I love you." He checked his watch. "I've been in here too long. I'll see you soon, babe."

He was halfway to the door when he called my name.

"Yes," I replied.

"One word of advice, baby girl," he replied with his back still turned to me.

"What?"

"Whatever you got going on with Sampson, don't get too comfortable. Aight?"

"Okay," I replied shakily.

"Love you."

Lonzo disappeared just as quietly as he arrived, leaving me alone with my own thoughts. The conversation lulled me into a dreamless sleep that was interrupted by Sampson placing a gentle kiss on my forehead. He placed a Target bag filled with sweets on the table. My belly growled involuntarily, eliciting a laugh from Sampson.

"Baby," I yawned. "How was your day? I hope you went home and got some rest."

"Nah, there was too much going on for me to even consider sleeping," he said, pulling another bag from the Target bag. I did an internal happy dance when I realized it was food from my favorite Spanish restaurant. "How was your day? Did you have fun with your friend?"

"I sure did have a good time catching up with my girl. We were on the outs for so long, I thought I lost her."

"What's her story? She come from good people?" Sampson asked.

"She did come from good people although she didn't get much time with them. Her parents died when she was young. They were killed at her tenth birthday party. Why do you ask?" I asked him, not in the mood to beat around the bush. "Have you two ever been acquainted?"

Sampson let out a chuckle. "Where on earth would I meet a girl that young? Our circles aren't one and the same. I just thought she looked familiar is all. Like the daughter of an old friend of mine."

"Unless that old friend is Apollo Monroe then you shouldn't know who she is. She's been living at her aunt's house since the entire ordeal. Stole her entire family in one day," I said, searching his face for even a hint of recognition. "You sure you don't know who she is? Not to call you old or anything, but that was around your time. I'm surprised you didn't hear anything about it."

"Nope," Sampson replied, placing a hefty plate of pernil with rice and beans in front of me. "Must've been when I was in Chicago."

On that note, I dropped the interrogation and began to eat my food. There was no way in hell Sampson could have never heard of Nubia's parents when the news of that massacre was all over the news. I researched the story when Nubia first told me because I couldn't believe it. Sure enough, there were plenty of articles on Nubia's family. Sampson was lying to me, and the only reason why I could think of was because he had something to do with one of the worst days of my best friend's life.

Maine

Ever since I dropped Nubia off at her place on Sunday morning, I went completely off the grid trying to figure out how I would keep her safe. My options were slim at this point: I could prolong my "search" for her until I was able to get her out of New York or I could kill a girl about her age and pass it off as a hit. I was on Facebook looking up girls with the last name Monroe when I saw a call from a foreign number come through on my MacBook. I patted my desk, searching for my phone before the caller hung up. A few seconds later the call did the exact opposite; it connected.

"What the fuck?" I muttered, rising from my seat and patting my pockets.

I closed my eyes and tried to remember where I last had my phone. I was on the phone with Salvador discussing drops and hopped into the—

"Estalita!" I shouted, banging on the bathroom door. "Estalita, open up the fucking door!"

"No," Estalita wailed. "No I'm not opening the door so you can call back your girlfriend!"

I snapped. Taking three calculated steps back, I kicked the bathroom door open, sending splinters of wood flying everywhere. Estalita screamed at the sight, hurling obscenities at me as she backed herself into a corner. As much as I wanted to punch her in the face, what I really wanted was my phone so I could find out who had called. I crouched down and told her as much, shoving my hand out.

"Who is she?" Estalita pouted. "She called you upset and crying like she knew you would be there for her. All the time we've been together and I've never been able to call you and feel like you'll actually be there for me. Who is she, Maine?!"

"Give me the goddamn phone!" I barked. I snatched it from her outstretched hand and looked at the number. "I don't know who this is, so you need to calm the fuck down."

"You might not know who she is, but she knew you," Estalita shot back sourly. "But she didn't know anything about me. She said it was the wrong number and hung up. I highly doubt you'll be able to get her again."

I stood to my full length, watching as Estalita shrunk away from me like I was some sort of monster. I turned to the mirror and saw that I looked like one: my eyes were dilated, my nostrils flared, and my lips were curled upward.

"Don't ever answer my phone ever again, do you understand me?" I growled.

"*Sí,*" she uttered contemptuously. "*Cabrón.*"

I waited until I was in the privacy of my office to call the number back. Like Estalita predicted, it went straight to voicemail. I knew I couldn't call her friend, who might speak on the situation to Sampson, which left me to hunt her down. I made a call to Vaughn since Cheyenne and Nubia were so close. I was prepared for an address, but what I got instead was something straight out of *Snapped*.

"Nubia did what?"

"Vincent showed up to her place, they had a huge fight, and she killed him. The cops locked her up because they walked in on her blacking out on his body. Cheyenne said she'd never seen Nubia look so angry. She's out now though; her uncle is a high-powered attorney so he did some investigating and got her released. Had he not came she might've been doing a bid based off of some he say/she say." Vaughn paused thoughtfully. "Why am I telling you this instead of Nubia?"

"Because Estalita tried to confront her and scared her off. I was hoping you could give me Cheyenne's address so I could talk to her in person."

"What would make you think I have Cheyenne's address?"

"Because I'm more than sure you heard about that lethal shit she do with her tongue and had to see if it was true."

Vaughn chuckled. "It was better than I expected. But yeah, I'll text you the address since I'm getting ready to enter the hospital to see Nia."

"What's Nia doing in the hospital?"

"Some crazy shit popped off with her, Shahani, and Donovan. From what she told me, Donovan forced her to set up Shahani. He was getting ready to kill her when someone showed up and fired shots. Word on the street is that it wasn't one of Sampson's people either."

"You mean to tell me there's a wildcard running around?" I said incredulously. "There's another thing we gotta deal with before this wedding in a few weeks."

"We? Maine, I know you still not tryna have me come aboard…"

"Vaughn, you're one of my closest friends; why would I not want you to have this position? When it comes to awarding someone a leadership role, you give it to the person who wants it the least."

Vaughn sighed. "I still think you need to consider Jodeci; he's the perfect fit for the job and you know it. Y'all mad at each other right now, but it's over something completely fixable."

"Me giving Jodeci that job is like stabbing myself in the back. He can't be trusted."

"You don't wanna trust him because you think he might try something shiesty when that ain't the case. All he wants is this position. Consider it," Vaughn recommended. "I gotta go; security is asking me to put my phone away. I'll shoot you Cheyenne's address right now."

"Aight," I said, bringing the conversation to a close. "Make sure you think of my proposition. I'm not playing. I will be following up."

"I got you. Now go check on your girl."

I took my mind off of business long enough to think of what I was going to say to Nubia when I laid eyes on her. With the magnitude of damage Estalita had caused, I knew there was no way I could show up empty handed with nothing but apologies. The night we shared had to be one of the best either one of us had experienced, and as of right now, murder and infidelity overshadowed it. No, I needed to show up with something that expressed how I felt for her.

"Welcome to Cartier, my name is Morgan, what can I get for you today?" the kind saleswoman greeted with a sweeping motion over the display cases holding everything from earrings to engagement rings.

"I'd like to look at your love bracelets."

Morgan led me over to the love bracelets and I knew which one I wanted immediately. It was 18k pink gold with diamonds in each space where each screw would've been. I tuned out the rest of Morgan's spiel, only thinking of how beautiful that bracelet would look on Nubia's wrist. When she was finished, I told her to wrap it up.

"While you're back there, can you throw in a really nice tennis bracelet? Something that says 'I'm sorry,'" I said, knowing it was best to return home with something shiny for Estalita to add to her collection.

I posted up against the display cases, staring at Nubia's new number, debating on whether or not I should give her another call. I knew it wouldn't hurt. Like I expected, it went straight to voicemail. Instead of hanging up, I opted to leave her a message.

"I heard about what you went through, and I want you to know that no matter what's going on in my life, you can always call me and I'll be there. I'll give you tonight to cool off because I know you're pissed, but I'm coming through to talk to you tomorrow." I sighed, unsure of what to say next. "Don't count me out until you've spoken to me, Nubia. I'll see you tomorrow."

As much as I wanted to go over there and confront the situation head on, I knew I had to give her time to digest this mess. Not only that, I had to make sure everything was straight at home. I found Estalita still in the bathroom, sitting on the floor silently crying. I let out an inward sigh of relief at the sight of her phone still sitting on the nightstand; she hadn't called her father or friends, which meant our relationship was still salvageable.

"Yo," I said from the doorway.

Estalita glanced up at me through her tears. "What?"

"You know you was wrong for answering my phone."

"There should be no secrets between us, Jermaine. My parents had none between them whatsoever. I watched my father love my mother until she took her last dying breath, and I always swore that when I married, it would be to a man who loved me that much." She stared up at me with hurt in her eyes. "You don't love me at all, do you?"

"You don't love me either," I countered. "This entire situation started because you got tired of living under your father's thumb. Once we got engaged, you got the freedom you always wanted."

"That's a lie!" Estalita shouted, clamoring to her feet. "I've always loved you! Why else would I have chosen you when I could've easily picked another man to inherit my legacy?"

"Because there was no other man. All these niggas are frightened of your father and can't none of them maintain all of this"—I motioned to the luxury penthouse apartment we lived in—"the way I can."

"That's what you think," Estalita muttered under her breath.

"Oh, you know someone who can?" I asked her, actually curious to hear the answer. "Hmmm? That's what the fuck I thought."

Estalita crossed her arms. "Did you really come all this way to start another argument with me?"

"No," I said, holding up the Cartier box. "I came back to apologize to you for how shit went down, but since you got someone that can do it better than me…"

Estalita leapt into my arms, wrapping her legs around me as she reached for the bag I was holding in the air. "There's no one else that can take care of me like you, papí. Now can I please have my present, *por favor?*"

"You swear to never go through my phone again?"

"I promise to never touch your phone again," Estalita purred, her eyes fixed on the box. "I swear. Now gimme."

I handed her the bag and watched as she deftly unboxed and unwrapped her gift. "A tennis bracelet! Pavé diamonds? Oh, Jermaine, I love it. Thank you, *papí*. Now how about I give you a gift."

Estalita slithered down my body, tugging on my pants on her way down. I knew this was how our fight was bound to end, and I would've preferred to decline, but if Nubia and I were going to work, I had to keep Estalita pacified. Literally. I was doing this for us, no matter how much pleasure I might've gotten from it.

******

Cheyenne leaned against her doorway, smiling at me for a split second before it dropped. "She doesn't wanna talk to you, Maine. She actually told me to tell you that when she's ready to speak to you she'll give you a call."

"I'm not going anywhere until I speak to her. I'll stay right in your hallway, scaring all your white neighbors, taking out your trash, ordering dinner to eat right here. You know I'll do it," I warned her.

"Then do it; my girl said she doesn't wanna talk to you and I respect it. So set up shop and be prepared for my scary ass white neighbors to call the cops by the end of the night..." Cheyenne had her door halfway closed when I placed my foot in the door. "Okay, Maine, I might be the one to call the cops on your ass. Move your foot from my door."

I reached into my pocket and pulled out five crisp bills. "You gon' let me in, or nah?"

Cheyenne snatched the bills from my hand. "Nah, now go away."

"Cheyenne..."

The door opened wide enough for me to enter. Cheyenne pointed to the back of her apartment as she covered herself with the door. "She's the last door on the left."

I followed her directions, slowly approaching the door with bated breath. I could hear a baby cooing from the other side, laughing and gurgling at nothing in particular. Taking a deep breath, I opened the door to find the bedroom empty save for a baby in a crib. I scoped out the entire room—observing the neatly made bed along with the absence of a jacket and purse—and knew I had been got. I turned to leave when I heard the baby whining. I knew the whining would soon turn to crying, and decided to be proactive.

"Here you go," I said, picking up the fallen pacifier and popping it back into the baby girl's mouth. She sucked on it hungrily and spit it out, her lip quivering. "Damn, you look just like your mother when she cries."

As a matter of fact, baby girl looked like Nubia all the way. She was light like Vincent for now, but her light brown ears revealed that she would have one more piece of her mother. She had Nubia's thick, curly hair along with her brown eyes. None of her father was present, and that was a good thing. I shrugged out of my jacket, cleaned my hands with some sanitizer, and picked the baby girl up. She quieted instantly, sucking on her lower lip as she stared up at me.

"You just wanted some attention, didn't you?" I said, gently rocking her back and forth. "They left you in here by yourself with nothing to entertain you."

She cooed in agreement.

"I was in the middle of making her a bottle when you knocked," Cheyenne said from the doorway. She held out the bottle. "You wanna feed her for me?"

I accepted the bottle. "Maybe when I'm finished you can tell me where Nubia really is."

"Of course I will…" she said, closing the door behind her.

"Cheyenne bugging the fuck out," I said as I slipped the bottle into the baby girl's mouth. "Oops, I shouldn't be cursing in front of you. But she is though. All I'm tryna do is talk to your moms and make shit work between us. I know I should've been a little more honest with her from the beginning, but I planned on telling her about my situation when the time was right."

Baby girl continued listening as she drank her milk. I spent my entire life holding in my feelings, and the moment I decided to speak on them, it was to an infant. Probably because she wouldn't interrupt.

"All I know is this: your mother is the first woman to have me thinking and doing different shi—stuff. She even got a nigga feeling different. Sometimes I start thinking about her and I forget all about work. Or how relaxed I am around her." I smiled down at baby girl's drooping lids. "Now I'm sitting here holding you, and I don't even like kids. I saw so many of them killed when they were your age I told myself I would never have any of my own."

Baby girl spit out the bottle and fell asleep on me. *She got what she wanted and now she don't wanna be bothered; I can relate,* I thought with a laugh. I sat watching her sleep, thinking to myself that if I wanted a relationship with Nubia I would have to accept her daughter as well. The bedroom door opening interrupted my thoughts. Nubia stopped short at the sight, her eyes traveling from the slumbering baby in my hand to the bottle sitting beside me.

"What are you doing here?" she asked, hanging up her purse and slipping out of her trench coat, revealing a barely there dress. "I came running all the way from work thinking something happened with the baby, and it's just you."

"You weren't answering my calls so I decided to pop up and talk to you in person."

"I said I needed space, why can't you respect that?"

"Because the more space I give, the better the chance you might let those crazy theories in your head start making sense."

Nubia scoffed. "Crazy theories? Like what? That you pursued me knowing you're getting married to another woman? That you know everything I've been through and made me believe—forget it," she said fanning the unshed tears in her eyes. "Put my baby down and get out of here, Maine."

"Finish your sentence," I demanded.

"You made me believe that there could be something between us," she choked out, pounding her chest. "I thought that after everything I've been through, I would have a chance at a healthy relationship. My hopes were all up, I was on top of the world, and then it came crashing down. I called you hoping you would be there for me, and got one of the ugliest truths I could ever get."

I stood up, approaching her slowly, hoping she wouldn't run from me. "What I have with Estalita is nothing more than a business arrangement. I don't feel anything for her, but unfortunately, I can't leave her. Yet." I gently held her chin. "Don't think about her when you think of us. That's a game, but this right here, this is real. One of the realest relationships I've had in my life."

"If you really felt anything for me, Maine, you would know how much it would hurt for me to be the other woman," Nubia said, her eyes locking with mine. "Whether it's a joke or not, you're getting married to her, which is a huge commitment. And for that reason, I need you to leave."

I handed over the baby, suddenly feeling cold and empty. "I understand. Can we at least be friends?"

"Sure, I don't see anything wrong with us being friends," Nubia agreed. She placed the baby back into her crib and turned to me. "I guess I'll see you around?"

"Yeah," I replied, shrugging into my jacket. My hand brushed against the Cartier bag in my jacket pocket. "I got you something as an apology."

"You didn't have to—"

I pressed the bag into her hands. "I didn't have to. I wanted to. I'll see you around."

Cheyenne was sitting on the couch sipping a mug of tea when I passed. "I tried," she mumbled. "Night, Maine."

I closed the front door without a reply. Nubia's rejection hurt me more than I wanted to admit. As I sat there holding her daughter, I had it in my mind that I could get used to living life at a slower pace, a pace that involved an insta-family. I was hoping Nubia would see me trying, and want to give us a try as well. My phone started buzzing in my pocket, interrupting my thoughts as I slid into my car.

"Wassup," I greeted Sampson as I pulled off into the brisk summer night. "Sorry, I been off the grid all day. I had some business to handle."

"It's not a problem. I got some good news I want to share with you. Swing by the shop."

"Bet."

Twenty minutes later, I was at the barbershop. It was empty save for Sampson, who was sitting in the last chair reading the newspaper. I took a seat across from him, my heart plummeting at the sight of Nubia's face on the front page of the paper. As much as I didn't want to believe this meeting was about her, I couldn't imagine anything else bringing Sampson this much joy.

"I don't know whether or not you heard, but my girl got caught up in some shit with her ex. I was visiting her in the hospital and you won't believe who I saw."

My heart skipped a beat. "Who?"

"Apollo's daughter. Her name's Nubia." Sampson had a Cheshire cat grin on his face. "You know what this means, right?"

"Of course," I said without a hint of hesitation. "The question is: how do I handle her without it looking like you had something to do with it?"

"Why would I have something to do with it?"

"You see her at the hospital and she pops up dead days later?"

Sampson scoffed. "Easy, Maine. I ain't say nothing about tomorrow or the day after that. However, I do need it handled before you walk down the aisle."

"Don't worry about it; I got you," I said with a shrug. "You got a picture of her or something?"

Sampson folded the newspaper he was holding and passed it to me. "She's right on the front page. She killed her husband in an act of self-defense. I heard from one of my buddies on the force that she looked like a demon when they arrested her. There's a lot of anger bottled up in that girl, and when it comes out…I feel sorry for whoever's in its path."

I couldn't picture little Nubia turning volatile, but there were a lot of things I never pictured in my life. Like having my own piece of the game. Falling in love. And picturing a future with a woman whose past I had destroyed. At this point in my life, anything was possible, including saving Nubia from Sampson's wrath. I would save her the way I hadn't been able to save Siabanda. I hadn't had the thought for more than a second when I saw him standing in front of the window of the barbershop.

"Sampson, get on the floor!" I roared as the hooded figure brandished a gun and popped off.

The window shattered as bullets sliced through the air, mixing with the shards of glass to create a deadly combination. I leapt out of my chair and hid behind a pillar, squeezing off a few shots of my own to cover Sampson, who tipped over his chair and rolled to the side of a station.

"I'll distract him with shots while you step out and go for the kill," Sampson shouted over the hail of gunfire. He pulled out his Glock from an ankle holster, took the safety off, and fired off his distraction shots. "Go!"

Sampson's plan worked perfectly; the gunman engaged in gunplay with him, leaving me with the opening I needed to go in for the kill. I stepped from behind the pillar and squeezed off two shots, one whizzing past the gunman and the other hitting him square in the chest. He bucked at the impact, his footing faltering a little before he took off down the street. I scrambled across the crushed glass, hopped out the window, and chased him, firing off shots every few feet. Sampson was hot on my heels, following me down the block and around the corner. The sound of tires burning rubber filled the dark street as a dark sedan pulled off into the night. I popped off a few shots just because, my chest heaving as I tried to make out the make and model of the car.

"Forget the girl for now," Sampson said from beside me. "I want that motherfucker dead and buried by the end of the week."

“Of course,” I agreed, thinking there was no way in hell a motherfucker could shoot at me and think it would end there. “If this wildcard wants a war, then he got one.”

Nubia

Cheyenne came creeping into my bedroom after Maine was gone. I appreciated her for waiting long enough for me to have one good cry and wipe my eyes. She took a seat next to me on the edge of the bed and pulled me into her arms, rocking me back and forth as the tears came again.

"Sweetie, might I ask why you're fighting your feelings for Maine? He's the trifecta: smart, handsome, and paid. You mean to tell me you're willing to let some bitch he don't even like ruin what could be a beneficial relationship for you?"

"Cheyenne," I said, removing myself from her embrace, "after everything I went through with Vincent, why would I put another woman through that? Vincent literally looked me in the eye and told me that Francesca was going to be his other wife. I can't imagine having Maine's fiancée have to live through something like that because of me."

"Who said he was going to tell her about you?"

"So now I went from side chick to dirty little secret? I'm not with it," I said, shaking my head. "I'm over the drama. All I'm focused on as of right now is making money and doing for my daughter. Speaking of which, I'm now behind because you called me down here for this fake emergency."

"Oh, girl, stop pouting; you act like you're not about to have a major come up off of Vincent," Cheyenne countered. "Remember, you're his wife. Everything he has now belongs to you. His family can fight it in probate court all they want, but I'm pretty sure you'll win, especially with snookums."

I waved away that absurd thought. "Like I told you; I don't have money for a high priced lawyer."

Cheyenne crossed her arms. "I mean…your uncle helped you out of that sticky situation. Call him and see if he can hook you up with a lawyer buddy of his."

"I'm not calling him back. I don't want anything from his ass."

"Don't tell me that he…"

"Right up until I moved in with Vincent. He got me pregnant, and that baby is the reason why Vincent resented me so much. That baby turned Vincent into a monster. He got me off because he thought it would get him some pussy. Now that he knows he won't be getting anything from me, I'm sure he'll refuse to help me out."

"You know what? There's a lawyer that shows up at the club at least twice a week, usually on a Wednesday and Friday. His name's Winston. Maybe you can talk to him and see if he might know someone that does pro bono work."

"Today's Wednesday and the funeral is tomorrow. I have no choice but to return to the club and see if here's there." I said, running a hand through my hair. "How do I look?"

"Like you just got finished having a meltdown."

"Fuck," I muttered, knowing I didn't have time to refresh my face.

"I'll just fix it at the club."

"While you're on your way, I'll call the club and see if one of the girls can keep him occupied until you get there."

I kissed Rhea on her head, reminding myself who I was doing this for. Fuck me, I would get by like I had been for the past year, but Rhea deserved a better future than I was handed, and having part of her father's legacy would make that possible.

******

The Pole Palace was still popping when I arrived. I spent five minutes preening myself and getting redressed before hitting the floor. Men grabbed at my hands, demanding a dance, but all I had eyes for was this Winston, who I was told would be in the VIP section popping bottles with a few friends of his. All it took was one walk around the floor to find Winston and his friends buying out the bar. Some of the baddest girls the club had to offer surrounded them, which would definitely make it hard to get close. You got this, Nubia, I thought as I fixed the cups of my bikini. I had barely taken one step when someone called my name. Not my stage name, Sweetie, but my actual name. A hand waved to me from a small section two seats away. T*his can't be happening*, I thought as I spotted Cornell's best friend, Bernard, sitting in the cut.

"Come here," he said, waving me over with a cheesy smile.

I approached him hesitantly, my eyes searching the vicinity to see if my uncle was going to pop up. Bernard must've known what I was thinking, because he quelled my fears immediately.

"You don't have to worry about your aunt or uncle; I come here by myself. It's my little secret," Bernard said, taking my hand into his. "Now it can be our little secret, right?"

I glanced back at Winston and back at Bernard. "Of course I'll keep your secret, but I need to speak to that man over there for a minute. It's really important."

"Is that Winston Price? What do you need to speak to a lawyer for? I thought it had been determined that you acted in self-defense?"

"This isn't about my criminal case; it's about probate court. I'm afraid that I might not receive anything from Vincent's estate because of the circumstances of his death. I figured I could talk to Winston to see how I might proceed and if he could refer me to a pro bono lawyer."

Cici, the madam of the place, gave me the eye; standing around talking to a client instead of dancing was a big no-no. I straddled Bernard, grinding up on him as he placed singles into the garter on my thigh, making sure to linger each time. The song changed, this one a much slower tempo.

"I can refer you to a pro bono lawyer," Bernard said easily. "There are quite a few that are members of the social club your uncle and I are a part of. However, I'm not understanding why you're in need of one with your trust fund."

"Trust fund?" I stopped dancing for a second. Bernard gave me a tap on the ass that brought me back to reality. "I don't have a trust fund."

Bernard let out a hearty chortle. "Nubia, I don't know much about your parents, but what I do know is that your father wasn't a broke man. At the time of his death, he had several business ventures.

Laundromats, dry cleaners, car washes, and even a strip mall that's still in business if I'm not mistaken. Your assets were placed into a trust, and they should be worth a pretty penny by now."

"My uncle or aunt never mentioned me having a trust or savings," I said, placing my hands on Bernard's shoulders and dipping low, grinding on him as if it would compel him to tell me more. "Have they been spending my money? Because I don't consider it a coincidence that they had a brand new house shortly after my parents died."

Bernard turned beet red, his mouth flopping open and closed. "I know your guardian received a sizable stipend for you every month. How-however, it's obvious that you never received any of those funds. If I had to assume, V-V-Vivica used those funds to pay the mortgage on her home. She and Cornell are doing pretty well, but that ten thousand dollars a month—"

"Ten thousand dollars? They've been receiving ten thousand dollars a month for me for the past ten years? That's—"

"Roughly $1.2 million," Bernard moaned, his eyes rolling into the back of his head. "Nubia, please slow down, you're gonna make me—aaah! Fuck!"

Bernard came all inside of his slacks, his limp dick twitching against my inner thigh. I hid my disgust, knowing I could get more information from him whenever necessary. He profusely apologized as he shoved the wad of singles in his hand down my bikini, and whatever couldn't fit he placed into my hand.

"That never happens. Especially not that fast," he apologized, looking around the club to make sure no one noticed his moment of ecstasy. He reached into his shirt pocket and whipped out a business card. "Give me a call some time tomorrow for the information on that lawyer. I'd like to have you dance in private for me as well. A few times a week if it's possible."

I rose off of him, rubbing my leg to make sure none of his kids got on me. "I'll be sure to give you a call. Thanks for the info, Bernard."

Bernard didn't clear the front door before I was already on my way to the dressing room. I was halfway into organizing my money when I felt my hands shaking. What Bernard pretty much told me was that I was sitting here shaking my ass and grinding on random men for money, when my parents set me up with more than enough. Breathe, Nubia, I thought as I continued fixing the money. One stack later, I gave up, thrusting all the cash into my purse, shrugging into my coat, and hightailing it out of there. I hopped into the first green taxi that came cruising down the street. Waiting for the morning to come would've been a smarter move, but fuck that. I had been playing the fool for too long and tonight was the night that would end.

******

I steadily pressed on the doorbell, ringing it until the lights flicked on. Cornell appeared, confused and half-asleep. I shoved right past him before he could make sense of what was going on.

"Nubia, what are you doing—"

"Where the fuck is my money?" I barked, crossing my arms and steadily tapping my foot on the hardwood floor. "You need to give me whatever papers and information I need to get my money."

Cornell shut the door behind him. He was not wide-awake, but still looked confused. "Money? What money are you talking about? Your parents didn't leave you any money; everything you had your aunt and I used to take care of you."

"BULLSHIT!" I roared. "Not only do I have an inheritance, I have a trust fund filled with money. Why on earth would my parents live lavishly and never leave anything behind for their child? How much sense does that make?"

Cornell held his hands up. "Where are you getting all of this information?"

"It doesn't matter where I got my information from! Where the fuck is my money? I've been paying for this nice ass house, your cars, vacations, and probably your daughter's education. Run me my motherfucking money."

"What's going on down here?"

Vivica appeared at the top of the stairs, clutching her silk kimono around her body as she surveyed the sight. I began to laugh, a deep laugh that came right up in my chest and bubbled out the hollow of my throat.

"Look at who it is," I said, clapping my hands together. "The woman of the hour. The queen of the palace, and by far, one of the most miserable bitches that I know. It takes a special kind of evil to rob someone's child blind."

"Excuse me?" Vivica asked, her lips forming a tight line. She made her descent down the stairs, never moving her eyes from me. "I know you didn't just walk into my house talking shit about me when I'm the one that saved you from the gutter."

"Bitch, you only saved me from the gutter for the fucking check! You don't love me! You ain't never gave a single fuck about me, Vivica! So spare me this bullshit about how I'm supposed to be grateful for ten years of living in a cold attic while your husband raped me!"

"Cornell would never! Stop saying that!" Vivica barked, her eyes growing wide as saucers.

I cackled at her reaction. "Cornell raped me a lot. So much, in fact, that he got me pregnant and begged me to keep the baby."

"Liar!" she hissed, her eyes wildly darting between Cornell and I. "You're nothing but a little liar like your mother was!"

Cornell grabbed me around the arm. "Nubia, you need to leave. Now!"

"No!" I screamed, shrugging out of his grip. "I'm not going anywhere until you give me what's rightfully mine. I'm being real nice about it, too. Because if you don't give me my fucking money now, then I'm coming back with a lawyer that will demand paperwork from the moment I stepped foot into this place and I'm pretty sure you'll lose a lot more than I will."

"Vivica," Cornell said tightly. "Give her the information she wants so that she can leave."

Vivica shot Cornell a withering look before disappearing upstairs. Cornell and I stood there in a tense silence, anger radiating off of both of us. Mine was white hot and ready to burn whoever, while his was a silent anger, bubbling to the surface and ready to boil over.

"Who told you all of this?" Cornell asked coldly.

"None of your business," I shot back with just as much venom.

Cornell snatched at my trench, revealing the skimpy outfit I wore. "Let me guess, you're out there shaking it for strangers like a common whore. Who do I know that likes strippers…Bernard told you, didn't he?"

"All I had to do was rub my body all over his and he was putty between my fingers," I crooned, smiling at the hurt expression on Cornell's face. "I liked having him touch me, grinding my pussy against him, feeling the heat from his body, unlike your nasty ass."

"I really loved you," Cornell hissed. "I was willing to give up everything for you—my wife, my career, everything—and you played me."

"Cornell, you never loved me, you loved controlling me because why else would a grown ass man fuck a child? A child that couldn't give consent, a child that was grieving her parents, a fucking child. Whatever you felt for me I've never felt for you."

Vivica came clomping down the stairs with a sizable envelope in her hand. I could see the dried tear stains on her cheeks, and judging by the way her lip quivered each time she glanced at her husband, she had finally accepted the fact that the façade she created was just that—a façade.

"Here," she said, holding the envelope out to me. I clasped my hand around it and gave a gentle tug, only to discover her hand still wrapped around it. I wasn't the least bit surprised. In a cold voice, she said, "Here is everything you'll need: your birth certificate, social security card, everything. In trade for this information, I don't ever want to see your face ever again. Whatever monies I need to pay to you will be sent through the bank. Do you understand me?"

"Why do you hate me so much?" I asked.

"Am I making myself clear?"

"What did I do to you to make you hate me so damn much? Or was it my mother?"

Vivica scoffed. "You still don't get it do you? The only reason why you had someone to come live with after that massacre was because I wasn't invited to the party. Vanessa knew there was no way in hell I would want to come to your birthday party to see the family I was supposed to have with the man I deserved. She stole him from me and she didn't even want him."

"Are you talking about my father?" I snatched the envelope from her hand with a sharp tug. "My mother loved my father. There was never a passionless moment between them. How dare you sit here and talk shit about her marriage while yours is falling apart? Don't worry, Vivica; you won't ever have to worry about seeing my face ever again. Trust and believe that."

I was halfway to the door when Vivica said, "Nubia?"

"What?" I asked, glancing over my shoulder to see her steady smiling.

"You're right; your father loved your mother."

I shot my middle finger up to her. "Love this, bitch."

For the first time in my life, I felt invincible. I had finally stood up to my aunt, told my uncle what I really thought of him, and walked out whole while they were patching themselves together. This was my biggest victory yet. Or at least I thought it was until I was in the privacy of my bedroom and opened up the envelope containing my legacy.

"Oh my god," I said, placing my hand over my mouth.

Sitting in my hands were titles to everything Bernard named and more. Then there was the life insurance policies on each of my parents that were untouched because they were in my name. Also inside of the envelope was the deed to my childhood home and the brownstone Vivica was living in. This bitch had been making me sleep in the attic of the house that I owned. It was cool though, because I also spotted a check from her for five grand, with the memo part written as "Rent." Yeah, payback was a bitch, and I would be getting a part of it every month for the rest of my life.

"Everything's going to be okay, baby girl," I whispered, kissing a slumbering Rhea on her forehead. "We've been blessed. No more struggling. You're going to live just as blessed as I was."

Shahani

I stood in front of the paper bag covered mirror, scared to look at the image that would be reflected back on it. Sampson wrapped his arms around me and nuzzled into my neck. He was the picture of patience, although I had been standing here for the past twenty minutes trying to find the courage to look myself in the eye. Or at least the one that was open.

"No matter what you see behind this paper bag, know that I will always love you, you hear me?" Sampson kissed me on the neck, being that my face was still settling down from the nose job I had a couple days ago. "Now let's remove this paper bag and—"

I placed my hand over Sampson's, holding on to the lie I had told myself for a few seconds longer. "I'll do it."

The paper bag crumpled in my hands as I snatched it from the mirror. I gasped at the sight. Initially, I thought Donovan had simply done superficial damage to my face, but once I was in the hospital with my entire face wrapped in a bandage, I knew it wasn't that simple. The bandages were gone and now I was stuck with the purple eyelids still slowly opening after being beaten shut, swollen but healing lip, and the stitched gashes on my face from Donovan's rings. A tear slipped down my cheek, barely making it to the curve of my face before Sampson gently wiped it away.

"Look at what he did to me," I cried, touching the mirror. "I'm hideous, Sampson."

Sampson shook his head in disagreement. "If that mufucka wasn't dead, I would kill him all over again for what he did to you. But he is, so all you can do at this point is heal and move forward. Nia is being released from the hospital. How about you visit her tomorrow?"

I hadn't mentioned to Sampson that Nia was in on the setup because I wanted to handle the bitch myself. Her biggest mistake at this point was surviving the shots Lonzo had pumped her full of because once I was through, she would be in deep shit. There was no way in hell I would allow her to walk around freely while I felt like a prisoner in my own body.

"Was that the door?" Sampson asked. "Were you expecting someone?"

"Yeah, I invited Nubia and the baby over," I said, leaning into Sampson and giving him the best puppy dog pout I could. I looked so pitiful it didn't take much by a long shot. "You don't mind, do you?"

"Of course not," Sampson said with a smile that didn't reach his eyes. "Let's not keep her waiting."

My main reason for inviting Nubia over was to make sure she was good after everything she had been through last week, but I also wanted to study Sampson so I could figure out what it was about her that made him so uneasy. She stood in the doorway full of smiles with her carrier right beside her. Sampson stepped in and assisted in carrying the baby into the house while I grabbed the baby bag slung over her shoulder. We set up in the living room, which was the second best place; I would've loved to spend some time outside, but I didn't want any of the neighbors seeing me like this. Sampson excused himself to grab refreshments and snacks, giving me some time to catch up with Nubia without him around.

"Someone's looking very nice today," I said, observing the Acme dress she wore. Nubia wasn't one for labels so I just had to know where she got it. "That's the Privacy Please dress, which is one of my favorites; I have it in four colors."

"I borrowed it from my girl, Cheyenne. I've been staying at her place ever since the 'incident.' I'm looking for a place as we speak, and I should be set up by the end of the month if everything goes right." Nubia hopped up and down in her seat as if she was brimming with news. She blurted out, "Shahani, everything's falling into place. Vincent's gone and out of my hair, Rhea and I are being awarded a large chunk of Vincent's estate, and…I got my inheritance two days ago."

My brows disappeared into my bangs. "Inheritance?"

"My parents actually left me a sizable inheritance, one that my aunt had been siphoning since she took me in…"

Nubia went on to tell me about how she stood up to her aunt, demanding what was rightfully hers after years of living in fear. I was proud of her for taking charge of her life the way she was. Being a mother definitely brought out a strength in her she didn't even know was present. I told her as much.

"You're doing it without anyone's help and that is so dope, boo. How did you find out about it anyway?"

Nubia scratched behind her ear. "I kinda found out while I was at work. Stripping at the Pole Palace."

"You were where, doing what?" I went to frown and nearly hurt myself. "Nubia, if you needed money—"

"I know, I know; I could've came to you and gotten a job or something. However, that wasn't bringing in the money fast enough. Plus, it served as a blessing in disguise. No need to worry; I already resigned."

Sampson reappeared with a tray of cookies, cakes, chips, and a pitcher of sweet tea. There was light condensation around the pitcher, which made me wonder how long he had been standing there listening to our conversation.

"Thank you," Nubia said, pouring out two glasses of sweet tea. She was working on a third as Sampson made his way from the living room. "Oh, you aren't staying for a few, Sampson? I barely got to talk to you at the hospital."

"Yeah," I said, scooting over and patting the cushion next to me. "Come and sit with us for a few, baby."

Nubia poured the third cup and placed it on the coffee table. "Shahani, it's so good to see you happy and with someone that loves you."

"I wish you could've seen me with a better looking face," I admitted, taking sip of iced tea. "Donovan did a number on me and I'm scared it might look like this forever."

Nubia shook her head profusely. "Of course it won't. Once the swelling goes all the way down, your coloring goes back to normal, and those cuts heal, you'll be good as new. One time my aunt hit me and

I fell right into the kitchen table. Split my face wide open. The doctor stitched it right back up and a few months later it was like it never happened."

"I keep telling her not to worry," Sampson co-signed.

"Exactly." Nubia dug in her pocket, glanced at her phone screen, and shoved it right back in. "Ugh, he is really trying my nerves right now."

"Who?"

"Maine. Apparently, the general manager can't approve my resignation so he wants to meet up and discuss it in person. I know it's nothing but an excuse to see me."

Nubia could act like she didn't want to see Maine all she wanted, but it was obvious by the way she was blushing that she couldn't wait. I called her on it and she tried shutting me down the best she could. We were in the middle of laughing when Sampson got a phone call.

"Jodeci's girl had the baby. I'mma meet him at the hospital," Sampson said, rising from his seat. He kissed me on the forehead. "I'll bring home dinner tonight. It was nice meeting you, Nubia."

"Same to you Sampson," Nubia said with a wave. She waited for the front door to close to say, "He's really nice. Plus, I can tell how much he really cares about you."

Yeah, when he's not hiding stuff from me, I thought, but said, "Sampson is definitely an upgrade. For him to see me like this and stay? Trust and believe that I ain't going nowhere."

"You never told me the entire story of what happened the night

Donovan attacked you."

"Nubia…Lonzo's not dead."

Nubia's eyes widened. "What do you mean your dead boyfriend isn't dead? Well if he wasn't dead, then where was he?"

I gave her the rundown on the conversation I had with Lonzo after Sampson left. While I felt confused after the exchange, Nubia was confident in her answer.

"He's playing you," she said without hesitation. "If there's one thing I've learned about people popping up in your life, it usually stems from convenience. You need to find out how a relationship with you would benefit him."

"You think? Lonzo and I have been through hell and back together. He took me in and gave me a beautiful life. I can't imagine him using me after everything we've been through."

Nubia gave my hand a gentle squeeze. "It's always hard to imagine those that we love having ill intentions. Fortunately, they typically show themselves sooner rather than later."

"You're right…" I accepted for the first time since Lonzo reappeared.

Six years had passed since we had been together. I had grown for the better, but who was to say that Lonzo did? With his talk of revenge, I couldn't guarantee that he was the same Lonzo who had picked me up when I was down. He might very well be one to knock me down if it meant getting ahead. I would keep an eye out and my heart close, especially since it belonged to Sampson. If there was one thing I learned from our relationship, it was to not give away my entire future for a "what if?"

Sampson

I sat in my car staring at Maine's phone number, contemplating on whether or not I should check him for this betrayal. On one hand, he could've been getting close to the girl to go in for the kill, but on the other hand, it sounded like they've known each other for a while. There was only one way I was going to get the answers that I needed, and that was by visiting the one person who knew him best. No matter how much they fought, Jodeci was like a brother to Maine—fuck that they were brothers—so I knew he would be able to let me know what was up with one of my most trusted lieutenants.

"Congratulations," I said to Jodeci, clapping him on the back as I entered the suite of Lenox Hill Hospital. "Congratulations, Ashanti."

Ashanti, who was perfectly made up despite having given birth hours ago, shot me a wide smile. "Thank you, Sampson. Would you like to see her? Jodeci, take him to see Michaela."

"You sure you gon' be good all by yourself?" Jodeci asked, walking over to his girl and giving her a kiss on the forehead. "I can wait for your parents to come."

"You don't have to worry, babe. They said they were parking the car when I last spoke to them, okay?"

"Aight," Jodeci replied, giving her one more kiss on the head. "Sampson, let's go see—oh shit, Mom and Pops."

If seeing Nubia again almost gave me a mild heart attack, then Vivica walking through that hospital door with her husband was liable to have me drop from a stroke. It had been over two decades since I laid eyes on her, and everything about her was still the same. Including that bougie ass attitude of hers. The holier than thou mask she wore was slipping with every passing minute; she had to be just as surprised to see me as I was to see her.

"This is my boss, Sampson," Jodeci said, motioning to the couple. "Sampson, these are Ashanti's parents, Vivica and Cornell."

I shook hands with Cornell and had to keep from laughing in his face when he tried to squeeze my hand extra tight. He was still a cornball ass nigga, which shouldn't surprise me because Vivica always had a thing for those. I could tell that she was looking for any little reason to get me alone so we could talk, but I wasn't having any of that; I left her alone all those years ago for a good reason. Talking to her would do nothing but dredge up old memories and a world of hurt; my eyes told her as much. She grabbed her husband's hand and walked him over to their child while Jodeci and I continued out the room.

`"Nice suite," I noted, motioning to the suite as we made our way down the hall. "Isn't it similar to the one Beyoncé was in when she gave birth?"

"It is; fortunately for me, Ashanti's parents paid for the suite while I paid for the birth. They've been real understanding with me getting on my feet and preparing to make some serious moves." Jodeci gave me a sideways glance. "They're actually cool with me being in the game as well. I never thought I would be able to get a girl like Ashanti's family to accept me."

Of course Vivica would approve of Jodeci; he was a hustler and I wouldn't be the least bit surprised to find out that she was living vicariously through her daughter. She was only with that square nigga because he was her third choice, with the other two being fed up with her bullshit. Yup, she wanted to turn Ashanti into the trap queen she could never be, and I wouldn't be surprised if she didn't push up on Jodeci in the process. She had a thing for getting with anyone's man on the low, blood or not.

"Of course they would accept you; you're one of the hardest workers. On top of that, you've got this hunger that won't quit. Ashanti gained a quality man, and I'm sure her parents can see it."

Jodeci shrugged. "If you feel that way, why won't you give me Maine's position? I know he has plans on giving it to Vaughn when he knows I'm more than deserving of it. His word ain't always bond."

"That's something I'm slowly starting to learn," I replied, digging in my pocket for the newspaper clipping I had from last week. I pulled it out and handed it over to him. "You ever seen this girl?"

"Yeah, this is Nubia. Her and Maine been on and off for the past year. They fell out over some shit that happened with her husband, but even then he's always had a soft spot for her. I wouldn't be surprised if they still messing around on the low."

We arrived at the nursery and Jodeci pointed at the beautiful baby girl front and center. She was slumbering peacefully, all wrapped up in a pink cashmere blanket. I was suddenly hit with the memory of when I first laid eyes on my baby girl, Ava. She was the prettiest baby

I had ever laid eyes on, and I swore that I would protect her from the evils of the world, and I failed her. I hadn't realized I had drifted off until Jodeci tapped my shoulder.

"I'm sure wherever Ava is, she's thinking about you, Sampson," Jodeci said, leaning against the window, watching his daughter. "Everyone knows you would give anything to have her back in your life again. That's how I feel about Michaela; I want her to have the best and know that Daddy is willing to do whatever it takes to make sure she's well taken care of."

I grabbed Jodeci's arm and lifted it until the picture of Nubia came between us. "Kill this girl, and the kingdom is yours."

Jodeci lowered the picture to reveal his game face. I felt chills up my spine; he reminded of me of how hungry and ruthless I was at his age. "Say no more, fam. I got you."

Nubia

Cheyenne came running down the stairs of the Bed Stuy loft house with a bright smile on her face. “Girl, this is the one. You have got to see that whirlpool bathtub, and the walk-in closets are bomb. Please tell me you're not thinking about looking elsewhere.”

With my finances set thanks to the huge blessing my parents left behind, I was now able to afford a place to live literally anywhere I wanted. So far, I had viewed apartments in Harlem, houses in Queens, and even dared to take my black ass to Staten Island. No matter what I had been through, Brooklyn would always be home; I just had to find the right one, and this wasn’t it. I told Cheyenne as much as we headed to the next spot with the real estate agent in tow. She knew my budget, and at the mention of so many zeroes, she was more than willing to follow me to the ends of Brooklyn if it meant she got a hefty commission.

“What are you looking for?” Cheyenne asked as we pulled up to the next house, a brownstone on a quiet Bed Stuy block. I thought the location looked a little familiar, but I could’ve been tripping. “You want it to be big, small, hella rooms, one kitchen, girl, please let me know so we can narrow down the options.”

“It’s hard to explain, but I want it to feel like a real place I can see myself raising Rhea. Right, pumpkin?" I said, kissing Rhea on the forehead before climbing out of the car with her carrier in my arms. "And somewhere that will make lugging this carrier a lot easier."

Cheyenne checked the time. "Boo, we got an hour before the girls get out of school. This is the last viewing we can do for the day."

"I know, I know," I said, taking in the view with each step I took. My feet had barely crossed the threshold when I felt a warmth come over me. "This place is beautiful."

While most of the homes had been remodeled, this particular brownstone still had that old school vibe to it. It was most definitely a fixer-upper, with the wallpaper peeling and the floorboards in need of a good buffing, but I could tell that it was lived in and loved. Cheyenne's face said the exact opposite; I could tell that she thought I was crazy for even entertaining such a place.

"What happened to the old owners?" Cheyenne asked the real estate agent. "They're still alive…right?"

"Yes, the house belongs to an elderly couple. While they're adamant that they can handle taking care of the house by themselves, their children aren't so sure so they moved them to Florida to be closer."

"How long have they lived here?" I asked, fingering the wooden banister as I made my ascent up the stairs.

"Thirty years," the agent replied, following right behind me. "The place is a bit of a fixer-upper, as the price reflects, but it's a beautiful home in an up-and-coming neighborhood."

I checked out each level, falling more and more in love with the place. My mind was completely made up when I entered a room with fading pink paint. The sun shined brightly inside, illuminating the room. I placed Rhea on the floor, picturing how great the room would look with a fresh coat of paint and furniture. Cheyenne stood in the doorway, smiling with her arms crossed as she watched me check out the room.

"So…how does this one feel?" she asked, although she knew the answer.

I dipped down and picked up Rhea, showing her, her future bedroom. "It feels like home."

******

After finding my dream house, nothing could kill my vibe. I sent Shahani over some pictures and she offered her tasteful eye to help decorate. Cheyenne did as well, and I couldn't wait to get two of my closest friends together. They were long overdue for a meeting, especially since I felt like they had so much in common: both were intelligent, outspoken, natural go-getters, and had my best interest at heart. While I was excited for the meeting, Cheyenne looked weary.

"I don't know…you already know that most females cannot stomach me for too long," Cheyenne said as we waited in front of the girls' school. "Plus, I don't think I'll ever not side-eye her for the way she played you."

"Cheyenne, I already told you we buried that hatchet. It's all good between us and I want the same with you two," I said with a playful nudge of my shoulder.

Cheyenne rolled her eyes. "Okay, okay, I'll play nice."

"Mommy!" Kiara shouted as she ran to Cheyenne.

I looked around for Marlee, who was usually right behind her cousin. "Kiara, where's Marlee?"

"She's over there talking to her dad," Marlee said, pointing to the other side of the playground.

I saw Marlee's mane of curly hair hovering in the air as a man held her over his head. Cheyenne was on it before I could move; I had barely picked Rhea's carrier up off the ground when she approached the pair, screaming the entire way. Everyone watched the scene with mild interest and I could already see school safety officers being called.

"Cheyenne, calm down before you get us locked up," I shouted as I jogged over to the pair. "School safety is on their way. Can we do this somewhere else?"

"No! Let school safety come so they can get a good look at this bitch ass nigga and make sure that he's never allowed this close to his child ever again," Cheyenne screamed. I went to tell her to calm down, but she continued on with, "Your daughter's mother is dead, Sullivan. She's been dead for nearly a year and you're just coming around to make sure your daughter is good? I always knew you were a piece of shit, but this is low even for you."

I turned to Sullivan and nearly swallowed my tongue. I wasn't sure if it was the ebbing pregnancy hormones or the lighting, but I couldn't help but notice how handsome Sullivan was. He was tall with Marlee's mocha skin, small eyes, and curly hair. The Nike hoodie he wore was fitted, stretching over his muscles, and complimented his muscular legs. On his feet was a pair of the latest Retro 13's so I knew he wasn't starving. Just by looking at his appearance, there was no excuse for him not attempting to find his child.

"Dead? I thought Precious was missing. You already know she's good for packing her shit and leaving," Sullivan said, glancing at Marlee. "I ain't believe she was dead."

"Girls, play in the playground for a few please," I said, pointing to the jungle gym filled with kids enjoying their after school festivities.

Once the girls were gone, Cheyenne spoke up. "Yes, she's dead. Her and that crazy ass boyfriend of hers tried to dead Jodeci on a pack."

"Word?" Sullivan said, rubbing his hands together manically. "I heard some whisperings of that being the case, but I never got a confirmation. I'mma handle that—"

"Are you fucking stupid?" Cheyenne barked, her eyes widening in disbelief. "Your daughter doesn't need two dead parents. She needs her father to take care of her and be the shoulder to cry on she's been begging for."

Sullivan hung his head in shame. "You're right, which is why I came here to see her today. I was thinking I could take her for the weekend or something."

"Nah, you can come by my place and visit her, but there will be no leaving with her," Cheyenne countered, rolling her neck with every word. "Marlee's birthday was also a little while ago and she could sure use a really nice present. Right, Nubia? Nubia?"

I nearly choked on a mouth full of drool, staring at Sullivan's fine ass. I swallowed it and replied, "Yeah, Marlee really wants you to be in her life."

"I promise that I'll be here for her here on out," Sullivan promised, licking his lips. He glanced at Marlee. "Can I give my daughter a hug and kiss before I go?"

Cheyenne nudged her head at the girls. "Be my guest."

When he was far enough, I asked Cheyenne. "How long have you known?"

"Known what?"

"Cheyenne…"

"I've known for a while now," Cheyenne replied with a shrug. "I know how shiesty my cousin can be, so I'm not the least bit surprised that she roped you into one of her shenanigans. Plus, she should've known better than to follow Paco's crazy ass. I don't know what you did to get out alive, but I don't blame you."

"So…you don't hate me?"

Cheyenne looked at me like I was crazy. "Didn't I just tell you that you're absolved of any guilt? You're a good person, Nubia. Even if I wanted to be mad at you, watching how you've looked out for Marlee makes that impossible."

My shoulders sagged in relief. "I swear holding that in was just… ugh. Cheyenne, as much of a good person I am, I can't be better than you."

"Well how about we celebrate this weight off your shoulders tonight? I already asked Donette, and she said she could take care of the kids. What do you say?" Cheyenne asked, batting her lashes at me.

"I'm down. Let's have some fun."

******

Something wasn't right. I had that inkling feeling from the moment I left the house with Cheyenne, who was amped up. She was looking gorgeous in a silver sequined dress while I was donning a pink silk gown with a daring split, and pair of satin Giuseppe's. My hair was a halo of curls and my makeup was natural yet flawless. Normally, I was all for having a good time, but tonight felt different.

"Cheyenne, I feel hella overdressed," I said, motioning to the classy dress I wore and her club-wear.

Cheyenne waved away my worries and handed me a glass of champagne. "You're nervous because this is your first time out on the prowl since your marriage ended and things fell apart with Maine. I saw you looking at Sullivan like he was a piece of meat. Trust me when I say it: the dick ain't worth it."

"Cheyenne, please don't tell me you fucked Sullivan."

"To be fair: he was my man first. When we broke up Precious slid into his inbox so hard I'm sure she smelled like burning rubber." Cheyenne cut her eyes at me. "That's another reason why that bitch couldn't be trusted. Oh, here we are."

The car pulled up to Savannah's, an upscale nightclub I had been to once with Vincent when we first started dating. The owner, Lucky Lewis, was pretty dope and made sure we were taken care of for the night. I already knew tonight would be a good night. Or at least I thought it was until we walked into the pitch-black club.

I grabbed Cheyenne's arm. "Girl, what's going—"

"SURPRISE!"

The lights flicked on, music began playing, and confetti rained from the air as we entered the club. Everyone was dressed in some variation of pink and white, which brought me back to the last time I even dared to wear the color. The stage of the club had been transformed into a throne, with a "Happy 21st Birthday Nubia" sign hanging right behind it. I stared at Cheyenne in shock, my eyes asking her where she got the time and money to pull off such a party. She didn't answer, and instead tugged me through the crowd and to my throne.

"Are you really not going to tell me how you planned all of this in such a short amount of time?"

Cheyenne popped the bottle of champagne sitting on a table next to me, pouring the foam out into the live crowd. "Nope! You'll soon find out. Now stop worrying about the little things and have some fun!"

Fun was exactly what I had for the next two hours. I turned up harder than I ever thought would be possible. The DJ kept playing all of my songs, the bottle girls were sending over nonstop drinks, and before I knew it, it was well after one. I was out of breath when I was greeted by Lucky, who wore a pink vest underneath his light grey suit. He motioned for me to follow him upstairs where I had a present waiting.

"A present? This party was a present enough," I said, feeling butterflies churning in my stomach with our ascent to the VIP section.

Lucky chuckled. "I'm glad you think so; I threw my wife a party this big last year and she still wanted to know where her present was. But Yulaney is a trip all on her own…here we are."

We approached a solitary door at the end of a secluded hallway.

Lucky opened the door and I received my second surprise of the night. Maine stood leaning against a table filled with pink and white gift boxes. He was dressed in a midnight black suit with a tie, pocket square, and socks the same color as my dress. Lucky winked at me and closed the door behind him.

"I know it's a little late but…Happy Birthday," Maine said rising off of the table he was leaned against and approaching me.

I took a few steps back, ending up pressed against the door, my heart racing as Maine closed the space between us. "It would've been happier if you came downstairs and celebrated with me."

"I didn't for your safety. There's a rumble in the streets that I don't want you mixed up in." Maine placed his hand on the door and leaned in close. "Are you enjoying yourself?"

"I sure am… *friend*," I said, making sure to emphasize the obvious. "I can't believe you went through this much trouble for me. The party, the dress…everything. You took one of the darkest days of my life and made it brighter, which is what I'm sure my parents would have wanted. I've never felt more special."

There was a flash of something behind Maine's eyes that I couldn't read. He replied in a husky tone, "That's what friends are for."

He continued to close the space between us, the smell of his cologne becoming intoxicating. I could feel myself growing weak at the thought of his lips claiming mine with the same amount of passion with which we had made love. They barely brushed against each other when I slid down the door and moved away from him.

"No, Maine," I said, shaking my head vehemently. "We aren't

doing this. Nuh-uh. I can't be with you knowing that you're going back home to her so that the two of you can…no, I don't even wanna picture it."

Maine sighed. "I've already explained to you that what I got going on with her ain't nothing more than business. I don't feel anything for her, Nubia!"

"But that won't stop you from marrying her!" I shouted. "That won't stop you taking her out in public while I remain behind closed doors like a dirty secret. I am tired of being treated like I'm something to be ashamed of! I want to be with a man that is proud to have me on their arm, a man that is willing to commit to me, a man that is able to love me without hurting me. And with you married to another woman, I don't think you can do that, Maine."

"No, I can't bring you out in public right now, but it has nothing to do with how much I care about you compared to her," Maine shot back. "I can't take you out because whoever's gunning for me wants to hurt anyone that I care about, with the only person falling into that category being you."

"Maine…" I started, and was silenced by his lips pressing against mine.

Maine pressed me against his body as he tongued me down, making my knees grow weak. My hormones kicked into overdrive again, and next thing I knew, I was grinding against his growing erection. All the shit I was talking minutes ago went out the window; I wanted Maine bad and I wanted him now. I let him know as much by snaking my hands to his belt and unbuckling it. As I fumbled, he opened my dress with one pull of a string, revealing my nude body.

"Damn, you gettin' real thick," he growled as he picked me up and carried me to the table of presents, where he sat me down like the most precious present of them all. "Where you been hiding all of this ass, 'cause I swear you ain't have it the last time I saw you."

I answered with a kiss, a sloppy one that muffled the moan that passed through my lips as Maine entered me with a sense of urgency. I wrapped my arms around his shoulders and matched his rhythm stroke for stroke. Every moment of hurt I felt for Maine was replaced by what felt like hours of ecstasy as we fucked. I had always thought of sex as being prim and proper, but here I was, being fucked on a table of tokens of affection as a celebration of my life happened beneath me.

"Why are you doing this to me?" I moaned in Maine's ear as he bounced me on his dick.

Maine answered my questioned with a kiss. Of course my reply was to kiss him with equal urgency as I locked my legs around his waist and rode him, matching his fervent pace. His legs buckled, and I knew I had him right where I wanted him. I made sure to squeeze my pussy muscles tight, the feeling enough to touch my G-spot and gave me one of the most intense orgasms I'd ever had in my life. Maine came right after and we fell to the floor in a heap.

"Damn," he chuckled, kissing me on the lips. "All I brought you up here for was to give you your presents. You came on to a nigga and shit…"

I playfully slapped him on the arm. "Oh please. You already knew me seeing you standing there in your crisp black suit, smelling like

Issey Miyake would have my panties wet. I don't think you planned to get it here, but you definitely wanted a taste of this birthday cake tonight."

Maine pulled me in for another kiss, this one sweeter. I could've laid there and kissed his lips forever. They tasted like mint, like he was chewing on it before I got here. *Oh, he knew he was trying to get some and my silly ass gave it*, I thought with a shake of my head as I freshened up in the luxurious bathroom. As I stepped out, Maine entered the room looking like his smooth self again. This time around, we focused on the presents, which I opened and thanked Maine for each one with a kiss. I had reached my beautiful fur jacket when there was a knock on the door.

"Nubia, they're ready to cut your cake!" Cheyenne called out.

I gave my hair one more tousle and gave Maine a playful nudge. "You got me a cake too?"

"It wouldn't be a birthday party without a cake," Maine replied with a kiss.

"Thank you for an amazing night," I said, holding on to the lapels of his suit. "I guess I'll see you around…"

"How about I escort you downstairs, you cut your cake, and we head out to a late dinner?"

"Maine, I don't want anything happening because of me…"

Maine placed a finger on my lips. "Don't you ever worry about any of that, you hear me? I got everything under control. Now let's go and cut this cake."

The party was still popping as we entered. Whereas people parted the crowd out of excitement when I entered with Cheyenne, Maine parted the crowd with his authority. I held my head high as Maine led me across the dance floor with a possessive hand on my waist. Men stared at me with longing while women eyed me enviously. For the first time in my life, I was the belle of the ball and I had Maine to thank for that.

"I see someone was unwrapping one of their presents," Cheyenne said with a smirk. "Hey, Maine."

"Wassup, Cheyenne. Good job on the party," Maine said, motioning to the festivities.

Cheyenne raised her glass to him. "With an unlimited budget anything is possible." She motioned behind us. "Especially a cake like that."

Two of the bottle girls appeared, pushing a six-tier birthday cake created for royalty. It was pink and white with silver butterflies all over. On top sat a tiara and several sparklers. Tears sprung to my eyes; this cake looked exactly like the one I had at my birthday party except larger.

"Alright, ladies and gentlemen, it's time to sing to the birthday girl," the DJ announced. "One, two, three!"

A chorus of "Happy Birthday" filled the club, the sound almost deafening. Maine stepped back half hidden by the cake, which allowed me to bask in the spotlight of such a special night while Cheyenne stood right by my side, clapping and cheering me on. They ended with a round of applause and some wolf whistles, cheering as I tucked my hair behind my ears and proceeded to blow out the sparklers. One of the bottle girls handed me a sword to cut the cake. I had barely plunged it into the cake when the shots fired, one of them piercing the sword and sending it flying out of my hand.

Chaos erupted in the club, with everyone trying to run out of the emergency exits. Maine's reaction was one of second nature; he jumped in front of me, squeezing off shots of his own as he backed me towards the exit onstage. Shots flew back, piercing the cake and whizzing past my face. Cheyenne opened the exit door and we entered with Maine taking the lead.

"Here," he said, reaching inside of his jacket and pulling out a gun. "Hold down the back while I handle the front. If anybody comes through that door shoot first, and ask questions later."

I kicked off my heels and did exactly as I was told to the tee, refusing to turn around until the spring air hit my back. Maine wrapped a protective arm around my waist and led me to the car waiting out back. We sped off into the night as the door busted open. I feared that it was the shooter, but the droves of people proved otherwise. I sunk into Maine's arms, shaking from head to toe at the thought of what would've happened had he not decided to join me onstage.

"What the fuck was that?" Cheyenne asked, her question cutting the tense silence like a knife. "Everyone knows better than to start some shit in one of Lucky's establishments. How did they even get in there and what were they doing trying to kill Nubia?"

"You think they were trying to kill me?" I piped up, my heart rate increasing again.

Maine dismissed the thought immediately. "Nah, their aim was off; they were aiming for me."

"But it was Nubia's party. How would they have even known you'd show up when I never mentioned—"

"They were aiming for me," Maine repeated and this time Cheyenne didn't object.

The rest of the ride was spent in silence. I placed my head on Maine's chest, listening to his heartbeat. While mine was steadily hammering, his was calm and cool, barely beating every few seconds. *He must be an athlete or something,* I thought to myself. I was halfway asleep when we pulled up to Cheyenne's place. She bid Maine a goodnight and left us alone to talk.

"I guess I shouldn't be surprised," I said, shaking my head as the tears began to fall. "Just when I thought I'd be able to celebrate my birthday without death and destruction, this happens. If I hadn't been such a brat and demanded an expensive party my parents might still be here."

"This wasn't your fault," Maine urged, pulling out his pocket square and using it to dab my eyes. "What happened with your parents wasn't their fault either. Sometimes shit just gets out of control. I don't wanna hear you beating yourself up over this anymore, Aight?"

"Okay," I sniffled.

"The one time I let my guard down and look at what happens," Maine said, tracing small circles on my thigh. "I think we need to put a pause on us until I handle this situation."

"You know what? I agree," I said, placing my hand over his and giving it a gentle squeeze. “I can't deny what this is, but I know right now isn't the right time for us to pursue it. Goodnight, Maine.”

Maine used his other hand to turn my face towards his. Our lips met for a gentle kiss, one that was filled with promise. This chapter between Maine and I may have closed, but I knew there was a future for us yet to come.

Maine

I watched Nubia enter Cheyenne's apartment building, smiling at the sight of her fat ass straining to be free of the dress she wore. She had put on a few pounds since I last saw her, but I was happy to see it went to all the right places. She gave me a small wave through the glass door and disappeared upstairs. The smile on my face was wiped clean and it was back to business as usual.

"Where we going, boss?" my driver asked, peering at me through the rearview window.

"Take me back to the block," I commanded.

There were a few recognizable people at the party tonight, and I knew if I made it back to the block within the hour I could catch a few people on their way home rehashing the events. Until then I would call my boy, Lucky, to see what went down at the club. He was known for having top-notch security, and if someone managed to penetrate it, they made an enemy out of him as well.

"How's your girl?" was the first question to come out of Lucky's mouth.

"She's Aight; a little shook up, but she's good." I took a deep breath and dove right in. "Lucky, what the fuck happened back there?"

"I got my entire staff present and I already let 'em know we ain't going nowhere until I get a name. Whoever it was that was firing shots was doing it from the premiere VIP section, which was closed for the night. We had it roped off, but security was supposed to keep watch of that area. I'm sorry about this, man," Lucky apologized. "You got my word that I'll get down to the bottom of this. I also got troops if you need 'em."

"I definitely appreciate that, bro. I'm getting ready to look into a lead right now. I'll get back with you by the end of the night."

"Bet."

My driver pulled up to the block, and of course, partygoers were walking into their buildings talking about the scene. I sat there for a full five minutes, waiting for someone to say a name, but for nothing. I knew I wouldn't gain any more information just sitting here so I made a couple calls, the first one being Vaughn, who picked up on the first ring. We made plans to meet up in five. My next call was to Jodeci so we could get the soldiers together and make a game plan. I wasn't the least bit surprised that his phone went straight to voicemail. Not one for leaving behind any virtual footprints, I hopped out and made a beeline for Jodeci's apartment building. His moms, Rosa, was still wide-awake when I knocked on the door.

"Hey, Maine," she purred, leaning in her doorway with her silk robe half open. Her black lace bra was on full display and I knew the longer we stood here talking the more I would be forced to see. "What brings you by at this time of night?"

"I was looking for Jodeci. Is he here?"

"Jody moved out a few weeks ago," she replied with a roll of her eyes. "That little bougie ass girlfriend of his got him spending all kinds of money and making big moves without his momma. I asked if I could move in with them to help take care of the baby and the little prissy bitch told me no."

"Damn, that's real fucked up, Rosa. You raised Jody all by yourself and for him to play you like that for his girl is crazy," I said because it was; I would give anything to have another day with my mother and Jodeci tossed his aside to suck up to a family that don't give a solitary fuck about him. "I know you already know him and I haven't been seeing eye-to-eye."

"And it's a damn shame because the two of you used to be so close. Like brothers." She shook her head. "I'm telling you that girl is to blame. She's the root of all evil. Won't even let me see my own grandchild because of some four week bonding time she wants with the baby."

"I bet she won't make her mother stay away for four weeks."

"Say that shit again," Rosa co-signed. She smiled up at me. "You always were a great listener, Maine. I can't give you a location on Jody, but is there anything else I can do for you?"

Rosa pulled the sash of her robe and it opened, revealing a pair of matching lace panties. Don't get me wrong—Jodeci's moms was built with a body that most strippers were paying good money for—but there was no way I could ever take it there with her. However, I knew if I was going to get any information from her I had to play the part.

Taking one good look at her body, l politely declined with a, "No, ma'am. Unless you can call him up on your phone for me. There's an emergency and I really need his help."

"Say no more," she replied, pulling her iPhone out of her bra. She called Jodeci on speaker and he picked up on the second ring. "Baby, I got Maine here on speaker with me. There's an emergency and he needs you."

There was a pregnant pause on the line followed by Jodeci saying, "Wassup, Maine."

"I need to get with you on some serious shit. Where you at?"

"I'm home with my girl and the baby. I promised her a full night's sleep so I can't make that trek to the block tonight," Jodeci said apologetically. "I can make all the calls you need though."

"I'd rather talk in person. Send me your address and I'll come through. I won't wake up your girl or the baby. I just need five minutes, aight?"

Jodeci sighed. "Aight. I'm sending you the address right now."

Rosa hung up and shoved her phone back into her bra. "Did you hear that shit? She got my son pussy whipped. Go talk to my son, Maine. Get him right."

"Trust me, I will," I promised, taking off down the hall. "I got plenty of get right for that nigga."

Vaughn was posted up on my car when I arrived downstairs. He took in my appearance with mild interest, cracking a smile at the sight. I already knew he would have a joke or two up his sleeve about catching me in pink, but instead he got straight to it. I gave him the rundown and like me, he was surprised that Jodeci was MIA during an emergency.

"You really think shorty got him on that tight of a leash?" Vaughn asked. "I can't see Jodeci not riding out because his baby moms said so."

"I don't think it's that he doesn't want to; I don't think he can."

It took Vaughn a couple seconds to piece together what I was trying to say. "Not Jodeci, Maine—"

"The only reason I can think of him not showing up is because he was there firing off the shots. I hit the shooter. I know I did because even though they had the upper hand they stopped shooting. If we get to Jodeci's house and he looks a mess, I know it's him."

"But you have to answer this question: what would he get from shooting you? In another week you'll be working exclusively for the Rojas Cartel. There's no need to kill you for your old position; what other reason could he have to want to see you dead?"

Because it wasn't me that was supposed to die, I thought to myself because I didn't dare let Vaughn in on my suspicions just yet. The battlefields taught me to look before I leapt, and tonight was one of the many times those lessons came in handy. Navigating unknown territory was the next lesson that came into play as Vaughn and I descended the stairs to the basement apartment. I knocked in rapid succession and was geared up for another round when the lights cut on and Jodeci appeared. He was dressed in a tee and sweats.

"I would invite y'all in but Ashanti is real finicky when it comes to allowing people into the house. We're doing this four week bonding and she doesn't want any germs around the baby," Jodeci said, slipping outside and closing the door behind him. "What's with the late night call?"

"Tonight someone was shooting at me while I was at a party for Nubia," I said, studying his face for the slightest hint of deception. "I need everyone out in the streets looking for whoever this muhfucker is. We riding out. You coming?"

"Absolutely not!" came a reply from the window. Ashanti pulled the curtains back so she could get a good look at us. "You must be out of your damn mind if you think you're gonna snatch Jodeci out of my home for some bullshit when you can't even give him a promotion."

"Babe," Jodeci said, rolling his eyes. "Close the window and get back to bed. I got this."

"No! They can't come here looking for your help at all times of the night yet they won't put you on. Fuck that!"

I squatted down so she and I were at face level. "I don't know who the fuck you think you are or what niggas been putting in your head, but you don't tell any one of my workers what they can and can't do for me. I'll snatch Jodeci out this yard and put him to work in nothing but his PJs, you understand me?"

"Maine, you ain't need to say all of that," Vaughn said nervously.

Jodeci let out a cold chuckle. "Nah, let that nigga keep talking out the side of his mouth 'cause tonight might be the night he finds out that he ain't the only one with some mean hands."

"Excuse me?" I said, rising to my full height. "I been real patient with you, Jodeci. And I been nice since we're in front of your baby moms, but don't get me fucked up with any of these other niggas—I only speak to give warning. Once you've been warned you gotta suffer the consequences. I want all the manpower you got on the streets searching for this gunman and dropping him at my feet when you got him."

Jodeci lifted his head to me, his eyes void of any emotion while a sur-de-soi smile played on his lips. "Say no more, fam. I got you."

This nigga was really standing here mocking me. It took everything in my power not to pull out my burner and murk his ass, but that would be too easy. If it was a war that Jodeci wanted, it was a war he was gon' get. I could promise him that.

Shahani

I stared at myself in the mirror for a full five minutes, trying to figure out whether or not I was ready to do this. My lips had healed and were already down to their normal size, my nose was coming along nicely, my ugly black eyes were slowly turning to an ugly yellow, and my teeth had been replaced. However, the scars from the attack were still present and they weren't going away any time soon. After an expert application of makeup, I should have been ready to walk out the door, except I had this crippling fear that everyone would see through my painted on armor.

"Come on, Shahani. You can do this," I said, giving myself a pep talk. "You can get out there and face the world."

I backed away from the mirror and left out the bathroom. I got halfway to my bedroom door when I doubled back, making a beeline for my closet. I threw a Gucci scarf on my head and a pair of matching oversized shades on to cover most of my face. Taking a look in the hallway mirror, I felt a thousand times more comfortable. *One step at a time*, I thought as I locked up the house and skipped down the steps to my car, a sparkling white Bentley jeep. Sampson surprised me with it yesterday as his way of luring me out of the house, and it kinda worked. The tint was perfect and I knew in the privacy of my car I wouldn't have to worry about anyone seeing me. I hooked up my music and jammed on my way to the salon. I was in the middle of bopping to Chris Brown's "Privacy" when a call from Nubia came through.

"Hello, lady," I greeted her with high spirits. "How was the party last night?"

"Morning! You knew about the party?" Nubia asked with a hint of surprise.

"Yeah, and I got fully dressed to come, took one good look at my face and couldn't bear going to the club. Lately I've been so self-conscious to the point where I'm almost ready to put the paper bags back over the mirrors at home," I admitted out loud for the first time. "I know; I'm pathetic as fuck."

"Of course you aren't. I didn't want to wear short sleeves for a long time when my aunt used to beat me. Time will heal those wounds: trust me. Plus, I'm happy you didn't come because someone shot up the party anyway."

Nubia launched into a story about how someone tried to shoot at her while she was cutting her birthday cake. I covered my mouth in shock because the first thought that popped into my mind was how strange Sampson had been acting over the last few weeks. Not to my face of course; he was a picture perfect boyfriend that catered to me, which was why it hurt to mentally accuse him of anything malicious like wanting to do harm to my best friend. It weighed heavy on my mind long after I disconnected with Nubia and arrived at the shop. A stream of applause knocked me out of my trance.

"Welcome back," Pinky announced, hugging me tight. "Shahani, you gave us a serious scare. Please don't go being a superhero ever again."

"Trust me, I won't. It's so good seeing all of you ladies are doing well and held down the fort in my absence. This is what real teamwork is made of," I said, giving them air kisses as I continued to my office.

"If there's anything you need let us know," Pinky called out.

I gave her the thumbs up and closed myself off inside of my office. Everything was still the same: my desk remained as untouched as it did the night I left it alone after finding my cooked books. Speaking of which—

"Let's get a look at this bullshit," I muttered as I snatched the ledger from the table and got a good look. "Oh shit."

As if by magic, my books were back to normal. The numbers were all in place without even a deduction in sight. I closed the book and placed it close to my chest, smiling from ear-to-ear at my discovery. Of course I couldn't contain my excitement and had to call Sampson immediately. He sounded equally happy to hear from me.

"I came back home for lunch and I see the car's gone," he said with a chuckle. "It's good to see you out and about."

"You know what else is good to see? This new ledger. Thank you for taking care of it," I replied, giving the brand new book an air kiss.

"When I got the call that you were in the hospital in near critical condition the first though that came to my mind was how I left things between us. I'm sorry for messing with your business, Shahani," Sampson apologized and I knew he meant it with all his heart. "I gave it to you as a gift and it should've never been with any ulterior motives. I won't lay a finger on it ever again. You have my promise."

"You have no idea how much that means to me," I said, wiping a few stray tears away.

Donovan wound never humble himself enough to apologize to me, even when he was painfully wrong. Sampson's accountability was a huge redeeming factor, and I knew that if he was able to be this open and candid with me about his wrongdoings, I could see a future with us. I told him as much and was warmed by his agreement.

"You're different than any other woman I've ever been with, Shahani. You make me wanna be different man—a better one than I was in the past. I love you."

"Love you, too. I'll see you when I get home," I kissed my phone and hung up. Taking a deep breath, I called Pinky into my office. "Pinky, you think you can find Nia for me? If you can't find her then Essence's slippery ass will do."

Pinky shot a couple of text messages out and had a hit five minutes later. "She's staying in the Marriott Downtown Brooklyn. Her other boyfriend's had her there since she was released. You can head out and I'll have the room number for you by the time you get there."

With Sampson and I on the right track, I thought it was time to tie up the last loose end in my life: Nia. It was one thing to fuck my man in my house—I was halfway out of love with him anyway—but it was another thing to get with him and set me up to be killed. *Me and Mercy are gonna handle her ass,* I thought to myself as I slid into my jeep. I was poised to turn it on when one hand grabbed mine while the other covered the scream that passed through my lips.

"Calm down," Lonzo whispered in my ear. "It's just me, Shahani."

I sagged in relief. "Fuck, Lonzo. You can't just keep popping up like this. A little warning would've been nice."

"I already told you I'm out here making shit hot right now. There ain't no room for warnings. Start driving before one of your bodyguards comes checking to make sure you're good."

I pulled off into the Thursday morning traffic, checking to make sure my bodyguards were still with me. The last thing I wanted was more bodies on my conscience because I decided to run off like a mad woman. I turned the radio on to 105.1 and began dancing to Wiz Khalifa's "Something New." Ironic how it came on as I was dealing with my old boyfriend interrupting my new life. A year ago I would've left Donovan in a heartbeat to be with Lonzo. Once upon a time I never thought I would find another Lonzo, but with Sampson taking care of me at my lowest, I was starting to think I had found better. My only problem was telling Lonzo as much.

"I've been coming to the shop everyday hoping you would show up but you been MIA. I thought your injuries weren't that bad," Lonzo said, interrupting my train of thought.

"They weren't, but my face. The swelling has gone down for the most part, but I still look hideous." I snatched off my sunglasses. "See?"

"All I see is the girl I fell in love with all those years ago. You are more than your face, Shahani, and don't you ever believe different."

Lonzo's sweet words warmed me; he always knew how to make me feel good about myself and today was no different. He had my best interest at heart and it wouldn't hurt to keep in contact with him for a little longer. Or at least I thought it wouldn't.

"So…what's new out on the block? I know you know with your

man being the big boss and all," Lonzo asked, sitting back in his seat and getting comfortable. "Any casualties? Takeovers? Anything out of the ordinary?"

"Sampson said someone shot up his barbershop…they got away before he could stop them," I mentioned, glancing at him through the rearview mirror. "My girl said last night someone shot up her birthday party. Your people hear anything about that?"

"The barbershop: I might know something about that," Lonzo said with a nod. "And the birthday party: that ain't have nothing to do with me, but I'll definitely put a bug out and get back to you when I can."

"I'd really appreciate that."

The rest of the ride to the hotel was spent in an amicable silence, with the radio providing background noise. Lonzo leaned forward in his seat and placed his chin on my shoulder.

"That spot you got back there is real nice, Shahani. I remember you always talking about how you wanted to open your own hair salon one day. That was my next move for us: to start building an empire. It's still my plan for us, except I gotta start from ground zero. That doesn't matter to me though, 'cause you're more than worth it." Lonzo kissed me on the cheek. "You think you can get away from your man next Saturday?"

I shook my head. "Nah, Sampson and I have a wedding to attend next Saturday."

"Who's getting married?"

"His lieutenant, Maine. It's going to be this big, swanky event at an exclusive hotel in the city," I said, recalling the expensive wedding invitation Sampson and I had gotten in the mail. "Knowing the bride, it's going to be an all day thing."

"Which hotel? Maybe you can sneak away for a drink or something at the bar?"

I shook my head in dissent. "Nah. Too much heat there. I already heard that the security is going to be tight as fuck. If you don't have an invitation or you aren't part of the hotel staff, you ain't getting in."

"Oh, that sucks," Lonzo replied with a kiss on the cheek. "Speed up and make this turn. You'll buy me thirty seconds to get out and be clear of the car."

I followed Lonzo's directions and he was gone as quickly as he arrived, leaving behind the smell of fresh soap and A&D ointment. *Sampson did mention that whoever shot up the shop got hit,* I thought to myself as I pulled into the hotel parking lot. I was torn between my old flame and new love, a situation that would have someone end up dead if I didn't do something. However, right now wasn't that time because I had a bitch to snatch.

"Room service," I called out in a professional tone, knowing Nia's greedy ass would have ordered something to eat by now.

A few seconds later the door swung open with Nia talking out the side of her mouth like she usually did. "It's about time because I've been waiting—Shahani? Shit!"

She tried to close the door but I was too quick for her, sticking my foot right in the doorway before her eyes could adjust. I shoved the door open as I whipped Mercy out from my purse, placing her right on top of Nia's collarbone. She placed her hands in the air as I backed her deeper into the room, closing the door with my foot.

"Hey, Shahani," Nia said playfully. "You're looking so good, girl. That eye? I would've never guessed that Donovan smashed it in. And your lips are looking much better too. Overall, I can say that you snapped back pretty well for someone on the brink of death."

I pressed the barrel of the gun deeper into her chest, knocking her onto the bed behind her. "Didn't I tell you that you were dead to me, bitch? I don't give a fuck how much you sit here and try to dick ride me, but that isn't going to stop me from shooting your head clean off your neck."

"You can't kill me right now, Shahani," Nia said, closing her eyes and pressing herself into the bed. "Think of all the cameras that saw you come up here. They'll have you within the hour. Am I really worth going to jail over?"

"With a decent lawyer I can plead insanity and get out with no trouble," I rationalized, shoving the gun so deep into her throat I could feel her swallow. "There isn't a damn thing you can say to me that would make me consider leaving you alive."

"I saw who killed Donovan," Nia choked out. "I didn't pass out right after being shot. I saw who killed him and I know that you haven't told Sampson. If you even think about killing me I have someone else that'll make sure he finds out."

Gone was the look of fear in Nia's eyes, replaced by her signature smugness. I refused to have her lay here thinking she had the best of me. I opened the right side of her robe, revealing her healing bullet wound. I dug my nails into it, shooting her a smug smile of my own as she screamed.

"You listen to me, bitch," I said over her pleas for me to stop. "If I find out that you have told anyone that Lonzo isn't dead, I will come back and finish what he started. You can't tell on me without telling on yourself and as far as everyone is concerned, I don't remember anything from that night. When it comes down to it, who do you think he'll believe, a miserable snake like you or his woman?"

"Okay," Nia garbled, her eyes pleading with me to move my hand. "I promise I won't tell anyone what happened. Please get off of my shoulder."

I eased up off of her shoulder, but didn't remove my gun. "This is a really nice room you got here. Your new boyfriend paying for it?"

"Why do you care?"

"I care because as much information as you have on me, I have on you. You go running your mouth about Lonzo and I can easily go to Vaughn and let him know the real reason why we fell out. Nubia and I are cool again so I'm sure she'll have no problem backing me up either. How's that for petty?"

Nia rolled her eyes. "Come on, Shahani. Get off of me."

I flipped Mercy over and popped her in the lip one good time, satisfied with the garbled scream that filled the room. I climbed off of her, and after watching her lying there crying like a big ass baby, I decided that it was time for me to get out of here before Vaughn showed up asking questions. Nia was a wildcard, and what I couldn't deal with right now was anyone that threatened to take away what I built with

Sampson. I had a choice to make and it had to be made sooner rather than later or else it would be made for me, with either result starting a war or ending in death.

Nubia

It had been a week since I had last spoken to Maine. After dropping me off home it was like he fell off the face of the earth. I tried calling and texting him a few times, only to discover that he had changed his number. For someone that was gunning to be with me, he sure did change his mind. I tried to act like I wasn't hurt by being blown off by him, but I was. The least he could've done was let me know what it was before completely ghosting on me.

"Sweetie, you're overreacting," Cheyenne said as she helped me carry the last box of my belongings into the short term rental I was staying in. "After the shit that popped off last week, I'm sure he's doing his best to protect you from whoever was tryna get at him."

"You mean me," I corrected her.

"You still think the shooter was trying to kill you? Girl, that's a huge reach."

I plopped down on the living room couch and kicked my feet up. "Is it really? Even you thought that the shots were meant for me until Maine talked you out of it."

"I mean, I did, but Maine's right: who in their right mind would want to kill you? You haven't done anything to anyone to warrant such a reaction. Unless…"

"Unless what?"

Cheyenne plopped down right beside me. “Unless whoever fired those shots wanted to hurt you, but only because they wanted to get to Maine. That would explain why he's keeping his distance from you.”

“So I’m supposed to sit here waiting for him to return to me when he's finished with his street war?” I scoffed. “You know what? I’m done thinking and talking about it. I already was opposed to us getting together and now the decision has been made for me.”

The conversation was officially ended by a knock on the door. I shouted that the door was open, and in walked Shahani with Rhea in her arms. She was always spoiling my little angel: holding Rhea whenever she made the smallest whimper, singing her to sleep, and sometimes sneaking her little tastes of juice. Shahani was glowing with baby fever and it was only a matter of time before she was trying to put a bun in her oven.

“We’re here,” Shahani announced as she set Rhea’s baby bag on the floor. “Look who it is, Mommy and…hi. I’m Shahani, you must be Cheyenne.”

Shahani held out a hand to Cheyenne, who gave it a polite shake. I could feel the vibes in the room change and for one good reason; both women were equally territorial and outspoken, so I knew they would bump heads a few times before getting used to each other.

“Nice to meet you, Shahani,” Cheyenne replied. “You look really familiar. Have I seen you somewhere before?”

“If you’ve been to my shop: Silk Tresses,” Shahani replied, taking a seat on the armchair adjacent to us; she had her guard up and was reading Cheyenne. “I've been open for a few months. We do a lot of advertising on Instagram."

Cheyenne shook her head. "I don't think that's where I know you from. You ever dance?"

No the fuck she did not. I wasn't too sure on how comfortable Shahani was with talking about her past, and Cheyenne purposely picking at it was liable to start a fight. I turned to Shahani, who sat there shaking with silent laughter.

"I used to dance over at Ahab's spot. Curves was the name," Shahani replied, shaking her head reminiscently. "That spot was wild as fuck. You danced there?"

"That was my very first club. I had to leave because my boyfriend found out and made it hard for anyone to wanna get a dance from me." Cheyenne pointed at Shahani. "You were my mentor in my head. I used to watch you all the time and copy everything you did. Had it not been for you, I don't think I would be half the dancer I am today."

Shahani placed a hand on her chest. "Thank you. I had no idea I was changing lives. All I knew was that the bills needed to be paid and it was either this pole or the corner."

"Who the fuck you telling? As cheap as these niggas are when it comes to paying for three dances and you think I'm about to be out on the corner haggling over the worth of my pussy?"

Shahani cocked her head to the side. "Imagine how much more difficult it is to haggle over someone else's. I stayed having to teach my girls to know the worth of their pussy."

"You used to pimp?" Shahani nodded her head. "Bitch, me too! I used to have a few hoes back on my old block. Taught them how to fuck a nigga and get that money!"

I watched with mild amusement as my two best friends bonded over stripping and pimping hoes. *At least they're not being catty*, I thought to myself as I made a beeline for the kitchen. I opened the refrigerator and sighed at the sad food choices. Since I just got the keys to the place yesterday, all I was able to grab was some juice, lunchmeat, and condiments. Looking back at Cheyenne and Shahani, who were both dressed head to toe in designer labels, I wasn't too sure how well a ham and cheese sandwich with a cup of Kool-Aid might be received.

"Shit, if they don't want to eat it, I will," I said to myself, popping open the package of sliced meat.

The stench that touched my nose was enough to have me retching. The women looked at me in concern, which I waved off. I threw the meat in the garbage and checked the fridge to make sure the temperature was up high enough. It was on the low side, proving it to be the culprit of the spoiled meat.

"Where are you going?" Cheyenne asked, her brows disappearing underneath her bangs as she watched me shrug into my jacket.

"The lunchmeat I had in the fridge spoiled. I'm gonna grab something for us to eat. Any suggestions?"

"Hardee's," both women said at the same time.

"Hardee's it is," I said, with a roll of my eyes. "I'll be back in like thirty minutes. You already know it stays packed in there, plus that walk is a bitch."

"Which is why you need to get your license already," Shahani shouted as I closed the door.

I was laughing right now, but I knew that Shahani was right; I needed to have a car before winter came creeping up like a thief in the night. I grew up being chauffeured around in some of the best cars that money could buy and I wanted the same for Rhea. There was no way in hell I could expose her to the bullshit of the MTA on a regular basis if could help it. I was finished with a majority of my planning by the time I reached the Chinese restaurant, which was packed. After mentally cussing myself for not making them call ahead, I stood in the line and patiently waited to be called.

"Hi, can I get three orders of freshly fried shrimp with pork fried rice and a side of dumplings?" I asked, reading off the text Shahani sent me. "And three eggrolls, and…lord, lemme get some sweet potato fries as well. These heffas are gree—"

"Nubia?"

I turned around slowly, and was greeted by one fine ass nigga. He looked like he stepped out of a page from GQ with his piercing green eyes, sandy-blond curls, and lean body. He wore a Harvard sweatshirt, giving me a clue as to who he might be but I wouldn't believe it until I heard the words come from his mouth.

"Hey…"

"Micah," Sundy and Bernard's only child said with a grin, revealing a perfect set of teeth. "How have you been? It's been what? Three years?"

"It has, it has," I said, painting an awkward smile on my face. Like everyone in the restaurant, I was wondering why Micah's fine ass decided to strike up a conversation with me. "I'm doing pretty well. I just had a baby a couple months ago. How are you?"

"I'm doing pretty good. I'm getting ready to enter my final year of school. Pre-med has been kicking my ass, but if it'll make my parents happy…"

I nodded my head sympathetically. "I feel you. So…what brings you to this side of town?"

While this part of Bed Stuy had improved with the introduction of gentrification, I didn't see Sundy and Bernard allowing Micah this close to the hood, which was literally a block away.

Micah waved away my worries. "I've been here the entire summer with my roommate. We didn't want to spend the summer under our parents' roof so we got a place down the block. How long have you been living here?"

"I just moved here from Crown Heights. I'm staying in a rental until I'm finished closing on my house, which isn't too far from here," I said, making a vague pointing motion down the block.

The cashier called an order and Micah grabbed his food. I expected him to end the conversation with an "I'll see you around," but he surprised me by asking a question.

"I know this is a little forward, but I was wondering if I could take you out to dinner? Maybe tomorrow night? I know that's really sudden, but I head out to the Hamptons with my parents on Sunday and from there it's back to school."

I nodded my head. "Okay, I'd love to go out."

After exchanging numbers, I stood there in shock. Was I really going to go out on a date with Micah? He was everything most women went for: handsome, smart, respectful, and he was going to be *a doctor.* So then why wasn't I as excited as I should've been? I knew exactly why. Because as much as I wanted to push him from my mind for the time being, a certain someone came shoving back to the forefront. Maine had me feeling sick to my stomach, or at least I thought it was him until I smelled someone's food as they exited the restaurant. This felt all too familiar, and one stop at Family Dollar would give me some piece of mind or make an already complicated situation worse.

******

I stared at the pregnancy test box for the past fifteen minutes, debating on whether or not I was going to take it. I hadn't had the time last night because my girls stayed until late. Now that I had the alone time to take it, I was wondering whether or not I should wait until tonight after my date with Micah. After staring at the box for a few more minutes, I decided it wasn't fair to Micah to bring my baggage along on our date.

"Someone looks gorgeous," Shahani noted as she rocked Rhea back and forth. "I can't believe you went to get Chinese food and came back with a date invitation from a doctor."

"He's not a doctor yet," I reminded her, as I slipped into my coat. "He hasn't even finished pre-med."

"Doesn't matter; from what you told me about him, he's going to become a doctor and you'll be a doctor's wife. I can't think of a better way to shut up any and all haters than to flash a blinging ring at them," Shahani said, wiggling her left hand. "Shoot, you deserve some normalcy in your life."

"My life is normal. Now," I said as an afterthought. "I purchased a house, I'm not running from my abusive husband anymore, I retired my position on the pole, and I'm raising my daughter in a positive environment. How much more normal could my life get?"

"You could meet a man with no baggage that likes you for who you are," Shahani replied. "With the title Dr. attached to his name. Now get out of here and have some fun."

"That I can do. See you tomorrow," I said as I dipped out the door and ran smack dab into Micah.

He was dressed smartly in a black Brooks Brothers suit, which matched the black satin bustier dress I wore. In his hand was a bouquet of red roses, which was so romantic. I smelled them all the way downstairs, only coming up for air when Micah asked me what I was in the mood for.

"Have you ever had French food?" he asked as he led me to his car, a Mercedes Benz convertible.

I slid into the passenger seat and smiled as he closed my door for me like a true gentleman. "I've never had it but I'm open to giving new things a try."

Micah and I spent the ride to the restaurant catching up with each other. While the past three years for him was filled with traveling the world when he wasn't in school, all I had to talk about was working at KFC and having Rhea. While I loved being a mother, I couldn't help but feel that my life was missing some major accomplishments. Micah could tell, and he tried to make me feel better over dinner.

"To be quite honest with you, I have no desire to become a doctor. It's what my parents wanted for me and I don't want to disappoint them. They've given me a better life than I could ask for, so it would feel messed up to repay them by pursuing something that's not as lucrative," Micah admitted with a nonchalant shrug, but I could tell he had been holding on to that secret for a long time.

"What do you want to be?"

"An author. I'd like to write Science Fiction. My parents never understood the appeal of writing books, but it feels like a calling. I have a novel that I recently finished, but I don't have the courage to turn it in."

"Do it," I said without hesitation. "I've lived a good chunk of my life afraid to stand up for myself and have a voice. Ever since I started doing what makes me happy, life has been a thousand times better. I'm not saying it's perfect, because I still have a long way to go, but if someone would've told me that I'd be sitting here a year ago I wouldn't have believed them. Sometimes you gotta step out on faith and go for what you really want."

Micah placed his hand over mine and gave it a gentle squeeze. "Like going for you? I always thought you were so beautiful, but I never really knew how to approach you. I couldn't let the perfect opportunity slip by me, and I'm happy that I acted on it."

"So am I."

As much as that pep talk was for Micah, it was also for myself. I was growing into my skin and there was no going back now.

******

"Tonight was amazing, Micah," I said as we arrived back at my door. “Maybe when you're back in town we can have dinner again?”

“I'd like that,” Micah replied, leaning in and kissing me on the cheek. “I'll see you around.”

Once he cleared the stairs, I danced into my apartment like a giddy little girl. Tonight was a perfect reminder that I could date a guy without any of the added drama. After dinner, Micah and I listened to music at a jazz lounge followed by drinks at a local spot. It was a pretty cool date with a really sweet guy, so why did I feel like something was missing? Maybe because I wasn't on the date with—

“Maine?”

Sitting at the end of my bed was Maine. His arms were crossed and only God knows how long he'd been sitting there waiting for me to return. I could see his jaw working and knew there was no way in hell I was going to end my night in peace like I thought I would. I kicked off my heels and went to make a beeline for the bathroom when Maine's hand shot out and yanked me into him.

“So that's how you gon' do me? Last week everything was good between us and then I gotta hear that you out on dates with cornball ass niggas? What the fuck is that about, Nubia?”

A whiff of alcohol tickled my nose. I shrugged out of Maine's grip, and surprisingly, he let me go without much of a fight. “Are you drunk?”

“That's not important,” Maine barked.

“Yes the fuck it is!” I barked back, nostrils flaring. “You think you can cut all ties to me and then come crashing back into my life like nothing happened? Then you got the audacity to come up in here drunk, waiting in the dark like my fucking father? You got a lot of nerve, Maine.”

"Oh, I got nerve?"

"A whole-fucking-lot of it, my nigga."

Maine rose to his full height, towering over me, everything about him alert despite the smell of liquor on his breath. "The reason why I haven't been in contact with you is because I been tearing apart this city looking for whoever shot up your party, which was the same reason why I cut my phone off and got a new number. You have no idea how much I'm risking by being with you, and you running off with some other nigga tells me so."

"Then let me know, Maine! I'm not a mind reader. I lost my parents when I was ten years old; all I know is abandonment because everyone I've ever loved is dead and the ones that hate me continue stringing me along," I said with tears streaming down my eyes. "I don't want someone coming in and out of my life when it's a convenience to them. I have a daughter now, and I want her seeing positive love. Not this."

I expected Maine to reply with one of his signature comebacks, but when he spoke it was filled with raw emotion I didn't even know the ever-cold Maine was capable of.

"I've lost everyone in this world that I've ever given a fuck about and you think I'mma just forget about the two people in the world that I do care about?" he asked, reaching out and placing an assertive hand on my waist. "I know this isn't your ideal type of relationship, but I want you, Nubia Monroe. This arrangement won't last forever. All I'm asking for is your patience; just let me handle this the best way I can and we'll be together."

I heard everything he said, except one part stood out to me. “Who's the other person you're talking about?”

“Rhea. No matter what went down between all of us, I could never make shit work with you without accepting your daughter.” Maine pulled me close and placed his head on my chest. “All I'm asking for is time, Nubia. Give a nigga some time.”

I agreed with a kiss, a simple one that set my entire body on fire. Maine's hands traveled from my waist to my face, creating a trail of heat along the way. The kiss intensified and my surroundings faded into the background—all I could think about was Maine's lips against mine and how alive they made me feel. Micah was a nice guy who took me out on a nice dinner and ended it with a nice kiss on the cheek, but he would never hold a candle to Maine, who was anything but nice. He was raw, passionate, a touch of crazy, with a hint of darkness that kept me coming back for more no matter how many times I told myself I would stay away.

“Stay the night with me,” I whispered against his lips. “She'll have you whenever she wants, but I need you tonight.”

Maine ran his hands down the back of my dress until he got to the end of it. I thought he was going to unzip it when he ripped it instead, the shredding noise echoing throughout the silent room. The pool of black fabric fluttered to the floor, leaving me standing there in nothing but my heels and the black lace panties I wore. Maine fingered them gently, tracing his long fingers around the edges for a few seconds before tearing them clean off of me.

I lay in bed basking in the multiple orgasms Maine had given me. A soft snore filled my ear and I couldn't help but laugh; Maine had gotten his nut and was fast asleep, mouth wide open and all. I placed my chin on his chest and watched him sleep, wondering when the last time was that he actually had a full night's sleep. He looked so…peaceful. I wished I could lay here all night and sleep just as easily, but I knew there was no way I would be able to without answering one particular question.

"Come on," I said, talking to the pregnancy test as I sat on the toilet. "What's the verdict…"

I wasn't sure which one was longer: a microwave minute or a pregnancy test minute. This had to be the longest ten minutes of my life, and by the time the timer went off, I was sweating bullets. With a trembling hand, I picked up the stick and looked at the results.

"Nubia?" Maine called out from the other side of the door.

I tossed the test into the trash with its box and covered both with toilet paper. "I'm good," I called out as I washed my hands. I opened up the door and found a fully dressed Maine standing there, his expression unsure. "You're leaving?"

"They'll be looking for me in another hour or so," Maine said as he wrapped me in his arms and kissed me on the forehead. "Today's the wedding and shit. Nubia, I really wish I didn't have to—"

"I'll be here," I told him, holding back the tears that threatened to fall at the news of him leaving me to marry another woman. "Do what you have to do and I'll be here waiting, Maine."

We stood there holding each other for what felt like an eternity, the only thing separating us was the buzzing of Maine's phone in his pocket. He accepted the call, and I heard Vaughn clear as day asking him where he was because Salvador came looking for him. Maine hung up with promises to be there soon. I knew I had to be looking a mess because Maine took my face into his and kissed each of my eyes.

"Don't stand here worrying about me," I told him with a shaky laugh. "Do what you have to do so you can get back sooner. Bring me back a souvenir wherever you vacation. I like key chains."

Maine kissed me softly on the lips, leaving the taste of promises of more to come in the future. "I'll be back as soon as I can, aight?"

"I know."

I closed my eyes, knowing it would make it easier for him to leave. They fluttered open at the sound of the front door closing like an exhalation of air. I trudged over to my bedroom window and watched as Maine hopped into his car and sped off into the bleary Sunday morning.

I gave my stomach a gentle pat. "There goes your daddy. Other than you and your sister, he's the only man that's ever made me feel complete. Who knows: maybe we'll complete him too."

Maine

The deeper I drove into Manhattan, the more alert I became; once I reached the hotel I knew there was no way I could walk in like I just got finished fucking after a long night of binge drinking. Salvador had spies all over the hotel keeping an eye on me, waiting for me to slip up hours before marrying his daughter. What he didn't know was that I had a few loyal niggas of my own that made sure I was able to slip out of my bachelor party without detection. I parked my car on the same block as the hotel and reached into the back seat for the bellboy jacket I borrowed from the bellhop that worked here. No one gave me a second glance as I slipped through the staff entrance, bypassing workers getting ready for work. I was back at my suite within minutes, where a nervous Vaughn sat waiting.

"Do you know how many of them cartel motherfuckers been looking for you?" Vaughn exclaimed as I shrugged out of the jacket and took a seat on the couch across from him. "Nigga, I had to tell them you were in your bedroom doing some African wedding ritual just so they wouldn't go barging in."

There was nothing I could do other than laugh at the absurdity of his statement. "And they actually believed you?"

"They ain't have no choice; I found some tribal music on Spotify and hooked it up to the speaker in your bedroom," Vaughn added, shrugging his shoulders at the incredulous look I gave him. "If you don't like how I handle shit, next time you'll find yourself back here on time. I said two hours—it's been seven."

"Nubia and I had a lot we needed to talk about."

"Sure you did…" Vaughn rose from his seat and stretched. "Now that you're back, I'mma head to my room and get some sleep. See you in a couple hours."

I laid down on the couch, figuring I could doze for another hour before I had to get up and start getting ready. Images of Nubia—her smell, taste, and the way her body felt against mine—swirled around my mind until I was knocked out cold. Banging on my door jarred me from my peaceful sleep. Wiping the drool from the corner of my mouth, I stalked over to the door and swung it open to find Vaughn standing there fully dressed in a crisp Armani tux.

"I've been calling you for the past hour. The service starts in thirty minutes, Maine," Vaughn shouted as he entered with my new barber, Supreme, in tow. "Hurry up and take a shower so we can get you lined up and ready to go before they come looking for you."

"My father's dead," I told Vaughn, but that didn't stop me from doing as I was told.

I took a quick shower, sure to rinse last night's party off of me, and was out in record time. Vaughn gave my cream Tom Ford tux a thumbs up; I wasn't a huge fan of bright colors, but the fit was perfect and had me looking like money on the outside, although I was dying on the inside. Half of it was a massive hangover I could feel coming along, and the other half was knowing that in a matter of minutes I would be marrying a woman that wasn't Nubia.

"Damn," Vaughn said, clapping me on the shoulder. "I can't believe you're doing this. Especially after what you told me last night."

"What did I tell you?"

"You don't remember? That's a first for you," Vaughn said with a laugh that I didn't return. "But like they say, a drunk mouth speaks a sober truth. I'm not telling you until I feel like the time is right, which isn't right now as you're getting ready to marry into a legacy most of us dream of."

I guess I didn't need to hear what I said last night. I had spent the past year watching Estalita plan this wedding with mild interest because I didn't give a fuck. It was nothing for me to stand up in front of a church full of people and make empty promises to a woman I felt nothing for. With Nubia it wasn't that easy anymore; the guilt I felt for choosing the game over her had me sick to my stomach. As I stood at the altar, all I could think of was the hurt look on her face at the mention of me leaving to get ready for my wedding day. Once the music started playing, I knew I had to lock those images away before I did something dangerous like walk out on Estalita and paint a huge target on both of our backs.

"She looks beautiful," Vaughn said, and the groomsmen, a mix of my soldiers and Estalita's cousins, agreed.

I could hear everyone gasping over the sound of camera shutters clicking. After what felt like forever, Estalita and Salvador finally made it to the altar. I turned around and saw the cause of the commotion; Estalita's ball gown wedding dress was a work of art that consisted of hand-stitched beading and a twenty-foot train. I could see her smiling at me through the thick veil and I gave her a rare smile back. After a year of fighting and arguing, we had made it. Who would've thought?

"You look beautiful," I mouthed, watching Estalita light up.

Everyone gushed at the moment like I knew they would. I heard Vaughn let out a small chuckle at their reaction; he had spent the better part of the week giving me tips on how to appear genuine enough to appease the cartel and so far, it was working. The murmurs of joy only intensified after I read the vows he had written for me, promising to love, cherish, and protect Estalita while treating her like the queen she is. I almost broke out into laughter at the absurdity, but kept it bottled up enough to make it to the end of the wedding.

"Do you, Jermaine Emerson, take Estalita Rosita Maria Bonita Ordonez to be your lawfully wedded wife?"

"I do," I said without hesitation.

"Do you, Estalita Rosita Maria Bonita Ordonez, take Jermaine Emerson to be your lawfully wedded husband?"

Estalita replied with a watery, "I do."

"By the power vested in me by the State of New York, I now pronounce you man and wife. You may now kiss the—"

Shots sliced through the air, turning what was supposed to be a special day into a bloody one. Guests jumped out of their seats as fixtures exploded and the men of the family whipped out heat of their own. I instinctively jumped in front of Estalita and motioned for security to get her out of here safely. I could see Sampson doing the same for his woman, firing off shots of his own at the lone figure peeking out behind the pillar on the far side of the wedding hall. Casualties dropped like flies, some elderly people caught up in the stampede while some were children. I snapped at the sight of the little small patent leather shoe peeking out from behind one of the aisles.

"Maine, get back before he kills you," Sampson shouted as he ducked low and squeezed off some shots of his own.

I started walked towards the figure with my gun raised, popping off shots. the gunman's aim faltered and he was hitting everywhere but me. His gun jammed and I used that as my opportunity to grab his ass. He turned around and booked it towards the emergency exits. I started running after him and was poised to enter the exit when Sampson stopped me.

"Fuck him!" Sampson shouted from the altar. "The cops will be here in minutes. Get rid of your burner so we can get to the hospital."

Hospital? I rushed over to where Sampson was bent over Vaughn, who was barely holding on as blood poured from his chest. I stripped out of my jacket and applied to his bullet wound.

"I went to grab my burner and he got me," Vaughn said with a chuckle. "I'm good though, you need to worry about grabbing that nigga before he gets away."

Vaughn's eyes closed for a split second and fluttered open, barely focusing. I looked up at Sampson, who was calm on the outside but I could see him panicking on the inside. There was no way in hell we could sit here waiting for the cops to show up. At the rate Vaughn was losing blood, he might not make it.

"Where's the nearest hospital?" I asked after a few seconds of mulling over my options.

Sampson pulled out his phone and after a few clicks he replied, "Twenty minutes away on foot. Five if we can get a cab."

"Fuck a cab; I'll carry him," I said resolutely as I stripped out of my shirt.

"What?" Vaughn said, his eyes widening in disbelief. "Nigga, are you crazy? You can't carry me. I got like a hundred pounds on you."

"Sampson, help him onto my back," I said, ignoring Vaughn. "Make sure my shirt is tied around him tight. I'm taking a big risk carrying him like this."

Sampson helped Vaughn onto my back and we were off, racing through the same exit doors as the gunman. For an old nigga, Sampson had no problem keeping up with me; he ran in front of me, shouting for people to move out the way so I wouldn't have to worry about nothing but Vaughn, who was groaning in my ear. People were screaming, cars screeched to a halt as we covered more ground in five minutes than an ambulance could on a busy Sunday morning in Manhattan. My muscles screamed in agony but I refused to give up; slowing down was the difference between life and death.

"It's right around the corner," Sampson shouted over his shoulder five minutes later. "I called ahead and they're expecting us."

I could see a stretcher right on the sidewalk with two nurses on either side. I picked up the pace, passing Sampson and only slowing down to keep from crashing into the stretcher. Once he was safely on it and whisked away to receive medical attention, the adrenaline start to ebb. I stalked into the hospital and took a seat in the waiting area.

Every muscle in my body screamed in relief as I relaxed.

"I've been through some wars in my day," Sampson said as he sat beside me. "Bloody ones where I was one of the last few standing. I've attended more funerals in the span of one week than most have in a lifetime. Sometimes I can still hear the gunshots in my sleep. But that, what you just did for Vaughn, was something I've never seen in my entire life. How many times have you done that?"

I thought of Foday, whose body was weak with malnutrition as I carried him through the forest until he took his last breath. "Once."

"Well it wasn't in vain; I've seen soldiers be carried into the hospital damn near dead and make it. He'll be fine," Sampson assured me.

I shook my head. "I'm not so sure about that. This isn't the first time this person has struck, Sampson, and I'm starting to think that even though I'm there all the time, it has nothing to do with me."

"You think someone showed up at your wedding just to get Vaughn?"

"And you, but they weren't expecting you to react so quickly," I said, watching Sampson for any type of indication that I was right. "If there's anything you know about the situation I'd prefer to find out now rather than later."

"What would make you think I would know something about this? Maine, you've been hitting for me for the past ten years. Me leaving out any information is the quickest way to put a target on both of our backs."

"Where's Jodeci? I haven't heard from him the entire time this went down. You been in contact with him lately?" I posed the question with the right amount of suspicion.

"You think Jodeci had something to do with this?"

"You don't think it's a coincidence that on the day Vaughn is supposed to become a lieutenant he's shot at my wedding?" Sampson let out a grunt of indignation. "If he ain't have nothing to do with this then he might know something about it. I'd call him, but he doesn't accept my calls anymore."

Sampson shook his head. "Sounds real familiar," he said with a sad laugh. "Me and my boy used to be tight just like you and Jodeci. He was my brother and we had plans to take over the streets together and build an empire. Everything was fine until he started changing. They were subtle changes, but nevertheless, he was changing and when I found out the reason was over a bitch I knew I couldn't fuck with him the way I once did. We started gunning for the same position and I refused to lose everything I dreamed of, to him and some bitch. In the end I did what I had to do."

"You killed them?"

"No," Sampson replied, shaking his head back and forth. "You killed them."

I had a feeling that was what he going to say. Whether he knew it or not, there was no way Jodeci was winning this war he started. After all these years of knowing me, Jodeci had to know he was playing with fire right now. The only reason I could think of him being this bold was because someone had given him the promise of no retribution. I glanced at Sampson and figured it all out at once. Luckily, my phone buzzing in my pocket kept me from calling him on his bullshit. It was Nubia and I knew she wouldn't call me right now if it weren't an emergency.

I rose from my seat and connected the call. "Wassup."

"Maine," Nubia whispered between sniffles. "I know you're at your wedding but I need your help right now. Someone's inside of my apartment. I'm hiding in the hamper and I don't know whether or not they're going to find me. I know it would've made more sense to call the police but I'm scared and I—ohmygosh. They're getting closer. I can't talk anymore."

"I'm on my way," I replied. "Even if you can't talk, stay on the phone."

"Everything good?" Sampson asked as I approached him.

"I gotta run somewhere real quick, but I'll be back. Call me with any updates on Vaughn."

"Of course," Sampson said, nodding his head slowly, his eyes never straying from my phone. I was halfway to the door when he called me. He shrugged out of his jacket and held it out to me. "You might wanna take this. You got Vaughn's blood all over your back."

I accepted the jacket with a curt nod. Sampson was always looking out for me like that, with his biggest gift to me being that he gave me a life when I was guaranteed insanity or death, and it kind of hurt to think he was hiding something from me. No worries though. I would get my hands on Jodeci and find out what was really going on behind my back before the knife sunk into it.

******

Nubia's place was trashed when I arrived. Her couch was knocked over, her coffee table broken to pieces, and a few chairs at her kitchen table were strewn haphazardly. Whoever broke in was trying to make it look like a fight happened when it was supposed to be far worse. I entered the bedroom and made a beeline for the closet, where the few clothing items Nubia had were strewn all over the place. The only thing that remained untouched was the large hamper with a box of wipes sitting on top of it. I moved the box and popped the top on the hamper to reveal a frightened Nubia. She started begging and crying until I bent down and tugged her from the tiny hamper.

"He was in here with someone else tearing everything up," she told me as I carried her over to the unmade bed. "I heard him calling out for me. He was in the closet when his partner called him over to look at something. They got a call and left."

"Did they sound familiar?"

Nubia nodded. "It was your friend…Jodeci. I know I only met him a couple times, but I know what he sounds like."

"Aight, you ain't gotta worry about him trying something ever again."

"Maine, I don't want you to—"

I took her hands into mine. "If I gotta choose between you and him, you'll always be the first choice, you hear me?"

"Yeah," Nubia choked out. "I'm just not used to having anyone to look out for me. The aunt I told you about? She ingrained in me that I'm not worth being anyone's anything. I'm working on getting out of that kind of destructive thinking, but Cornell and Vivica did a number on me."

I could see her venture off somewhere far, and when she returned it was with a wilted smile. "You want something to drink?" I asked.

"Please?"

While I was grabbing Nubia something to drink my phone started buzzing. In a haste to get Vaughn to the hospital, I had completely forgotten about Estalita. She was sobbing on the other end of the phone as she cussed me out in Spanish. We had tied the knot hours ago, and that was the only reason why I approached gently with any regard to her feelings.

"Everything happened so fast, one minute you were there and the next you were gone. Where are you, Jermaine? I'm at the hospital with Sampson, Shahani, and the rest of Vaughn's family."

"I'm out tracking this nigga down," I lied. "I'll be back at the hospital in a few, aight?"

"Okay, *papí*. Stay safe."

"I will."

Nubia sat at the edge of the bed playing with her fingers, her head hung low. She accepted the glass of water with trembling hands, and gulped it down quickly. A burp escaped her, which she apologized profusely for, although I found it cute.

"Everything is okay now, Maine. I can go over to Cheyenne's place. You can get back to your wife and wedding celebration," Nubia replied with a sad smile. "I shouldn't have called you in the first place."

I silenced her with a kiss. "You can call me anytime, day or night, and I'll be there. Don't ever hesitate to reach out for me." My phone started buzzing again. "Lemme take this call real quick."

I stepped into the bathroom and balked at the caller ID. *Who in their right mind would be calling me private,* I thought as I connected the call. I was expecting Jodeci, but was surprised with someone completely different.

"I ain't mean to fuck up your wedding like that, my nigga," the wildcard said to me. "It was one of those rare opportunities where almost everyone I wanted was in the same room."

"Who the fuck is this?"

"I can't give you that information yet, but I can let you know that my beef ain't with you unless you want it to be. Step aside, lemme murk these niggas, and you ain't gotta worry about being caught in the middle of this shit ever again. You already got your territory and all I'm looking to do is take back what's mine."

I took a seat on the toilet, mulling over how to approach this next. "Give me one good reason why I should sit the fuck back and mind my business."

"Because had I not shot Jodeci at the club your girl would dead."

I was convinced the reason why Jodeci stopped shooting was because I got him, but if this wildcard was telling the truth then it might be better to work with him than against him. At least until I got what I wanted and popped him.

"Leave Vaughn out of this; you keep gunning for him and you'll find a real enemy in me."

"I think I have room in my heart to make a call like that. He wasn't the leader anyway."

"Who was? Jodeci?"

"Ask my girl, Shahani," the wildcard replied before hanging up.

I stared down at my phone in shock. "What the fuck does Shabambam have to do with this?"

This shit was getting beyond complicated. I had one best friend trying to kill my girl, the other fighting for his life, and I had a pretty good feeling my mentor knew more about the situation than he let on.

Nia

"Nia!" Essence screamed at the top of her lungs. "Nia, wake the fuck up! It's an emergency!"

I stared at my phone and placed it facedown on my pillow. "Bitch, what is it?"

"Girl, Vaughn has been shot!"

I bolted upright, straining my stitches. "What?" I screamed in agony as I picked up my phone. "What the fuck do you mean Vaughn's been shot? Where? When? Don't tell me you called me with half assed information, Essence!"

"He got shot at Maine's wedding. It's all over the news. Maine carried him to the hospital on his back and everyone is talking about it. Just Google 'Butta shot.'"

I placed her on speaker and inserted Vaughn's stage name into Google, gasping at the search results. An armed gunman snuck into a prominent Mexican businessman's daughter's wedding, and let out a hail of gunshots. Five people were killed, including one of the flower girls, and several were injured. My jaw dropped at the pictures and videos…oh the videos. I knew Maine wasn't normal by any means, but he had to be superhuman to carry Vaughn so far without breaking his stride.

"You see it right?" Essence brought me back to reality. "Are you going to the hospital?"

"Of course I am; that's my man and he needs me."

"Want me to meet you there?"

"Sure, girl. Just in case Drea's annoying ass decides that she wants to show up and start some shit. I'll see you in a few."

I swung my legs over the king-sized bed in my hotel suite and trudged to my closet. Normally, I would be mortified at the idea of anyone seeing me look like less than my best, but I knew all television outlets would be posted out front and I needed to look the part of the concerned girlfriend. I skipped my usual makeup routine and threw on a pair of sweats along with an oversized T-shirt with Vaughn's picture on it. I grabbed my purse, shades, and rushed from the room, calling an Uber on my way downstairs. It pulled up as I reached the front of the hotel, and proceeded to take me on one of the longest rides of my life.

What started out as a relationship of convenience between Vaughn and I sprouted into something more. Sure, he was with Drea because she was mentally unstable, but that never stopped him from checking in on me every night. We wouldn't always fuck either; sometimes we would watch TV, play card games, or even eat out at a local restaurant. People always made assumptions about me being with him for the money, but when I woke up in the hospital with Vaughn by my side, I knew he was someone I could see myself with indefinitely.

That is, if Drea moved out of the fucking way.

"Nia," Essence called out as my Uber pulled up in front of the hospital. "I just got finished talking with the receptionist and she said

Vaughn's out of surgery. I got the room number and everything."

I followed Essence through the busy hospital. There were murmurs through the crowded lobby and I could see the flash from a few cameras go off. *Of course fans would post up in the lobby just to get pictures to post on MediaTakeOut and World Star,* I thought to myself as I studiously ignored the whispering. Essence did the exact opposite; she made sure that the camera caught her good angles as we made a beeline for the elevator and didn't stop posing until we were safely inside.

"Really, bitch?" I asked her once the doors closed.

"What? My future husband could be on the blogs and I always gotta stay ready. Unlike you, I don't have a rapper to fall back on."

I rolled my eyes. "I'm not falling back on Vaughn. We're actually working on getting me into the studio and everything."

"You got bars, bitch?"

"I might!" I retorted, nearly killing myself to squeeze through the elevator doors to get away from her. "But now is not the time to be discussing all of that. I need to make it to Vaughn."

My heart was hammering against my chest as I approached Vaughn's room. I could see that it was filled with people. He was always telling me about his family, but we decided to wait a little while longer before I met them. As I saw them gathered around him I wished we would've reconsidered. I felt awkward as his parents and sister clocked my entrance. Vaughn's mother was gorgeous, with rich brown skin and his hazel eyes, and his father was even darker, but I could see that Vaughn was a splitting image of him. Like Vaughn, his sister was a perfect mix of her parents, except she had the same skin tone as them. They all smiled politely at me as I crept into the room with Essence backing me up.

"I'm sorry, dear, you must have the wrong room," Vaughn's mother said kindly.

I shook my head. "No, I'm here to see Vaughn. I'm his…friend."

"Friend?" his mother's eyes lit up in recognition. "Oh…you're the 'friend' that came between Drea and my son. Get out. Now. Before I call security and have them drag you out of here like the trash that you are."

"Excuse me?" I barked.

"You heard my mother-in-law: get the fuck out!" a cold voice said from the doorway.

Drea stood there with a wide ass smirk on her face, shaking her head from side-to-side as she approached me. Essence went to jump in the middle of us, but I placed a hand on her chest; this bitch had been trying me for the longest with her social media smear campaign, and she was about to get these hands, hospital or not.

"You know damn well Vaughn would want me here by his side when he wakes up," I said to her, motioning to the bed where Vaughn was recuperating. "You might be the one in public, but a piece of his heart belongs to me."

"Because you stole it!" Drea shot back. "You aren't the one that has spent countless nights up with Vaughn editing and rewriting his verses, booking venues for his appearances, setting up photo shoots, scamming him clothes so he could look good all the time. But you wanna come in here while the momentum is hot and he's gaining a name for himself? The only reason why Vaughn is still fucking with you is because I allow him to. He knows that without me he wouldn't be half the man he is, and that is why I got the ring!"

Drea waved her left hand in my face, revealing a gorgeous two-carat diamond ring. I refused to let this bitch one up me in front of everyone so I rubbed my stomach and replied, "You may have the ring, but I have the baby."

"You're lying," Drea accused, her eyes flickering to my stomach and back at me.

"Am I?" I walked by her, making sure to brush my stomach up against her. "Or are you mad that he chose me to carry his child over you?"

Drea shook her head, a devious smile lighting up her face. "You don't get it, do you? With Vaughn in the hospital recovering, it's up to me to pay for your hotel room, approve the payments you make with the card he gave you, and everything else you rely on him for. I was going to be nice and maybe keep on handling those bills, but I think you need to learn not to bite the hand that feeds you, so consider yourself burned. Your room is paid for up until the end of the week. By then, you need to find somewhere else to be."

"You can have as much power as you need to while Vaughn is recovering because once he wakes up, all that mouth will be no more. I'll be right back, Drea. The only way you'll ever get rid of me is if I hear the words from Vaughn's mouth," I said loud enough for Vaughn's family to get the idea as well. "C'mon, Essence, lets get out of here before I fuck around and really hurt some feelings."

"Damn, Nia," Essence exclaimed as we headed back to the elevators. "You read that bitch her rights. She didn't wanna admit it, but it was obvious that she's shook. I can't believe his family really tried to play you like you haven't been on his arm for months. That was shady as fuck..."

I tuned Essence out as she went on and on about the situation, reliving it from everyone's perspective. As much as this might be petty drama for her, I had to figure out what the fuck I was going to do by Friday morning. All the money I had went to Donovan, and his family had already drained his accounts before his body was cold. I had not a single dollar to my name, I burned my bridges with Shahani, and it would be nearly impossible for me to fuck around with any of these niggas without ruining my developing reputation. There was no way in hell I was willing to go from being Butta's girl to an escort.

"Oh shit, Roderick is calling," Essence said, making a dash for the exit so she could answer the phone for her new pimp. I stepped outside just in time to hear, "Hey, Daddy. I met up with Nia at the hospital because her boyfriend was shot... Yes, Daddy, I'll be there ASAP."

"That nigga really makes you call him Daddy?" I asked once she hung up.

She rolled her eyes. "He damn sure does. I never thought I would live to see the day where I missed Donovan's crazy ass. He had his ways, but they were nothing compared to this old country bama. I swear if the money wasn't good I'd go right back to stripping."

"You need to, and give that tired ass pussy a rest," I joked.

Essence gave me the finger as she hailed a cab. "Whateva, bitch." She lifted her shirt, revealing her perky 34 DD's, which nearly caused a car accident as three taxis skidded to a halt. She hopped into the first one and said, "I'll see you later, boo."

"Later," I said with a wave.

With Essence gone, I was able to let down the mask I had been wearing. Tears got to falling and next thing I knew, I was sitting on the floor crying my eyes out. For the first time in my life I was left without a backup plan because it was lying in critical condition. I knew I couldn't call Shahani, I couldn't sell my pussy, and I couldn't sit around waiting for Drea's bitter ass to lower the boom.

"You're the last person I would've expected to be sitting out here crying because some bitch punked you in front of your man's family. Get up off the floor and stop crying," someone said from beside me.

I looked up and found Alonzo sitting right beside me. He was still as fine as ever, looking like a tall Larenz Tate. Giving him my best cold shoulder, I said, "You got a lot of fucking nerve coming to sit next to me after you tried to kill me."

"Nia, both you and I know that if I wanted you dead, you'd be six feet under."

"So then why did you shoot me?"

"Because you deserved it. You set up your cousin to be killed."

I scoffed. "Like I said, I didn't know he was going to actually kill her. I thought we'd beat her up, hoe her out a little, and send her back to Sampson."

"It doesn't matter what your intention was; you set up your cousin and I had to punish you for it. Your wound healed, right?"

"Yeah..."

"Aight then. Consider it water under the bridge."

I cut my eyes at him. "You must be out of your damn mind to think that just because you came over here with some rationalizations that I'mma just move on and forgive you. Give me one good reason why I should."

"Because I can give you a place to rest your head."

I rolled my eyes. "I can get that anywhere. My girl has an extra room I can use."

"I can hit you off with ten stacks on the spot to start."

"Ten stacks ain't shit to a bitch like me," I lied through my teeth, knowing even one stack was needed right now.

"How about this: you help me with my situation, and I'll handle the one you got up there."

"What do you mean by 'handle'?"

"Whatever you want, consider it done." Lonzo held his hand out. "We got a deal?"

I got a good look at Lonzo: he was still fine as ever, except there was this hunger in him I never saw while he was with Shahani. *Maybe I could hustler hop myself into something better,* I thought as I placed my hand into Lonzo's large one.

"You got a deal."

Sampson

I watched as Maine rushed from the hospital with that murderous glint in his eye. If the timing was correct, then his girlfriend should be dead by now. I told Jodeci to play with her a little before he killed her, give her some time to spend on the phone with Maine before she was reunited with her parents. Vanessa spit that girl out; they were twins and once I laid eyes on her I was hit with a strong whiff of nostalgia. After the nostalgia wore off, I recalled how that pretty face and those mysterious eyes did a number on me. No, that girl had to go, and Shahani would be sad for a little while, but I had something to take her attention off of it.

"Sampson?"

Shahani stood in the middle of the emergency room looking around. I rose from my seat and held my arms out to her. She rushed into them, nearly knocking me off of my feet. My baby was passionate, but I had never seen this side of her before. She was sobbing into my chest, rambling about how she was worried sick.

"Everything happened so fast. My last memory of you was you jumping in front of me to protect me and I just couldn't bear the thought of 'what if that's the last time we saw each other?'" Shahani cried.

"Calm down, baby," I soothed, taking her face into my hands.

"I'm not going nowhere, you hear me?"

She nodded. "Yeah."

"How about you take a seat and let me get you something to drink, okay? How about a cup of tea?" Shahani nodded. "All right, I'll be right back."

I barely cleared the automatic doors when my phone started buzzing in my pocket. It was Jodeci, and if he knew what was good for him, he would have some good news for me.

"Maine just left out of here in a rush, presumably to find his girlfriend's body. Am I right?" The pregnant pause on the other end let me know that wasn't the case. "Jodeci—"

"Sampson I couldn't do it!" Jodeci exclaimed. "I got there and we started trashing the place like you told us to. It gave shorty enough time to get into the closet. We got in the room and I was in the closet getting ready to fuck shit up when I saw—"

"I don't give a fuck what you saw," I barked, scaring passersby. "I gave you one fucking job, Jodeci, one job and you can't seem to get it right. This is the second time you've fucked up—"

"I already told you what happened the night of the party. Someone was up there and they got a shot off before I could get the girl!"

"All I keep hearing from you is excuses, and you know what? Since you can't seem to get this shit right I guess I'll have to handle it."

"Sampson I could've handled it right then and there but I think there's something you should know—"

"I don't need to know nothing except the girl's location. Have it within the next few hours and I'll show you how a real nigga gets shit done," I said, hanging up before he could ply me with any more excuses.

I was so heated Shahani's large tea felt cold as I carried it back to the hospital. She wasn't alone; Estalita was there along with her security detail. She had changed out of her wedding gown and was wearing a demure dress, probably what she had planned to wear on her honeymoon. Shorty was looking behind me and to the sides of me in search of her husband, who went off to be with another bitch before even checking to make sure she was good. I felt sorry for the poor girl, but not sorry enough to ever betray one of my own.

"Where's Maine?" she asked, covering her mouth as a sob escaped her. "He wasn't hurt, was he?"

"No, he went to handle some business for me," I lied, placing a consoling hand on her shoulder as I led her back to her seat next to Shahani. "All the soldiers are out there looking for the motherfucker that did this or any word on him. I don't mean to scare you but…this isn't the first time he's done this. He shot at Maine and I a few weeks back while we were at the shop."

Another sob passed Estalita's hands. "Someone's trying to kill Jermaine? *Ay dios mio*. And he's out there trying to find the person himself? I need to call *Papí* and—"

"No, sweetheart, ain't no need to call your daddy; this happened on my territory and we'll have it handled promptly."

"It happened at my wedding, which makes it the business of my family," Estalita shot back.

I leaned in and said to her, "You have no idea who you married, do you? Maine is a savage. No matter how much of your family joins this fight, they'll never have equal to even half of his manpower. He's playing nice right now, but you just wait until the sun goes down. Everything will be handled."

"So I'm supposed to sit here and let him handle his business by himself?"

"That's exactly what he would want."

Estalita simmered herself down and kept Shahani company as we waited. I paced the emergency room, hoping we would get an update soon. If I was going to handle my business tonight then I needed to be out of here before dusk. No sooner had the thought came to me did the surgeon come out asking for Vaughn's family. Time stood still as the surgeon waited for all of us to gather around. Vaughn's family, who had only arrived an hour ago, silently cried at the surgeon's presence.

"Your son lost a lot of blood but we were able to stabilize him, remove the bullet, and perform a transfusion. He's going to be out for a day or so, but we're expecting a full recovery."

There were shouts of celebration throughout the emergency room, with strangers clapping and a few whistling. Shahani and Estalita were hugging each other tight, and I could see a friendship blossoming between the two of them. Let them hang out few more times, and she might not even notice the fact that her friend is missing.

"Today was a long day. I just wanna go home and soak in a bubble bath and forget all of this madness happened," Shahani said on the ride home. "Sampson?"

"Yes?"

"Why would someone do something like this, and to Vaughn of all people? He's as harmless as they come. According to Nia, he isn't even in the game."

I shrugged. "Sometimes bad shit happens to good people. Don't worry about none of that though; I'll take care of this. We're going to war."

The rest of the ride was quiet, with Shahani sleeping peacefully. She looked so beautiful I didn't want to wake her up once we arrived at the house. I picked her up bridal style and smiled as she wrapped her arms around me without waking up. As we crossed the threshold into the house, I could picture myself carrying her like this on our wedding night.

"Damn, I'm really falling for you," I whispered as I placed her gently into bed and watched her curl up into a ball.

Her eyes fluttered open for a second, gazing around until they focused on me. "Aren't you coming to bed?"

"I gotta handle some business," I replied, leaning in and kissing her on the forehead. "Get some rest and I'll see you in the morning."

"Okay. I'll make breakfast. Some waffles and stuff…" she murmured before falling right back to sleep.

I was halfway to the bedroom door when I felt it. We weren't alone. Someone snuck into my house thinking they would bring harm to me and my woman. I made a beeline for the closet, dipping through and checking every cabinet and drawer before making my way to the bathroom. Everything remained untouched down to the spot I left my cologne before leaving out to the wedding. *Nah, someone's here,* I thought to myself as I dropped to my knees to check underneath the bed. There was only one person I could think of that would be able to be in my house and evade me.

"Jodeci," I hissed into my phone as I slipped out of my bedroom. I went to the next bedroom and searched it just as thoroughly. "Did you find out where the girl is staying?"

"She's at Cheyenne's house. You'll need to be buzzed up, so there's no element of surprise," Jodeci replied hesitantly.

"I don't plan on doing anything in the building," I said. "Now send me the address and apartment number."

"Bet."

With that out of the way, I proceeded to search my entire house from top to bottom, not missing a crack or crevice. I was irritated, exhausted, and ready to take my Black ass to bed when I thought of how this needed to be nipped in the bud tonight. My phone lit up with the address and it was game time.

Maine's little girlfriend would die tonight, and if he wanted to jump in and save her he could eat a bullet too. I brought him into the game and I could certainly take him out.

******

Cheyenne looked me up and down, licking her lips as she opened the door a tad bit wider. "Hey, Sampson," she said, drawing my name out. "Long time no see."

"I can say the same," I replied, eyeing the T-shirt and panties she wore. "I'm looking for your girl, Nubia. She here?"

"She sure is. Come on in…"

I entered and took a seat on the couch. Two little girls sat at the table eating dinner. Their curious eyes followed me on my way there, studying my rumpled clothes and tired eyes. I didn't want to kill any kids, but there was no way in hell I could leave anyone in this house alive if Nubia didn't comply. The warm smile on her face told me I probably wouldn't have to worry too much.

"Hey, Sampson," she greeted cheerily, plopping down in the armchair across from me. "Cheyenne said you wanted to see me. Is everything okay with Shahani?"

"I don't know if you heard, but earlier there was a shooting at Maine's wedding. Shahani is pretty shaken up by it and she could use someone to keep her company. I was thinking maybe you could come by the house tonight and keep her company since I won't be around."

Nubia shook her head. "I can most definitely stop by tomorrow morning, but tonight I really can't. Rhea is coming down with a slight cold and I don't want to carry her back and forth."

"I can slip Cheyenne a stack to take care of your daughter for the night."

"I'm sorry…I'll call Sha, check in with her tonight, and make plans to meet up with her tomorrow morning. That's all I can do right now." She paused hesitantly. "I'm not supposed to be talking about this, but earlier someone broke into my apartment. Fortunately, my daughter wasn't home, but I can't help but think: what if she was? I need to spend tonight with my baby, and if Shahani knew what happened, she would be more than understanding."

Her smile dropped as mine grew. "I was trying to be nice about this because the kids are here and your baby is in the next room, but I guess I gotta shoot straight. You are leaving with me. Right now. Call Cheyenne over here and tell her you need to come with me for the same excuse I gave you."

"And if I don't?" she had the nerve to shoot back.

"Then I'll slaughter everyone in this house," I shot back, my eyes telling her that I included her child. "Now do what the fuck I said, and quickly."

"I need shoes."

"There are shoes right by the door."

"Cheyenne," Nubia called without taking her eyes off of mine. When Cheyenne arrived she went back to her pleasant self. "I have to make a real quick run with Sampson to check on Shahani. You mind watching Rhea for me?"

"Of course not. Does she need a bottle or anything?" Cheyenne asked, her eyes flickering between the two of us.

"Nope. She should be good for a few hours. I should be back by then," Nubia replied rising from her seat. "Can I borrow your sneakers?"

"Sure. Just make sure you don't mess 'em up 'cause if I have to call my sneaker plug to get me another pair he's gonna have a fit. Can you bring home some toilet paper?"

"I'll be sure to bring the big bag. There's no point in bringing a little bag because it seems like you be eating it," Nubia joked on her way out the door. We barely cleared the door when she said, "Do whatever it is that you need to do to me, but leave them out of this. They know how to keep quiet. You won't have to worry about anyone saying anything."

"I'll make that decision," I said, pushing her into the elevator. "Now be quiet and only speak when you're spoken to."

Nubia crossed her arms and not another peep was heard out of her until we were safely inside of my car. The doorman didn't even bother to give us a second glance as we passed him by. So far, everything was running smoothly. All I had to do was get the little bitch to the warehouse, handle my business, and I would be home before the sun came up. I shot Jodeci a quick message telling him to meet me so he could see how ruthless you needed to be in this game.

"So you're the one that's been trying to kill me," Nubia said after a lengthy silence.

"Didn't I tell you to only speak when you're spoken to?"

"The least you could do is give me a reason why you kidnapped me."

"I don't have to do a damn thing," I snapped. In a calmer voice, I replied, "you'll find out everything you need to when the time is right."

"If you kill me, Maine is going to kill you. Gut you like a fucking fish. Snatch your intestines out your body and strangle you with them. Cut you up piece by piece and feed you to yourself before you die."

I let go of a hearty chuckle. "If you think Maine is going to turn on me after everything I've ever done for him, you're stupider than I initially thought." My phone lit up from the cup holder. I placed it to my ear, refusing to give her little smart ass the satisfaction. "Talk to me."

"Wassup," Maine said casually. "I'm tired'a than a muhfucker."

"Same here. This shit with Vaughn got me exhausted and the night ain't even over. Where you at right now?"

"Eh…riding around trying to clear my head. Ain't so bad though cause I got company. Right, friend?"

"Sampson, what the fuck is going on?" Shahani shouted in the background.

Nubia's head snapped towards me. "What the fuck is Maine doing with Shahani?"

"I knew you were in my house," I growled. "Where?"

"Right on top of your shelves looking right at you search all over the place. That's your problem: you're very farsighted. What would make you think I would allow you to get this close to Nubia without some type of plan? You wanna fuck with my woman, I can do the same thing with yours. So where we meeting up at?"

"The warehouse," I said, and hung up before he could get another word in edgewise. "Your boyfriend has my woman."

"And you have his! What were you going to tell Shahani about me disappearing, huh? She's like a sister to me, so if you thought she was gonna just let it go and move on with her life, you thought wrong."

"Sister? You stopped speaking to her over your boyfriend. Some sister she was to you!"

"You don't know anything about that situation to even speak on it! You don't know a damn thing about me!"

"I know that you remind me of your mother; she couldn't shut up to save her life either," I barked, my chest rising and falling with anger.

Nubia's eyes widened, then turned to slits. "You knew my mother? I met you how many times and you never mentioned knowing my mother." She swallowed loudly, preparing both of us for the next question to fly out of her mouth. "You had her killed, didn't you?"

I sighed. "How you know I wasn't the one that did it?"

"You're too big. The person that did it was smaller," she replied. "I replay that moment in my mind every single day and I always wondered, why? Why did they have to be taken from me so soon? Why did you kill them?"

What was I supposed to tell the girl, that I killed her father because he stole my territory and my woman? That my bruised ego wouldn't allow me to let Apollo Monroe walk the streets with my girl? That I had the both of them killed for a come up? I didn't know what to say so I said nothing at all. Nubia had grown quiet as well. She sank into her seat and cried the rest of the way to the warehouse. I didn't even get a peep of dissent as I grabbed her out the car and placed my gun to her back. Jodeci was inside smoking a cigarette when we arrived.

"You were part of this too?" Nubia asked through her tears. "Maine is like your brother. How could you do something like this to him?"

Jodeci turned his head away in shame; as much as he pretended to not give a fuck about Maine, shorty's words hit him where it hurts. I knew that had to be the reason why he punked out. If he killed her then he knew there was no way him and Maine would ever be close again.

Too bad he ain't know that didn't matter, because tonight Maine would become an enemy whether Nubia was dead or not.

"Sampson, there's something I need to tell you about her," Jodeci urged as I led her to the tarp set up in the middle of the floor. "Shorty's pregnant. That's why I didn't finish the hit."

I faltered for only a split second before continuing towards the tarp. "Why am I supposed to care about that?" Jodeci was at a loss for words. "That's what I thought. Now stand here and watch how an original gangsta handles shit. Get down on your knees, girl."

Nubia stepped onto the tarp and dropped to her knees. "Make it quick. Don't leave me to suffer like my father did."

I slowly stalked around her until I was facing her. "He deserved it. Your daddy was a thief that got exactly what he deserved. You're right; I'm not the one that killed your parents. But if I ever had the chance to go back in time, I would be the one to pull the trigger and that would've included you. Don't hold your head down," I said, taking my gun and lifting her head all the way up. "Look at me when I'm talking to—"

The lighting in the warehouse changed and there, underneath Nubia's chin, was a star-shaped birthmark. It was perfectly centered like it was tattooed. The only other people to ever have those birthmarks were my two children and myself. Mine and Jr's were covered, but on my baby girl? Hers was bright as day. Jodeci, who knew Ava, had seen it on plenty of occasions. Like me, he was rooted to the floor in shock.

"Yo, Sampson," he said after a minute of us staring. "Is that what I think that is?"

I removed my gun and placed it into my pants. Nubia lowered her head and began grabbing at her neck. She stared between the two of us, her expression going from fearful to confused.

"What?" she asked. "Why'd you put your gun down?"

I stared down at her, taking a closer look at how we had the same lips, eyebrows... hell, she even had the same teeth as me. That birthmark opened up Pandora's box, and now it was painfully obvious that my desire for revenge kept me from seeing what was right in front of me.

With the calmest voice I could muster up, I replied, "Because... I'm your father."

Maine

Shahani sat in the passenger seat sick, sweating, and squirming. The tension between the two of us was thick enough to slice with a knife. I guess that was to be expected when you woke someone up with a gun to their head. Of course there had been some resistance, but once I mentioned Alonzo, all the fight Shahani was inflated with disappeared. She was the perfect hostage, slipping into her shoes, grabbing a coat, and following me out of the house. If there was one thing the game taught me was that it's easier to control people with your words than a weapon. Tonight was no different.

"How much did Alonzo tell you?" Shahani asked, breaking the awkward silence.

"He told me to ask you why he was popping off everywhere. So… what's the story?"

"I barely know it my damn self. All I know is the night he was 'killed,' involved a robbery. We were coming home from dinner when a couple men robbed us. They took my engagement ring and Lonzo's jewelry. He went off to find them and never came back. I always heard it was a setup by his old partner that wanted to sell their territory."

"What's the partner's name?"

"Blue."

"Sampson used to do business with a Blue way back in the day.

That nigga moved up out of the hood about six years ago. Took his whole family with him and everything," I said, recalling the expansion. I also recalled one night in particular when Vaughn and Jodeci went to run an errand for Sampson while I stayed behind because I wasn't feeling well. "I know why he's doing all of his. He wants everyone involved in the robbery and taking of his territory. Ain't no asking for that shit back either; Sampson owns it."

"Which is why he's been trying to get rid of him too," Shahani finished. "Which is why he asked me what I was doing this weekend. He knew Vaughn would be at the wedding so he showed up to take his shot. This is all my fault. How could I have been so stupid?"

"You been stupid, Shakazulu. You should've told Sampson about this when it first happened. This nigga would've been dead a long time ago."

"So he could accuse me of being with the shits? And my name is Shahani," she finished irritably.

"Whatever you say, Shake Shack."

"Shahani!"

"Shalalala-boom-boom-she-lay."

"Fuck you, Maine," she shot back, giving me the finger and returning her attention to the window. "I can't believe Sampson would pull some shit like this, and to all people, sweet Nubia. I…I loved this man. After this entire situation I don't think I can look him in the eye."

I clutched the wheel tight, thinking of how I would soon find myself in the same predicament. With all of this coming out, there was no way the truth could be hidden from Nubia much longer. She would put two and two together soon enough and find out that I played a large part in the worst day of her life. I knew I would have to come clean one day, but I never imagined this series of events being the catalyst. It was all I could keep my mind on for the rest of the trip. It was going on midnight when we arrived. Two cars were parked out front, one belonging to Sampson and the other belonging to—

"Fucking Jodeci," I muttered under my breath as I pulled my piece from my pants. "I got something for his ass."

"I thought we were here to make a safe trade. There was no mention of shots being fired," Shahani said as I gripped her up and placed my gun to her head. "This ain't for nothing but leverage. You stay calm and you don't have to worry about me shooting your head off your shoulders."

We crept quietly into the warehouse, overhearing the conversation from afar. I saw Nubia kneeling on the tarp as Sampson spoke to her. I removed my gun from Shahani's head and was prepared to hit Sampson at point blank range when Nubia rose to her feet and backed away from him, shaking her head at whatever he said. My eyes traveled over Sampson and Jodeci's body language; neither one was armed and they were staring at Nubia like she was a science project.

"Father? You're my father?!" she screamed at the top of her lungs. "No, you're lying. Ain't no way in hell my mother would ever get with a lowdown snake like you."

"Father?" Shahani echoed, turning all the attention to us.

I removed my grip on her, and followed her over to the stricken Nubia, who was still shaking her head. Shahani hugged her tight, smoothing her hair as she cried. I stood in front of the two with my gun still drawn; both of these niggas were once blood to me and now I had no idea where I stood with either one of them.

"Ain't no need for all of that," Sampson choked out. "She's mine."

"Yours?"

Jodeci motioned to his chin. "She's got the mark. All Sampson's kids got a birthmark and she has the same one. This beef? It's over."

"Ain't a motherfucking thing over," I retorted, aiming my gun at Jodeci. "You tried on two separate occasions to kill Nubia."

"He didn't want to," Nubia piped up. "He could've killed me back at the apartment but he didn't. Leave him alone and let's just get the hell out of here."

Shahani started pulling Nubia towards the door. Sampson called out to her, only to get the middle finger thrown up at him. I don't know what made him think her reaction would be any different with her knowing he was getting ready to slaughter her friend. I told him as much and had it thrown right back in my face.

"And what? You think you and her are gon' live happily ever after once she finds out your role in this entire situation?" Sampson countered. "With some time I might be able to fix my relationship with Shahani, but you? Once she finds out what you did she'll never forgive you."

He was right, and there was no reason for me to tell him so just to stroke his ego. I lowered my gun and followed the women out of the warehouse, knowing neither man had the heart to shoot me in the back. Nubia and Shahani were in the backseat when I climbed in. I pulled off and tried to zone out, but listening to Nubia recount her night broke my heart.

"I was back at my birthday party again. He had me get on my knees and I remembered my mother down on hers, begging for her life when all I heard was…pop"—I winced at the feeble pop that passed her lips—"I always wondered why my parents were chosen and knowing it had to do with some fucked up love triangle…it hurts so bad."

Shahani continued soothing her. "Honey, I know how you're feeling. We're gonna get through this, I promise you. The most important part is knowing that you don't have to worry about him trying to hurt you again."

"How about I put y'all up in a hotel tonight. The last thing you want is to go home and scare everyone," I suggested, stealing a glance in the rearview mirror.

Nubia remained silent so long that Shahani answered for her. "You know what? I'm not going back to Sampson's place so I'll need somewhere to stay for the night. A hotel sounds perfect."

The rest of the ride was spent in silence, with the only sound heard being a sniffle here and there from Nubia. I was relieved when we finally pulled up to the hotel. Nubia was out of the car before I could come to a complete stop. Shahani shot me a "I don't know what's wrong with her" look, but I had a feeling what was going on.

"Book three rooms," I told Shahani, handing her the debit card to my old bank account. "Tonight is gon' be a long night."

I rolled up my window and made a call to Estalita, who I was sure had to be waiting by the phone. She picked up on the second ring, wide-awake from the sound of it. I expected her to start whining, but was pleasantly surprised when all she did was ask me how I was doing.

“I'm Aight, but it's about to get crazy out here, which is why I need you to do me a huge favor: I need you to go on our honeymoon without me,” I said, removing my ear right before she went off.

Spanish profanities filled the car for a full minute followed by heavy sobbing and some cussing in English. I was honestly amazed at how she didn't even take a breath through her entire diatribe. When she was finally out of gas, I spoke my piece since I knew she wouldn't be able to interrupt me.

“There is no way on earth I'll feel safe with you being in NYC while all this shit is going down. Enjoy seeing your family back in México. Take some pictures, send me videos, and have a good time. Invite your friends if you want. But I need you gone first thing in the morning.”

“If that's what you really want then I will oblige; you are my husband and I will respect your wishes. I love you, Jermaine,” Estalita replied. “*Hasta luego.*”

“*Hasta luego,*” I replied.

Truth be told, I only wanted Estalita out of the country so I could spend some time cleaning up this entire mess with Nubia. I couldn't do it if I had a wife at home waiting on me and crying over my every move. With her squared away, now I could focus on shit that mattered. But first, I needed a hot shower.

******

Nubia was sitting in the center of the king-sized bed wearing nothing but a towel when I came in. She wore a towel around her still moist body and one wrapped her hair tight. I watched as she stared at her toes in deep thought. For a second I thought she was ignoring me, but the longer I stood there, I realized she was in a trance. I sat at the edge of the bed and gave her ankle a gentle shake, which scared her half to death.

"I ain't mean to scare you," I apologized. I held out a duffle bag filled with some clothes from her birthday gifts. "I thought you might need something to put on."

"Thanks," she replied drily, accepting the bag and placing it next to her. "I guess I'll see you tomorrow?"

"Nubia, why don't we talk about what has you upset—"

"You mean how you knew who was trying to kill me this entire time and thought it wasn't worth me knowing? Maine you looked me in the eye and swore that those shots from my birthday party weren't for me and I believed you!" Nubia exploded. "Had you been upfront and honest with me I could've made extra precautions for myself and my child!"

"I made the precautions!"

"Yet, Jodeci managed to get into my building and damn near kill me," Nubia countered, deflating after her outburst. She sunk into the pillows and stared at me. "If you could hide something like that, what else are you hiding from me? Hmmm? Did you know that Sampson had my parents killed?"

I remained silent.

"Maine...please don't tell me you knew Sampson had killed my parents and smiled in my face this entire time."

"I didn't know until you told me the story of how your parents were killed," I admitted. "I wanted to tell you but..."

"But what, Maine? What's your excuse for not telling me something like this?"

"Because I was in love with you and I knew that if you knew the truth you would hate me."

Tears slid down Nubia's cheeks. "You love me?"

"Of course I love you. Everything I've done from that point was to protect you, Nubia. I didn't tell you about the shooting because I didn't want to worry you with something I would personally handle."

"I love you, too," Nubia said, grabbing my hand and propelling herself into my arms. She planted a salty kiss on my lips. "I know we don't have the most conventional relationship, but how do you expect it to work when you keep on hiding things from me? First it was Estalita, and now this? Maine, I'm not a fragile flower. You can be real with me."

I replied with a kiss, the last one I knew we would share once I dropped this bomb on her. "I promise to from here on out...which is why I need to tell you something."

Nubia sat back in her spot. "What now?"

"Yes, I knew that Sampson was the one that ordered the hit, but there's more to it."

"How much more?"

"I already told you stories about my childhood, but I didn't tell you what happened later on. When I was ten, I was drafted into the Sierra Leone Civil War. I didn't spend much time in it before being rescued, but what I did certainly never left me. After some time in an orphanage, I was given the opportunity to come to America to start a new life. I accepted and was brought here to work for Sampson. Impressed by my skills, Sampson sent me on my very first mission, which was to kill a rival dealer and his family."

"No," Nubia cried, shaking her head back and forth. "Maine, please don't tell me what I think you're telling me."

"If there was one thing I learned from the war, it was to follow orders. So I went to the party and did what I was told." I found it harder to speak over Nubia's cries for me to stop. "I killed Apollo Monroe, his mother, his wife, uncles, cousins—"

"Shut up!" Nubia howled, slapping and punching me, uncaring of either towel falling off of her. "Shut up! Don't you dare say his name!"

I ate her punches, knowing it was only right that she get her frustration out. "The only person from the family I didn't kill was his daughter."

"You should have!" Nubia screamed, her face nothing but a mess of hair and tears. "You should have put a bullet in me because what you left me with was worse than death, Maine! Do you know what I went through after that? I ended up stuck at my bitter aunt's house where she beat me because she hated my mother. And my uncle? My uncle made me his sex slave. I spent my entire childhood underneath a grown ass man while living in the attic of the place that was supposed to be my home! You're the reason why I am the way I am, why I let Vincent beat me because I thought I wasn't worth loving, and why I haven't been able to love myself."

"I'm sorry—"

"Just get out! Get out and don't come back!" she stared me down with hate in her eyes. "I don't ever want to see you ever again. Stay away from me, you monster!"

I was halfway to the door when she called my name. I glanced back at her and was greeted with a harsh, "I hate you."

Taking a deep breath, I continued to the door, numb from Nubia's harsh diatribe. I opened it to find Shahani standing there with her mouth wide open. She went to touch my arm, but stopped short at the look on my face. I closed the door behind me so I could ask her a quick question, which she answered the best she could.

"I don't know much about them other than the fact that they're really well-known. Her uncle was the one that got her out of prison," Shahani replied. She pointed to Nubia's door. "Now if you'll excuse me, I gotta check on my girl."

I handed her the room key and entered mine to play detective. It took all of five minutes to find out that Nubia's uncle and aunt were not only well-known, but familiar. I spent the rest of the night laying out a plan that had to be one of my greatest yet. I had given Nubia flowers and other tokens of my affection as Maine, but for the next few days I would have to bring out Saidu, the savage in me, who would show Nubia the meaning of true love.

******

I watched as Vivica took a sip of the tall skinny latte with a double shot of espresso. She swished it around in her mouth, popped the lid off of the drink, spit it back into the cup, and handed it to the Starbucks employee.

"That is absolutely disgusting," she said, frowning up her face. "You would think after coming here every single day you all would manage to get my order right just once. Is Dave here? Because I swear all of you only have some act right when the general manager is on duty."

An older white man dressed in an apron came buzzing at the sound of his name. "Mrs. Wright, had I known you were out here I would've made sure to personally prepare your drink."

"I know, David. You always hook me up," Vivica said coyly, touching the man's hand as she smiled at him. "Make sure to add a little extra vanilla, mmkay?"

"Of course," David replied with a grin.

I looked around to see if anyone else was catching any of this freaky shit they were shooting back and forth. Like true to life New Yorkers, everyone was engrossed in their phones or checking out the new products on display in the large coffee shop. With no audience, I decided that today would be the day to start phase one. Vivica accepted her cup from David, their hands lingering for longer than necessary, and she went about her business. As she cut through the other customers waiting, our eyes locked, and she shot me a warm smile, which I returned with a head nod. She kept it moving, making sure to add an extra dip in her hips as she exited the shop. I kept it cool and waited for my drink to be made, knowing her thirsty ass wouldn't be too far. And she wasn't. I spotted her outside on her phone like she was making plans. She placed it into her Celine bag and approached me with no shame.

"Look who it is: Jermaine Emerson," she announced, rubbing her hand on my arm.

I glanced down at her disinterestedly, grimacing at the over-the-top greeting. "Don't be shouting my government out here."

"I'm sorry; it's a really bad habit of mine," Vivica apologized. "You see, I'm a politician and part of the job is recalling names. I figure if I start out with them I don't have to recall halfway through the conversation."

"Good for you."

Vivica watched me sip my green tea lemonade with a special focus on my lips. "What are you doing at Starbucks? You never struck me as the type to like brewed green tea."

"I don't," I lied with a nonchalant shrug; Vaughn's bougie ass put me on to this Starbucks and I had been a fan ever since. "This shit nasty as fuck."

"I guess if it's not a forty it's not good enough, huh," Vivica replied, taking a long sip of her drink.

I stared at her dumb ass long and hard before heading towards my car. "I don't know what type of old head niggas you got in mind, but I don't drink none of that bullshit."

"That doesn't take away from the fact that you need a real woman to show you the better things in life," Vivica said, following behind me like I knew she would. "You can keep on playing like you don't want me, but I see the exact opposite, Maine. Let me mold you into the man I know you can be."

"I don't think so."

I slid into my car and was nothing short of shocked when Vivica slid her happy ass into the passenger seat. This bitch was making it hot, and the fire engine red pantsuit she had on didn't exactly help the situation. She reached over and began stroking my leg, her hand growing closer to my dick with each rotation. My stomach churned in disgust at the feeling; there was no way in hell that she would ever arouse me knowing that she abused Nubia. I took a deep breath and turned off my emotions, finding the feeling slightly more tolerable.

"I saw you on television yesterday. Everyone has been talking about how much of a hero you are for carrying Butta all the way to the hospital. That was one of the bravest things I had ever seen, Maine. Do you have any idea how we can capitalize off of that fame? Books, movies, endorsements—I can turn you into something amazing if you let me."

I knew there was a possibility that there would be some pictures and videos of me on the internet, but I didn't think it would make it to the news. This made shit trickier. I had to be careful about where I was seen with this bitch with my image fresh in viewer's minds.

"I'm not about that life. The spotlight ain't for a nigga like me so you might as well dead all them plans you making," I countered, staring her right in the eye. "And who told you to get in my fucking car?"

Vivica opened her mouth to give me one of her dry ass replies when her phone started ringing. I didn't even need to steal a peek at her phone to know who it was—her eye rolling and teeth sucking as she picked up said it all.

"Hey…I'm on my way to the office…can't that wait until I get home? If that was the case then why didn't you let me know this before I left? Fine, Cornell, I'm on my way back to the house." She hung up and leaned her head against the headrest. "I know you barely know me, but do you think you can drop me off at my place? It's only ten minutes away. My car is in the shop and I hate having to depend on Ubers to get everywhere."

I didn't argue; this was definitely an easier way to find out where she lived. If I played my cards right, I could be on to phase two by the end of the week.

"You don't sound too happy to hear from your husband," I noted. "Is that why you're over here tryna fuck with me?"

"I'm not using you because of my issues with him. Trust me, I've liked you long before I got tired of Cornell's trifling ass. I'm ready to divorce him, but he's refusing to let go without a fight. I want my half of everything because I damn sure earned it. He wants me to take a pittance and claims that I'm the reason why our marriage is over, when it's obvious that other parties were involved."

"He cheated on you?"

"Yup. He was fucking around with my niece and got her pregnant. How he expects me to stay with him after doing some foul shit like that is beyond me. I have been nothing but a good wife and that's how you choose to repay me? I literally walked in on them fucking and she tried to play the victim. No, little bitch, I caught you and now you're sorry just like my bitch ass husband." Vivica noticed how tight I was gripping the steering wheel and asked, "Are you okay?"

"I'm good. I just can't believe that he would do you that way. Maybe you should give him a taste of his own medicine. Maybe that's how he'll understand that you're ready to move on."

"You mean like him walking in on me fucking someone?"

"That's exactly what I mean."

Vivica's hand found its way back to my thigh. "I hope since you made that suggestion that you're going to volunteer yourself."

"All I need is a time and date."

"Say no more," Vivica got to clicking in her phone and five minutes later she came up with, "My place this Friday at ten. Cornell will be out with some friends so I can expect him home around eleven. I want him to come home on top of the world and have it crash down right before his eyes. You promise to put on a good show for me?"

I had succeeded in having Vivica plan her own death. It was nothing for me to reply, "I'll give you a show you'll never forget."

******

My thumb hovered over Nubia's number for the umpteenth time this week. It had been four of the longest days of my life, but if I handled my business correctly, there might be some dialogue between us by tomorrow night. I dropped my phone back into the cup holder and stared at the time. With a heavy heart, I hopped out of my rental and walked up the street. It was pitch-black and deserted for a Friday night, with barely anyone walking the Fort Greene streets. I took that as a good sign. I pulled the fedora on my head low and adjusted my leather gloves one final time before ascending the steps. Vivica answered on the first ring of the doorbell, wearing nothing but a burgundy teddy with a matching silk robe.

"You're right on time," she noted as she accepted my wool coat. "And well dressed. I honestly was expecting you in something a little more…hood."

"There's a time and a place for all of that," I replied, scoping the place out for any possible cameras before handing her my hat.

"I'm happy to hear you feel that way. Are you hungry? I made dinner."

"Nah, but I could use a drink. Scotch on the rocks if you got it."

She shot me a wide smile over her shoulder. "The longer we talk the more impressed I become. Here I was thinking you were like Jodeci when you're so much more refined. Why don't you wait for me upstairs in my bedroom? Follow the rose petals."

As I climbed the stairs, my thoughts strayed to Nubia, who told me she lived in the attic of this beautiful home. *They treated her like a fucking animal,* I thought to myself. I was tempted to forgo the entire charade and strangle the bitch where she stood, but no. These two monsters had to know why they were getting ready to take their last breaths.

"I brought the good stuff," Vivica said with a shimmy as she entered the room with a platter filled with fruits and liquor. "Cornell's sacred single malt scotch that he's been sipping on for the past year. It's fifteen grand a bottle. Make sure you save him a drink because when I'm finished with him he's going to—did you hear that?"

I did hear it; someone was entering the house and doing a loud job of it. Vivica looked stricken by the possible entrance of her husband. I could tell that she thought of this all week, but when the moment came she was still feeling out of her element. She shook away any worries she might have and began kissing and rubbing my neck. I slipped a pair of cuffs out of my jacket pocket, readying myself to pounce when Cornell grew close enough. He made it too damn easy with all the noise he was making on his way up the stairs. The bedroom door opened and there he stood, blinking a few times to make sense of the scene.

"What the—" Cornell started but it was too late; I pounced on him, cracking him in the back of the neck and knocking him out instantly.

Vivica watched in horror as I carried him over to the armchair sitting in the corner of her room. "What are you doing?"

"I thought we could make it more interesting," I said, cuffing Cornell to the chair and stuffing his mouth with his own pocket square. "Let him get a real good look at you fucking another man. Doesn't that turn you on?"

Vivica nodded vehemently. "Yeah, Daddy."

I slapped Cornell across the face, jarring him awake. His eyes narrowed at the sight of me, then widened in shock. "You remember me from Jodeci's party, don't you?" Cornell nodded. "I'm here tonight because your wife wants you to see how a real nigga puts in work. Right, Vivica?"

"Sure do."

I walked over to Vivica, who was sitting in the middle of the bed on all fours. I climbed on the bed and whipped out my nine with a brand new silencer attached. Vivica opened her mouth to scream, and was silenced by the barrel of the silencer traveling deep down her throat.

"Suck it," I commanded, grabbing her by the throat so she couldn't move.

Vivica did as she was told, sucking on the metal that was warmed from my body heat. Cornell screamed from the sidelines at the sight; I bet out of the years they were married he never got some top from her.

"Don't get all shy now; do all that shit you was telling me you wanted to do the other day. Flick that tongue. There you go," I coached as she continued deep throating the barrel. "You ready to get some of this pipe?" Vivica shook her head. "Too bad because it's ready for you."

I shoved Vivica off of the barrel and flat onto her back. She begged and pleaded for me to stop, but I was on a roll now. The night was young and there was still a lot of fun to be had. I dragged her to the edge of the bed so a now crying Cornell could get a good look at his wife before she met her maker. With one fluid rip, she was naked from the waist down.

"I don't know why you're doing this, but please don't hurt us. We have money, status—we can give you anything you want if you stop right now. We'll pretend none of this ever happened, right Cornell?"

Cornell nodded his head, though his eyes said otherwise. "See?"

I placed my lips against Vivica's lips. "Shhh, no more talking. Arch that back and get ready for this pipe Daddy's got for you."

Vivica cried as the cold metal entered her. I thought of Nubia being placed in this same predicament and entered her deeper, pulling the gun in and out as she silently cried.

"This doesn't feel good, does it? I don't think it felt good to Nubia either when your filthy ass husband used to climb on top of her and violate her every night." Vivica stopped crying at the mention of Nubia's name. "Yeah, bitch, this was about more than some dick. This is about you taking in your sister's child and allowing your sick ass husband to rape her."

"I see she's got another nigga to cape for her, huh?" Vivica shot back contemptuously. "I was wrong, okay? I was wrong for the way I let Cornell treat her, but I didn't know how to make him stop. All I could think about was the way Vanessa had done me and I let that hate in my heart take over. If I could go back in time I would make things better between us."

"What happened to you walking in on her fucking your husband so you beat her ass? You knew he was raping her, didn't you?"

"Yes, I knew he was raping her; I've known all along, but what was I supposed to do? End my marriage and face the scrutiny of everyone? I stayed quiet because of my pride. Because I'm beautiful and there's no way in hell my husband should ever choose a child over me!"

"And there was no way in hell you should've chose your husband over your niece. Now I get to make a choice and this time you'll get to come first."

Vivica grabbed my hand as I plunged the gun deep inside of her. "No! Please don't—"

I squeezed off two shots, watching Vivica's skin ripple as the bullets tore through her body and came out of her head. Blood splattered all over the bed like morbid confetti. I stared at the permanent look of surprise on her face with satisfaction. A rattling to the left of me reminded me that my work wasn't done yet. I extracted my gun from Vivica's corpse and held it at an arm's length, careful not to get blood and pussy juices on me.

"No man should ever leave this world without getting some pussy, even a sick bastard like you," I said casually to Cornell. I pressed the gun to his neck and hissed, "I hope you're ready for this, muhfucker."

I uncuffed Cornell from the chair and ripped the pocket square from his mouth before escorting him over to Vivica's body. He stood in front of it and went from angry to miserable. "You killed her, you fucking savage."

"No, you killed her by not being able to keep your dick in your wife and out of little girls. But I'm feeling a little generous tonight. Since you like fucking so much I'mma let you fuck your wife one last time."

"I don't want to—"

"Drop your pants and fuck her."

Cornell sobbed as he unzipped his pants. It was too late for all that sobbing shit. I always found it crazy how people didn't start to feel sorry for all the fucked up shit they did until it was time to pay for it in full.

"I'm so sorry, Viv," he cried as he entered her. "I shouldn't have cheated on you the way I did. I shouldn't have touched Nubia, but I just I couldn't help it. She wanted it; she told me so with her eyes and like the weak man that I was, I divulged."

I stuck my gun into his ass and squeezed his throat to keep him from screaming. "This is what you did to Nubia every night, you sick bitch. She didn't want shit from you, and the fact that in your sick mind it was okay to rape her, I know you don't mean shit you just said."

I squeezed off another pair of shots. Cornell fell on top of Vivica as he held on to his private parts, or at least what was left of them. I hit him with a head shot that stilled him instantly. I stood there admiring my handiwork, thinking to myself that maybe this would be the first step to getting Nubia to forgive me. With these two monsters gone, she could heal and begin to officially move on with her life. Even if it didn't involve me.

Nubia

I stood in front of the barbershop watching him through the window. He was laughing and smiling with his peers like he hadn't rocked my entire world four days ago. I shouldn't have been surprised; he spent the past ten years not giving a fuck, why should he now? I patted Shahani's gun in my pocket. She was home watching Rhea while I claimed I was going for a walk. She wouldn't notice her gun missing for a few hours. But she might notice that I stole her phone. I sent Sampson another message from it telling him that "she" was down the block so he needed to clear the shop out. Not even a minute later, the shop was cleared out save for Sampson sitting in the last chair, patiently waiting for my girl to arrive. The smile on his face widened as I entered.

"I should've known it was you," Sampson said with a sardonic grin. "When Shahani came to my house she told me she never wanted to see me ever again. Part of me was hoping she came back to her senses, but no, it's just you."

"Yeah, it's just me: the woman you tried to kill until you found out she was your blood. Why didn't you just kill me when you had the chance? It's not like you give a fuck about me anyway," I shot back.

Sampson eyed me long and hard before saying, "You're right; I did try to kill you, but it had nothing to do with you. I was trying to erase the pain that your mother had caused when she cheated on me and left me for Apollo."

"My mother wouldn't do something like that. She loved my father."

"Oh did she?" Sampson replied with a hearty chuckle. "Or was she simply chasing the nigga with the biggest bankroll? I gave Vanessa everything: my heart, my time, and every dollar that I had. I promised her a life where she would live like a queen and she shitted on me. Ripped my heart out of my chest and stepped all over it. You mean to tell me that you ain't never have someone that you loved unconditionally throw their new life up in your face? How did that make you feel?"

I thought of Vincent and Francesca, using me to satisfy their every need while I lay there like used trash. "I felt like a piece of garbage. I put my everything into our relationship and to have him bring her in the mix like I was nothing, it hurt me then but now it makes me—"

"Mad?" Sampson egged me on. "So mad that you just want to—"

"Kill him," I said shakily, wiping my eyes. "I wanted to kill him and I did. I was like a soda bottle, shaken and shaken until I lost control."

"I lost control too, Nubia. Vanessa announced that she was pregnant but I never saw you all those years. Had I known you were mine I would've never did what I did, but there's no going back in time." Sampson eyed my purse, noticing the way I was clutching it. "You came here on some revenge shit, didn't you? I would do the same fucking thing if someone ever came for my family. However, now we are family."

"We ain't shit," I said, pulling Shahani's gun from my purse.

Sampson shook his head. "If firing off some shots is what you need to do then by all means, do it. But it's not bringing back your mother. Take it from a man that's put a lot of niggas in a grave: killing me won't make you feel better."

I whipped out the gun and planted it right underneath his chin. A guttural sob escaped me, racking my entire body. "Everything in my body is telling me that I should kill you, that I should make you feel the pain I've felt since that day ten years ago. But my heart? My heart is telling me not to give you the satisfaction. You're not worth me going to jail. You aren't worth Rhea growing up without me. You aren't worth any of the bullets in this gun. I hate you—I hate everything about you—but God will take care of you better than I ever will be able to."

"Trust me, he's already at work," Sampson promised.

I withdrew the gun, placing it back inside of my purse before I changed my mind. As much as I didn't want to admit it, standing there with every opportunity to kill Sampson didn't feel right. God was telling me to wait on it not because he deserved it, but because he knew I needed no more blood on my hands. I was pregnant, and it would be nothing short of disrespect to my unborn child to put it through the trauma that comes with taking a life.

"Have a nice life," I said, making a break for the door.

"Nubia, wait."

I glanced at him over my shoulder. "What?"

Sampson shook his head. "I understand you being mad at me, but leave Maine out of this. He didn't do anything but follow my orders like a soldier should. When he got here, he didn't speak a lick of English and had this dead look in his eyes. I thought of him as more of a weapon than a kid. I sent my best weapon to handle business for me, and by some rare stroke of humanity, he saved you, and he's been saving you ever since. He left his wedding to protect you, and he turned on me to make sure you were saved. That man loves you. He is in just as much pain as you are. Hear him out."

"Whatever, Sampson. Have a nice life," I said, but took every word he said to heart.

I knew for the sake of my unborn child that I would have to figure out where Maine and I stood. Whether I made that decision tonight or ten months from now, it still had to be made.

******

Sampson's words followed me home, and pervaded my every thought. As much as my heart wanted me to hate Maine, my body wouldn't allow me to; I spent days picturing us together and nights remembering his touch. When I wasn't thinking of him and I, my thoughts strayed to him holding Rhea. Maine once spoke of her with fleeting interest, but when he held her in his arms, I could tell that he cared about my baby girl. As I sat here staring out the window at traffic passing by, I knew I would never find out exactly how much.

"Hey there," Shahani said, holding out a mug of tea. "How you doing?"

I took a sip of the warm chamomile tea, which was perfect for this foggy Monday morning. "I've been better. Is Rhea okay?"

"I just put her down for a nap."

"Thanks, Shahani. I don't know what I'd do without you."

"I can say the same; without you letting me crash here I would be stuck in a hotel until I find a place."

"Why don't you move into my house with me? It's not like I won't have the space. The place is huge. It's really homey too." I smiled at the thought of Shahani and I being roomies again. "It reminds me of my life growing up. My parents really looked out for me. Did I tell you the full story of how I got my inheritance?"

"Nope, and I've been patiently waiting to find out."

I told Shahani the story of how I found out about the large estate that my parents left me. Her eyes were shining with unshed tears when I told her about how I stood up to my aunt and uncle as well. I beamed with pride as she gave me a round of applause, which I accepted with a mock bow.

"The crazy part is that my aunt told me that my father loved my mother. The bitch knew it was Sampson all this time and never bothered to tell me," I said, recalling the showdown between the three of us. "I can't believe my entire childhood was based on a lie."

"Nubia—"

"Then my relationship with Maine was too. What am I supposed to do, Shahani? I have every reason to hate Maine yet—"

"You can't stop thinking about him," Shahani finished. "It's only natural. What Sampson did to you was absolutely fucked up, and I don't want anything to do with him, yet I keep thinking about him. I know I'm not going back but still…"

"We're all fucked, aren't we?" I joked.

"Damn sure are," Shahani replied as she scrolled through her phone. "But not as fucked up as this couple. Apparently some well-known defense attorney and his congresswoman wife were raped and murdered in their Fort Greene home."

"What?"

Shahani turned her phone to me and there, posted up in a picture from one of the various banquets they attended, was Cornell and Vivica. I took the phone from her and skimmed the article, which read like something out of a horror story. Apparently, after not hearing from either one of her parents all weekend, Ashanti finally went to visit them, only to discover them brutally murdered. Cornell was sodomized and shot while Vivica was raped and shot through her vagina. The rest of the details had my stomach churning. Who the fuck in their right mind would murder my aunt and uncle in such a violent way?

"Maine," I said aloud.

"Maine what?" Shahani replied. Her brows disappeared underneath her bonnet. "Maine did this?"

"I mean he could've. I told him what they did to me when I was a child and all of a sudden they're dead?" I bit my bottom lip to hide the smile threatening to grow. "Should I call him?"

"You should, but not on your phone. Use mine," Shahani said, rising from her seat. "I'll check on Rhea while you make that call…"

Maine's phone went straight to voicemail. I was tempted to hang up, but opted to leave him a voicemail.

"The way we left everything was pretty fucked up, but I was wondering if we could meet up and talk. How about Brooklyn Bridge

Park tonight around nine? See you then."

I hung up the phone and placed it on my stomach. I still hadn't told anyone about the baby because I knew that once I fully acknowledged it, I would have to figure out where to go from here. There was a lot of damage done between Maine and I, and adding a baby on top of this madness was likely to bring more problems with little solutions.

******

It was nine o'clock on the dot when Maine appeared out of thin air. He was dressed in all black everything; from his black Balenciaga trainers to the hoodie he wore. He posted up a foot away from me, giving me the space I needed, or at least I thought I needed. The cool summer air ran over my skin, giving me goose bumps and I could've used Maine's warm embrace. I rebuked the thought immediately and instead turned my attention to the matter at hand.

"I saw the news this morning," I started, leaning against the railing and staring out at the view of lower Manhattan. "I tell you about Vivica and Cornell, and days later they end up dead, but not before being raped."

Maine shrugged. "I hope you're not expecting me to play all coy and shit. How could you think in your right mind that I would hear what they did to you and just let it go? Fuck that. I killed the both of them and if I had to do it all over again, I would."

"Is that supposed to fix this entire mess? Yes, they were scum of the earth and I'm happy they're gone, but that doesn't take away from the root of the problem. You destroyed my family, Maine! You are the cause of the road my life has taken—"

"And you played a part in it as well!" Maine fired back, getting up in my face. "From the day I have met you I've tried to give you back the worth you lost and you never thought you were good enough for it. I have saved you over and over again, Nubia, more times than you've ever tried to save yourself. I might have been part of breaking you, but you can't look me in the eye and tell me that I haven't tried to put you back together."

I turned away from Maine, crying because as hard as it was for me to admit, he was right. Despite his one wrong done to me, there were so many rights in his corner. His onyx eyes were studying me when I turned back. A gun was in his hand with the grip facing me. He held it out to me, pressing it into my chest.

"What do you want me to do with that?" I asked, staring down at the gun.

"Kill me," Maine replied. "It's the only way we'll ever be even. I don't have any family for you to kill so you'll just have to take my life."

"Maine—"

"Nubia, I can't take this back and forth much longer. I can't bring your parents back, I can't right every wrong in your life, but I can at least give you some type of justice. An eye for an eye. You kill me, and you'll get some type of closure."

"No," I cried, clapping my hands against my mouth and shaking my head. "Are you crazy, Maine? I'm not killing you!"

"Then what did you bring me here for?"

"I brought you here to tell you that I'm pregnant and as much as I hate you…I love you too. This is a big ass mess that we'll have to get through, and I want us to start over again. From the beginning."

"Pregnant? By who?" Maine asked, and I thought he was deadass serious until he cracked a smile. "I'm just playing."

"Gimme that gun," I playfully commanded, motioning for him to hand the gun over. I smiled at his smile, a lump of guilt in my chest. At the thought of Sampson's words, that feeling faded. "I won't kill you but I might whip your ass."

Maine let go of a hearty chuckle, doubling over in a round of genuine laughter. I don't think he would ever know how beautiful he was when he smiled. He calmed down after a few minutes and held out his hand.

"To starting over?"

I shook it, the warmth from his fingers permeating mine, bringing me back to life after days of feeling so dead on the inside. "To starting over."

Shahani

I was half-asleep when Nubia walked through the door. She had a small smile on her lips, like she was replaying the events of her meeting with Maine repeatedly in her mind. I couldn't even be mad; the heart wants what the heart wants and there was no getting around it. I wanted to tell her as much but feared that it would be received wrong since, well, I was in love with her father. Who was I to go around telling people what to do with their love lives when mine was a mess?

I patted the sofa cushion next to me. "How was the meeting?"

"The meeting went better than I expected. Yes, Maine was the one that handled my aunt and uncle. He said it was his way of trying to even the balance between the two of us. When he felt like that didn't work he told me to kill him."

"Did you? You did take Mercy the other day without my permission..."

Nubia playfully rolled her eyes. "As much as I wanted to kill him, there's no way I can harm the father of my child."

It took a full minute for her statement to sink in, but when it did I nearly pounced on her ass. "You're pregnant! How long have you known? Bitch, why didn't you tell me?"

"Well for the most part out of embarrassment; Rhea's nowhere near one and I'm already expecting another baby. Can you say hot in the ass? Plus, I wanted to tell Maine first over a fancy dinner, but that idea was ruined."

"Aww," I said, giving her belly a rub. "Look on the bright side: this pregnancy is going to be much easier. You've got a baby daddy who cares—"

"Who's also married—"

"A strong support system—"

"Does that include my murderous father?"

"And you've got ME!" I clapped. "I didn't have the grace to be there with you for your first pregnancy, but this time around we're going to do this right. No stress, no worries, just all about taking care of you and baby."

"You are way more excited about this than I am."

"That's because you've got a lot of heavy stuff on your mind," I reminded her, but she was right.

I wasn't excited because I would be around for Nubia this pregnancy. I was happy to have someone to help me get through mine.

******

I would never knock another bitch for getting pregnant by a fuck nigga ever again. As I sat in the doctor's office on the examination table kicking my legs, I now understood how you could fall in love with someone and they just change up. Then you find out that you're pregnant and stuck with the choice of getting an abortion or earning a lifetime of headaches. That's what I was debating when the doctor walked in.

"So, Doc, shoot straight with me. I took a pee test last night and it was positive. Now all I need to know is the results for the blood test."

Dr. Housman smiled at me. "Congratulations, Shahani. The results came back positive."

My first reaction was a strained smile; I just got out of this relationship with Sampson and now I had to figure out how I was going to co-parent with him. Or even if I planned to co-parent with him at all. After all, his last baby mother didn't make it out of their situation too well and he tried to kill his youngest. Plus, I wasn't even sure how to break the news to Nubia. Last night I was excited at the possibility, but when the doctor gave me the news, it made everything so much more concrete. I was still mulling over my choices on the way home, and became so caught up in my thoughts that I didn't even notice the black sedan that pulled up beside me. The passenger window rolled down and there was Lonzo with a cheesy ass grin on his face.

"Lonzo, get the fuck out of here while I'm in a good mood," I spat, continuing my trek to the supermarket. "I don't have shit to say to you."

"Well maybe I got something to say to you. Get in so we can talk," Lonzo urged.

I stopped walking and shot him an incredulous look. "Like I said, I don't have a motherfucking thing to say to you, Alonzo. I know that was you at Maine's wedding. Do you have any idea how many innocent people you killed? Even worse, you involved me in it by asking me about the wedding. Had I known you planned to do something so fucked up I would've—"

"You would've what?" Alonzo barked. "Told your boyfriend? Oh, I forgot; you can't because by telling on me you tell on yourself. I been hunting all them niggas down since I came back and you've known about it. What type of loyalty is that, Shahani? Oh that's right: it's called disloyalty."

"No, it's called stupidity. I was nothing more than stupid for even entertaining your bitch ass when Sampson has been nothing but good to me. Stay far away from me, Alonzo, because unlike you, I got good aim."

Alonzo didn't follow me after that; I made sure to hit his ass where it hurt. He never did have great aim and that probably was the reason why we got robbed so easily. They knew that the only time to be scared of Alonzo was when he was aiming for the person next to you. As of right now, I felt like I had painted a target on my back and with the way Lonzo was popping up, he might fuck around and get lucky.

******

Nubia and Cheyenne were lounging on the sofa when I got back. Cheyenne was all smiles as she took in my appearance with those curious eyes of hers. I had on a sundress that fit like a glove with a pair of sandals, which was perfect for the dwindling summer weather. I was expecting a compliment on maybe my clothes or the cute little Furla bag I was carrying, but the next words to come out of Cheyenne's mouth nearly sent me into cardiac arrest.

"Someone's glowing," she announced. "Lemme find out there's a bun in the oven and we're about to have another little Sampson running around in these streets. Byron was something else when he was living out here..."

"You fucked Byron?" I asked as an attempt to change the subject.

"Like once or twice, but never on some relationship type ish. He was always hell bent on making a name for himself in Chicago and I wanted to raise my daughter here. Now that I think about it, I should've made the move because other than Nubia, I ain't got shit out here. I wonder how he's doing."

"He's married. To my homegirl."

Cheyenne placed a thoughtful finger on her lip. "I think I saw some of their wedding pictures on IG. That's wassup…I wonder if Yajé is still single, with his fine chocolate ass."

"He was available the last time I saw him," I said, giving her an air high five.

With the conversation successfully changed, I was able to stop worrying about Sampson or any of our problems. We were all in the middle of making dinner plans when my phone went off. It was an unknown number, which could only be one of two people. Since Sampson wasn't one to hide behind private calls, I knew exactly who it was.

"How may I help you, Lonzo?"

"I'm sorry."

"Sorry for being an asshole in general or…"

"I'm sorry for the way I came at you earlier. I'm also sorry for putting you in the middle of old beefs. Can I make it up to you with dinner?"

I may have rolled my eyes but there was no way I could stay mad at Lonzo, especially when he wasn't afraid to be wrong. "Promise me that you'll never use me to settle a personal score ever again."

"I promise."

"I guess we can do dinner."

"How about tomorrow night?"

I bit my lip; while I was ready to forgive him for being a dick to me, I wasn't too sure I was ready to be seen in public with him. "I'll have to look at my schedule and let you know."

"Aight. I'll talk to you later."

Nubia was giving me the eye when I came to the table. I stuck my tongue out at her and asked why she was looking at me like that, to which she replied, "I don't know, maybe because Cheyenne's right; you're glowing."

"It must be my makeup. I put on too much highlighter."

Nubia shook her head. "No…it's an inner glow."

"Like the same glow our little baby machine over here has," Cheyenne said, studiously ignoring the dirty look Nubia gave her.

"I was trying to save this news for a better time but…I'm pregnant," I admitted with a shrug. I shot Nubia a sympathetic look. "I know it's not ideal, but I'm going to have to tell him."

Nubia thought long and hard about what she was going to say next, and it surprised me. "I hate him, and there's a chance that I'll never forgive him for what he did to my parents, but if you feel like you need to tell him for your safety then by all means, please do."

"It won't be any time soon; I still don't know if I'm keeping it."

"The only thing Vincent blessed me with was Rhea. Don't give up your blessing over some misplaced hate."

"Same goes for me and my daughter. She looks just like her father, but I wouldn't trade her for the world," Cheyenne co-signed. "The farther along you get the better sense you'll make of the situation. Trust us from experience."

"You're right."

We spent the rest of the night making plans for Nubia's new house, which was halfway done. I accepted her offer to move in and was looking forward to rooming with my girl under better conditions. We didn't have Donovan or Nia around to cause unnecessary drama, and this time there wouldn't be any secrets between us. Things were looking up for me, and I knew once I made it over this small hurdle, I would be unstoppable.

******

I woke up the next morning feeling slightly under the weather. This baby made its presence known overnight and I had a feeling this was going to be the longest pregnancy ever. Nubia seemed to be feeling the exact opposite; she was bubbling with joy as she made us mugs of tea.

"With my first, I was always sick as a dog. With Rhea, it was much more controllable. This little one right here though"—she gave her stomach a pat—"I have all the energy in the world. I'm up early, I'm spending all the time I can with Rhea, I'm also checking in on the businesses that I have to make sure everything is running smoothly. I'm a brand new woman."

"It must be some of that African pride. With a father like Maine, that baby is gonna come out ready for the world," I joked. My phone buzzing interrupted the conversation. I spotted the name on the caller ID and was mildly surprised. "Hey, Sharita, you are going to live too long. I was just thinking about you last night."

"You must've sensed me touching down at JFK last night," Sharita laughed. "I'm here for a week, boo. What do you have planned today?"

"I was hanging with my girl, running some errands…"

"Can you put a pause on the errands and please work those magic fingers on my hair? I have no problem with your friend coming, too."

Nubia, who could hear the conversation from across the table, mouthed, "Go. Have some fun."

"Okay, I'll meet you at the salon in an hour."

Sharita was sitting in my private room reading a magazine when I arrived at the salon. I texted Pinky to shampoo and condition her while I was on my way. Her kinky, curly hair was sitting on her head in a pouf, waiting for me to silk press it. We caught up with hugs and kisses, and then it was right to work.

"What brought you to New York?" I asked as I sectioned her hair and applied my handmade balms. "Is Byron here on business?"

"Yup, we wanted to give Sampson the news in person that he's going to be expecting his very first grandbaby."

"You're pregnant?" I exclaimed. I clicked on the blow dryer to prevent her from hearing the strain in my voice. "Congratulations. How many months are you?"

"Three. We wanted to wait until we passed the three-month mark to tell everyone. We're having a small dinner tonight and we'd love it if you can come."

"Sharita…Sampson and I broke up last week. As much as I would love to be there when you give him the news, I don't think it would be appropriate," I apologized.

Sharita reached up and touched my hand. "I know, boo. Sampson called and told me about the whole situation. He wanted me to come and see where your head is so—"

"So what, Sharita?" I shot back, spinning around so she could look me in the eye when I asked her my next question. "Did he tell you what he did? He kidnapped my best friend and was ready to kill her in cold blood, all while acting like nothing was out of the ordinary. There is no way in hell I could even consider being with him again. Not even because of this baby!"

"What does my baby have to do with you and Sampson?" Sharita asked, her eyes wide in fright.

"Well…you want me to come to the party to hear about the baby…I can't be in the same room as him because of the baby," I covered up real quick, but I wasn't sure whether or not Sharita bought it. "The bottom line is: he looked me in my face and lied to me. It wasn't even a little lie either. It was an 'I'm going to kill your friend and pat your back at her funeral' lie."

"Did Nubia tell you they had a conversation?"

"Yes, she did, and she ended the conversation with I might not kill you today, but I might come for that ass tomorrow. But that's beside the point; my issue with him may stem from the situation with Nubia, but it's also its own separate one. How on earth can I be with a man that I don't trust?"

Sharita sighed. "I'm not condoning what he did, but what I will say is that you at least owe him some type of conversation on the matter. Don't have him thinking if you stay gone long enough to forget you'll eventually come home. If you don't want to be with him tell him to his face."

"At your 'party'?" I replied incredulously.

Sharita nodded profusely. "Yup. It's the perfect place: there's plenty of people around to keep the drama at a minimum, plenty of liquor, and you can bring plenty of friends if that will make you feel better."

"I highly doubt Nubia will want to show up to this event."

"She might want to meet her brother."

I wasn't too sure that Nubia would want to meet Byron, who grew up with both of his parents while she made due with none, but I replied, "I'll run it by her but I can't make any promises. The same goes for me."

"That's all I'm asking for. Now can you please slay my hair for tonight? Just because Sampson played himself doesn't mean I have to show up to this party looking like a show poodle," Sharita said with fake anguish as she pointed to her hair.

Sharita and I made light conversation while I did her hair, but my mind kept floating to tonight. I was scared of seeing Sampson again because I knew it would open up my still scabbing wounds, and even worse, he might tell me that he couldn't live without me and I might believe him.

******

Nubia stared up at the expansive Long Island mansion and back at me. "I can't believe I agreed to come. Would you judge me if I stuck a piece of fish in a vent?"

"Nubia…I mean if you must, I would recommend one that's properly hidden," I said with a shrug as we walked up the walkway.

Sampson's house was packed; I was expecting some people from the block, but all I saw in attendance was Jodeci. He inclined his head at me, to which I replied back with a nod. Nubia didn't notice the exchange; she was too busy studying everything her eyes came across—family pictures on the walls, guests who were sneaking peeks at her, and anything that passed us. She slowed down when she spotted Sampson across the room talking to Byron. His lips formed a thin line and he whispered something to Byron, who looked over at us. After their exchange, both father and son began to cut through the crowd, making their way towards us. I started searching for Sharita so she could mediate this entire situation before shit went left.

"Shahani," Byron greeted, pulling me in for a warm hug. "It's good seeing you. How's everything going?"

"I'm doing pretty good. My shop is as well," I replied. I motioned to Nubia, who was wearing a faux bored face. "This is my best friend, Nubia."

Byron, who was usually smooth with the ladies, stood there trying to figure out how to greet the cold Nubia, who was bobbing on her heels. He settled with extending a hand. "It's nice to meet you, Nubia. I'm Byron…your brother."

I expected Nubia to throw shade at Byron, but the word "brother" seemed to have a surprise effect on her. "Nice to meet you, Byron," she said sweetly. "You're married, right? I'd love to meet your wife…"

The pair disappeared to find Sharita, who I spotted in the kitchen chatting up some of her relatives. I watched as Byron introduced Nubia to Sharita. They shared a hug and brought Nubia into whatever conversation they were having. Sampson motioned for me to follow him outside where only a few people were lounging around the pool. He asked them to politely leave, and they obliged with haste. T*here goes the safety of the public Sharita promised me,* I thought with an eye roll.

"She might not like me now, but she'll get over the entire situation after a while," Sampson said, interrupting my people watching. "When that happens, do you want to be the only person still holding on to old feelings?"

I glared up at Sampson. "Don't be too sure of that; she barely spared a glance in your direction. Nubia might learn to tolerate your existence, but if I were you, I wouldn't hold on too tight to the idea that the two of you might develop a bond."

"Because you young people have no patience. I don't search for fast fixes when it comes to long-term goals. That's how you end up roaming the streets wreaking havoc with no real plan in sight," Sampson said, and I felt like that was a jab at Lonzo. "If you really want something, you have to be willing to wait for it."

"So you want a relationship with Nubia?" I asked for clarity.

Sampson replied with an affirmative nod. "She's my blood; whether she likes it or not, we're bound for life. I know what I did was fucked up Shahani, and like I told her, had her mother told me she was my daughter none of this would've ever happened."

"But it did happen. And if it wasn't her then it would've been some other innocent girl," I said, holding him by the shoulders and staring him in the eye. "You brought an innocent person into a beef and it was wrong. A little girl watched her parents die in front of her eyes and grew up to be so broken that she settled for anything. It took her husband nearly beating her to death for her to understand that she was worth having a life. At twenty-one-years-old she is now learning to love herself, when that is something that should've been taught to her by her father. You stole a lot from her and you treat it with such a cavalier manner that as I sit here pregnant with your child, I honestly don't think I'm ready to bring another person into this world that you might possibly break over your hurt feelings."

I went to move my hands from Sampson's shoulders, only to have him keep them in place. "You're pregnant?" he croaked.

"I am," I choked out. "I'm also gearing up to raise this baby by myself unless you can prove to me that you're not the malevolent father I think you are."

I snatched my arms away before he could stop me and headed back inside where I found Nubia having a good time with Byron and Sharita, who frowned at the sight of the frown on my face.

"I take it that your talk didn't go too well?" she asked hesitantly.

"Not by a long shot. All I wanna do is go home, take a long shower, and sleep tonight away. You ready, Nubia?"

I could tell that Nubia was having a good time with Byron and

Sharita, but I had to get away from Sampson. "Of course I'm ready. Will I see you guys tomorrow for dinner?"

"Of course. Just text me with the address and we'll see you tomorrow night."

"Look at you being all friendly with your brother. And you thought tonight would be a waste," I said once we were comfortably situated in the back of our Uber. "It looks like you and Byron clicked real easy."

"We did. I know this will sound kinda lame, but when I was younger I always wished I had another sibling. I begged my mother for one. To be quite honest, I think that's what the big surprise was that she had for me on the day of my party." Nubia stared wistfully out the window. "Byron was so nice, and I felt like he really cared about me, and not in that fake way people care about you when they wanna know your business."

"Do you think you'll ever feel that way about your father?"

"I don't know. It's like, I don't think he fully understands what he did to my life, and if he doesn't get it then how can we ever really coexist?" Nubia took my hand into hers. "I'm sorry my issues broke up your relationship, Shahani."

"I don't blame you for any of this," I said, and I meant it.

I blamed Sampson for having me think there was such a thing as true love, only for him to step all over my heart with lies and deceit. Then in turn, I kicked his around with my own deception. Now we're stuck trying to come together for the sake of a tiny human being that feels doomed before it's had the chance to arrive. This was the bad side of love; the side I thought I was going through when I was with Donovan, except with this pain tearing my heart apart, it felt much more real.

Maine

Ever since I found out that I was going to be a father, I started doing weird shit like trying to stay alive, which was unusual for me. I was even trying to make amends with people I would've once killed with no remorse, like Jodeci, who was standing in front of his old building smoking a blunt. He called me asking if we could have a parlay. This was the first time we'd seen each other since everything that went down at the warehouse. It was still hard to believe the nigga I once felt was a brother to me now felt like a stranger, and all over some power.

"I ain't think you was gon' show up," he said, taking a thoughtful pull of the blunt before ashing it on the gate he was posted up against. "Actually, I did. Just much farther away, you know, staring at me through a sniper rifle or some shit like that."

"Nah, you know I like to kill up close and personal," I replied, reaching in my jacket pocket and pulling out a blunt of my own.

"You sure do…" Jodeci said, and I could hear the double meaning behind his words.

"So…what'd you call me out here for?"

"I wanted to talk about what happened last week…"

"There's nothing to talk about. I put the pieces of the puzzle together. Sampson offered you the position you been gunning for in exchange for you killing Nubia. You almost got her the first time, but what stopped you the second time around?"

"Because my boy showed me the pregnancy test. As much as I wanted that spot, I wasn't ready to get it by killing an innocent child. If it was Ashanti and someone killed her knowing she was carrying my child, I wouldn't rest until I found the person and..."

"Something we can finally agree on," I said, taking a pull and offering him the blunt, which he accepted hesitantly. "Although, back at home many pregnant women were killed without mercy. I remember this one time we came across this home that the rebels had invaded. You could smell the death before you opened the door. We entered the house and saw the remains of two small children. Upstairs we discovered the mother tied to her bed naked. Her flesh had rotted off of her body and there, in her once protruding stomach, was the remains of her child."

Jodeci closed his eyes and took a long pull from the blunt as if trying to erase the image from his mind. "How did you see fucked up shit like that and not kill yourself?"

"Who says I didn't try?" I countered. "There were two reasons why I didn't want you to have the job. The first one is that you give responsibility to the person who desires it the least."

"Which is why you chose Vaughn..."

"Exactly. Sampson needed someone he could mold. I'm not saying you can't be molded, but we both know that sometimes you like to handle business your way without taking everything into account."

Jodeci rolled his eyes. "You might have a point there. What's your second reason?"

"The story I just told you. It made you sick to your stomach. Of course you've done enforcement work for Sampson, but what if there was a situation where you needed to go into someone's home and kill with no remorse? I don't think you're mentally prepared for it. Nubia still being alive is proof of it."

"So if I would've killed your girl that would've made me perfect for the position?" Jodeci asked incredulously.

"You say it like it's a bad thing. There's nothing wrong with humanity. I got a kid on the way and don't even know how to get the rest of mine back."

"Yup, 'cause I'm sure killing Ashanti's parents set you back a ways…" Jodeci trailed off, waiting for my confirmation that I was behind the deed.

"Damn sure did," I co-signed. "Took me right back home for a few minutes. You mad?"

Jodeci shook his head. "Nah. I saw those pictures, bro. If they did what those pictures imply then I can't even be mad. To be honest, the death of her parents has actually brought Ashanti down to earth. She also got a big ass payout from the insurance company so I ain't gotta worry about killing myself to provide her lifestyle for her. Which brings me to the point of this meeting: I want us to get into business together."

"What?"

"Ashanti and I have the legit money to open up a business. I'm sure you don't trust all your money with the cartel, so why not allow me to launder it for a fee? Plus, you need a way to get money to Nubia without them noticing. How about it?"

I stared at Jodeci for a full minute before replying, "This is the nigga that I grew up with. This is my brother."

"Is that a yes, *Jermaine*?" he asked, mocking Estalita.

"Hell yeah, bro."

I held my hand out to Jodeci, but instead, he pulled me in for a brotherly hug. This time it felt real, like we were back to shooting the shit as we cracked on niggas walking by and caught up on life since our beef. Jodeci gave me my props on my trek to the hospital with Vaughn, which reminded me of my reason for agreeing to this meeting in the first place.

"Alonzo is back."

"Is that who shot at me and damn near killed Vaughn?" I nodded. "So instead of going after the king, he's choosing to eliminate pawns? We were fucking kids at the time. If he really wants to get revenge he needs to go after his 'business partner,' Blue."

"I heard that Blue was found dead a couple months ago, and his stash was stolen," I said, recalling the call I got from one of my cartel contacts I put on the case. "If he's keeping with the same pattern he'll try for Sampson again. You'll be right after. I'll slip right in because I'm guilty by association. Let's handle this wildcard before he tries to come for the family again."

Jodeci held his fist out. "For old times' sake?"

I dapped him. "For old times' sake."

******

While I was hanging with Jodeci, he mentioned something about Nubia that bothered me. Last night she left Sampson's party with Shahani and they hopped into an Uber. The more I thought about it, the more I realized that Nubia never drove anywhere and was always in the passenger seat of Cheyenne or Shahani's car. With our child on the way I wasn't having that, so I saw no other solution than to teach her how to drive. After scouting parking lots all last night, I lucked out when I found an empty one over in Sunset Park and called her early the next morning to link up.

"Wake up. We got business to handle," I shouted into the phone, chuckling as she groaned in annoyance.

"Maine, what are you talking about?" Nubia huffed. "Today's Saturday. The only business I got today is with my bed and Netflix. We're getting into a marathon of The Punisher."

"If I gotta come upstairs and drag you out of bed I'm gon' punish you."

"Maine, what could we possibly have to do today that is so important?"

"Come downstairs and find out. I got breakfast waiting, too."

"A baconeggandcheese?"

"With an orange juice."

"Why didn't you say that before?"

Twenty minutes later Nubia was sitting in the passenger seat inhaling her breakfast sandwich and sipping on her orange juice like she hadn't eaten all day. She caught me looking and covered her mouth as she laughed.

"I'm sorry. Lately I've been hungry as hell in the morning," she said as she finished the rest of her sandwich at a slower pace. "So... where are you taking me today?"

"To a parking lot so I can teach you how to drive. We aren't leaving until you can drive, brake, and park."

Nubia rolled her head towards me. "I hope you have all day because I'm terrified of driving. It gives me anxiety."

"So then what were you going to do when the baby came?"

"Me, Rhea, and the baby would just get on the train."

I shook my head. "Nope. It ain't even going down like that. All the crazy shit that happens on the train and you want to get on with two little ones? We nipping that shit in the bud today."

Nubia looked like she wanted to argue, but instead turned her attention to my sandwich. She finished wolfing mine down as we pulled into the expansive parking lot. I hopped out and popped the trunk to the Toyota Camry I had rented for the day. I set up some cones for us to practice with once she got the hang of things. For someone that wasn't too excited to be driving, Nubia certainly found herself in the driver's seat when I returned.

"Buckled in?"

"Yup."

"Did you adjust your seat?"

She reached down and fiddled with the knobs until she was

comfortable. "Yup."

"Checked your mirrors?"

"All adjusted."

"Aight, place your foot on the brake…" Nubia placed her foot on the brake and waited for further directions. "Now put the car in drive."

Nubia placed the car in drive and took her foot off the brakes too quick. We lurched forward and she screamed. I tried to hold my laughter in but I couldn't. She pressed on the brakes again, jerking us to a stop.

"Maine this isn't funny! I just saw my entire life flash before my eyes, I almost went into premature labor, and I think I peed on myself." She slowly turned her head to catch me silently laughing and started hitting me. "This isn't FUNNY!"

"But look at you with your foot on the brakes," I noted, nudging my head at her controlling the car and beating me up at the same time. "You only think you can't do it because you put it in your head that you can't. Trust me when I say no one just hops in a car and starts driving with no problem."

"So you weren't good at driving when you first started out?"

I shook my head. "Of course not. My very first time driving I hit a parked car. Jodeci teased my ass about it until the following week we got into a shootout with some Brownsville niggas and I drove like a Nascar driver. I just hopped in and we were off. It was all good until we got home and I ain't know how to park. After that, I went and took some driving lessons. I've been good ever since."

"You hit a parked car?" Nubia laughed.

"That's all you got from my story, bro?"

"No…but I couldn't stop picturing you running into a parked car and I didn't catch the end of the story. I'm just playing," she said, holding her hands up in mock surrender. She placed them on the steering wheel and said, "You're right; I'm just psyching myself out. I got this. I can do this."

I reached out and squeezed her hand. "You got this. I believe in you."

Nubia took a deep breath and we started our lesson over. After the first hour Nubia had made a great amount of progress, and by noon she was driving through the cones like a pro. Her parallel parking would need a few more practice sessions, but she did well enough for me to spring her surprise on her.

"Maine," she said as she stood blindfolded in the middle of the Mercedes Benz dealership, sniffing the air that was thick with new car smell. "I know I'm not where I think I am…"

"Remove the blindfold and see."

Nubia pulled the blindfold from her eyes and squealed at the sight of every make and model of the 2018 lineup. "Which one?"

"Whichever one you want."

Nubia spent the next hour playing with each car. She looked like a kid in a candy store and I couldn't even control the smile she brought to my face. After much debating, she narrowed it down to the G550 and the S550.

"We'll take both," I told the associate.

Nubia turned back and looked at me like I was crazy. "Maine," she mouthed. "Both?"

"What I told you about acting like we broke in front of these white people?" I joked, playfully nudging her. "You need two cars anyway. One for when you have the kids and one when you're running errands. Now I've given you motivation to get your license, huh?"

"Damn straight. I'm about to practice every chance I get. Out there like 'skrrt skrrt.' My only problem is finding somewhere to hold the cars until that happens…"

"I was thinking my place in Jersey. You and your girl can stay there for the time being. I would take you house hunting right now but that can't be done until I handle some loose strings."

Nubia shot me a mischievous grin. "There's no need to do any house hunting. Now, it's my turn to surprise you, Maine."

I never did like the unknown element of surprise, but the pure joy on Nubia's face at thinking she could surprise me was enough for me to play along. Except when she tried to blindfold me. I was trusting, not crazy.

******

I pulled up to a brownstone in the middle of Bed Stuy. It was under construction but they appeared to be making some progress. Nubia leaned against me as she stared up at the house.

"I remembered growing up in a house filled with love and I've always wanted the same for my baby girl. Now I want it for both of my babies," Nubia explained, intertwining our hands as she spoke. "My parents left me a sizable inheritance with a little bit of everything, including my childhood home I grew up in, plus a home they had planned for us. One I can't bear to go back to because of the pain and the other, the one Cornell and Vivica lived in, it's nothing more than a bad memory. Instead of trying to live in either one, I found a new home where I could make memories of my own. It needs a little work, but once it's done, it's going to be what I've always wanted: a home."

Crazy part was, ever since I came to America I had been searching for a home, and it was probably the reason why I never found true comfort when I rested my head anywhere. I met Nubia and found peace whenever I was with her, and in some strange way, she became home for me. As she stood here watching her home, I wrapped an arm around the waist of mine, praying that it never left me.

Nubia

Seven months later...

You wanna know what's better than being happy? Being pregnant and happy. My first two pregnancies were filled with nothing but anguish and loneliness, which made it nearly impossible to thrive, but for my current nugget life was good. I didn't get to see Maine often, but when I did, we made the best of our situation. That included looking up baby names, doing some serious online shopping, and taking trips to the park so Rhea could enjoy outdoors. She was a precocious nine-month-old that stayed in everyone's conversations, including Maine, who was her father without the official paperwork. I wasn't sure what I would tell Rhea when she was older, but as of right now I was leaning towards the idea of erasing Vincent's entire lineage from my mind.

"I mean he wished death on her, treated me like shit when I was carrying her, and to top it off, tried to steal her from me and have another woman raise her," I told Shahani as we looked around this cute little baby boutique in the mall. "Should I really remind my baby of what a monster her father was? Or should I let Maine step in and be the man she needs?"

Shahani fingered a cute little princess onesie; I could tell that she was fiending to have a little girl. "Coming from the person that has been here from beginning to end, I say you let Maine be in her life as a father figure. Didn't Vincent's deadbeat ass family stop hitting you up when you and Rhea were awarded the bulk of his estate?"

"They sure did. I had Rhea with me thinking they would want to see her since it had been a couple months, but no, they didn't even spare her a second glance," I said, referring to the probate court meeting I had with the Morris family.

"Then fuck them. Personally, I don't think they should've gotten a single, solitary dime. They knew what he was doing to you and did nothing. If I could have my way they would be under the jail. There needs to be a new law stating that if trifling ass parents know their child is abusive and fail to warn any future spouses they should be—Francesca?"

I had noticed from the moment we entered the shop one of the sales associates had been acting really funny. At first I thought she might've thought we were stealing, but I figured that would be near impossible since I was rolling through with a limited edition Bugaboo stroller that had cost an arm and a leg. Now I knew it was because she didn't dare show her face to me after going to the media and acting like I was a deranged psychopath. I owed her an ass whupping and she was beyond lucky that I was pregnant, or else my foot would be up her ass. I could tell Shahani was thinking the same exact thing as we approached the now skittish Francesca.

"Hello, Nubia and Shahani. Welcome to the Nursery Barn: what can I get for you?" Francesca greeted with a fake ass Becky accent.

I cocked my head to the side. "Really, bitch. That's how you're gonna play this? Like you didn't get with my husband, take my place, and amp him up to come for my child? Hmm?"

Francesca held her hands up in defeat. "Nubia, please I don't want any problems right now."

"Don't 'Nubia, please' me, bitch. What happened to my 'please' when I was abused by Vincent? Where was my 'please' when he made me eat your pussy, huh? I didn't get a please then."

"I know and I'm sorry—"

"I don't think you are," I shot back. "Because if Vincent was still here you would be walking around on that high horse of yours looking down on me. You went to the news outlets and did interviews calling me guilty! You almost had me sent to jail behind your bullshit so please try to explain to me why I should be quiet up in here?"

Francesca placed a hand to her mouth to keep from crying. "Nubia, without Vincent I have nothing. His family blamed me for his death, saying that I should've stopped him from going up there, which I can now admit I should have. I was kicked out of his house with nothing but the clothes on my back. Vincent may have treated me nice, but he was tight with his wallet; I got what he gave me and on the day he died all I had was $500 in my account. He didn't leave me anything in his will either, so I've been living in a shelter until I get on my feet. This job is all I got!"

"And I was all I had," I hissed, getting right up in her face, close enough so that our noses touched. "You're looking for pity from me when I have none to offer you. You saw how Vincent treated me and believed that it made you better than me. That he was your man and you would always have his heart. Well good job for you because you did have his heart, and in the end, his wife got his wallet. I also got blessed with a good man and more fortune than I could ever ask for, not even including the money I got from Vincent. And now, I'm going to take that good fortune to another store because I refuse to pay your bills directly or indirectly. Have a nice life."

Shahani clapped and wolf whistled me out of the boutique, chanting my name on the quiet street. When we were outside, she hugged me tight. "I'm so proud of you, boo. You've come such a long way and it shows with everything that you do."

"It's these babies," I chuckled through the tears spilling down my cheeks. "They're pushing me to be better. And they're making me a little crazy too."

"Crazy and respected. Life is out here blessing us and humbling plenty of these bitches," Shahani replied, holding out a napkin she pulled from her purse. I watched as her eyes traveled behind me and narrowed. "Speaking of bitches that need humbling…Hello, Nia."

Nia was walking through the mall wearing a pair of chinos with a black button up. The black moccasins on her feet were a stark contrast to the usual designer heels she wore. I guess Francesca wasn't the only person to fall on hard times, because judging by her entire outfit, Nia was on the hunt for a holiday position.

"Hi, Shahani," Nia said, slowing to a stroll. "Hey, Nubia."

"What brings you to the mall, you little Grinch? I know it ain't to buy nobody nothing," Shahani said, her eyes steadily raking Nia's appearance.

Nia rolled her eyes. "I'll have you know I'm here looking to get a job for the holiday season. It's too dangerous to get back into the life and my relationship with Vaughn is still on ice as he heals."

"His girlfriend is still keeping him away from you?"

"Fuck that nigga; he was a bitch ass little punk anyway. Waking up to Drea and his family surrounding him made him all soft, so they got back together. It doesn't matter to me, though, because he's talking all that shit now because he just got out the hospital. I give him another month and he'll be right back sniffing around me."

Shahani shook her head. "You still don't get it, do you? Why don't you find a man that belongs to you instead of chasing everyone else's? Stealing someone's man is what got you into the situation you're in right now, and you still don't give a fuck."

"You're right," Nia mumbled.

"What?" we both said at the same time.

"Shahani, I said you're right. You know how I was raised so what makes you think I would act any other way? I have to look out for #1 because it's either kill or be killed out here. I'm not you, with the cute little dreams and the ability to make hustlers fall in love with me. I'm the bitch that only knows how to get what she wants by using what she has."

Nia broke down in tears, full on sobbing in the middle of the mall. Shahani was watching her with an impassive expression. I knew her cousin had cut her deep and there was no way in hell she would comfort the woman who had set her up to be killed. However, she did offer her some words of encouragement.

"Now that you're aware of why you are the way you are, do something about it," Shahani said, grabbing the handlebar to Rhea's stroller and taking off, leaving Nia standing there looking like a raccoon with her mascara running down her face.

I handed Nia one of the tissues I hadn't used and kept it moving. Shahani had tears welling in her eyes when I caught up to her. My girl wasn't used to being so cold, and I could tell that she wanted to help her little cousin out but knew nothing good would come of it.

"These pregnancy hormones got me all in my feelings," Shahani admitted after a few minutes as she dabbed at her face. "I'm over here acting like a straight up punk and you're the one reading bitches for their rights with no mercy. My how the tables have turned."

"If you want it's not too late for me to go back and tell her how I really feel…" I joked, halfway turning around only to be pulled along by Shahani.

"No, you can be the best pregnancy buddy in the world and eat some ice cream with me. Look, there's a Haagen-Dazs stand right over there…"

Shahani, who was farther along than I was, took a seat while I ordered our ice cream. My phone lit up with a call from an unknown number. I didn't have the best history with those, but I picked up anyway just to make sure it wasn't important.

"Hey, it's me…Sampson."

"How'd you get my number and why are you using it?"

"I wanted to see how Shahani was doing other than her weekly texts telling me she's good. I also wanted to get your opinion on some stuff for the surprise baby shower I'm throwing her."

I groaned. "Why don't you call Sharita? I'm pretty sure she can help you throw a real bomb ass baby shower."

"I want the person that knows her best helping me out."

"How about you cut a check and I'll get everything done?" I proposed, knowing I really wasn't trying to be in the same vicinity as Sampson.

"I want to be a part of the planning for my next child's baby shower. I know I'm a villain to you, but I've been nothing but good to my other children, and you can blame your mother for you not experiencing that."

"Blame my dead mother?"

There was a pregnant pause on the other end. "Nubia—"

"Just send me over pictures of the stuff. Actually, send me all pictures from now on," I said and hung up.

I took a calming breath and moved up a pinch in the line. I wasn't mad with Sampson because of what he said about my mother…I was mad because he was right. I had this perfect image of my mother in my mind and to hear how she did Sampson had me conflicted on where I stood with him. Her honesty would've saved everyone involved in this situation. That wasn't the only part of this situation that was unfortunate. I glanced over at Shahani, who was playing with a now awake Rhea. She was going through her pregnancy without the father of her child while I had my relationship with Maine. My phone lit up with pictures of color schemes for the baby shower with the caption, "Which one would she like the most?" I gave each scheme a fair look and knew the aqua color scheme was right up Shahani's alley. I could suck it up and plan this shower for my girl when she had already given up so much for me.

Nia

I stood there watching Nubia and Shahani eating ice cream, laughing like the best of friends like Shahani ain't lie in that bitch face for years. So she was to be granted forgiveness for her hoe tendencies while she couldn't forgive me for mine? Okay, so I went along with Donovan and his plan, but I honestly had no idea that he wanted to kill the girl; I thought we were gonna trick her out a few times and send her back to her man. To be quite honest she needed to let it the fuck go, having me put on a show in front of all these damn people. I thought I had softened her fat ass up some but no; she was still playing games. I told Lonzo as much on my way back to the house.

"You've been following them all day long and you mean to tell me that you haven't found anything we can use to get what we want," Lonzo said incredulously. "Nia, these niggas are closing in on me and if I don't find a chink in their armor soon then we're all assed out."

"Listen, all them bitches did was walk, shop, and eat ice cream. It's been like this for the past seven months; they walk their fat asses around eating food, shopping, and going to the doctor all the damn time."

"What?"

"I said they're walking around eating food—"

"I heard what you said, but why didn't you tell me sooner? Nia, you sure they're not pregnant?"

"Of course they're pregnant. Shahani looks like she's going to go in any day now and Nubia's a little behind her. Them hoes were busy," I replied nonchalantly.

"YOU STUPID BITCH WHY DIDN'T YOU TELL ME THIS BEFORE!"

I rolled my eyes so hard they damn near got stuck in the back of my head. "Because this is my first time seeing them like this, that's why. You told me to stay far away from them so I have, and part of that is only seeing them when they hop out the car to go into places—while wearing coats. This time I decided to go into the mall because I wanted to see if anyone was hiring so I could get into some workers' comp money. There they were with no coats, looking big as houses."

"I ain't mean to snap on you like that, but how long have we been plotting? This makes it so much easier. These niggas will risk it all for their bitches, but their kids? They'd risk way more than that. I feel something brewing in my brain. I'll share it when you get home. Bring dinner."

Lonzo hung up before I could get a word in edgewise. I tossed my phone on the passenger seat of the car, shaking my head as I asked myself what I ever saw in his ass. When he was with Shahani, Lonzo was like a god; his respect spanned the entire hood and there wasn't a nigga crazy enough to go against him. For someone with all that power he was humble as fuck, which made him so damn sexy. This new Lonzo was paranoid and annoying as hell; if he wasn't talking about Shahani and winning her back, then he was going off the deep end and getting in the mood to murk everyone. I had to stop him from shooting up plenty of places a few times. To be honest, I knew the girls were pregnant but didn't tell him until now because I didn't want him to do something premature that would get the both of us killed. I guess it was too late to be thinking of that, because by the time I got back to the apartment I'm sure crazy ass would have a plot ready for me to go over.

"Damn it smells good in here," I said as I entered Donna's Soul Food; he might've had his ways, but Lonzo had put me on to some good food spots, with this being one of my favorites.

Or at least it was my favorite until I saw Drea and Vaughn sitting at my favorite table chopping it up. I hadn't fixed my makeup so I was looking paler than usual and my once crisp chinos were wrinkled. All in all, I looked a hot ass mess and had to see my ex nigga looking good as ever with his old bitch. Drea eyed my stomach and covered her mouth as if to hide a laugh. No, I wasn't pregnant, but I damn sure was glad not to be pregnant by a spineless little bitch like Vaughn, who focused on his phone so he wouldn't look at me. I placed my order and took a seat on the other side of the compact restaurant. As Drea started running her mouth, I wish I had laughed in her face when she showed up at the video set because now she was getting on my last damn nerve with all her loud talking.

"Vaughn, please tell me that you confirmed our tickets for the Bahamas," Drea said, her shrill voice carrying through the restaurant. "I already held up my part of the deal and booked the hotel for the next two weeks."

Vaughn sighed. "I already told you I handled that earlier this week, Drea."

"I'm just making sure, baby. This is our honeymoon we're talking about," Drea simpered.

Honeymoon? As in they were getting married. I pulled up Instagram and went straight to Drea's page before recalling that she had blocked me ages ago when I was on Vaughn's arm all over. To my surprise, she unblocked me; her page was wide open and showed various pictures of her planning an extravagant wedding. I closed the app and looked up to see Drea sitting real pretty, smiling at me as she held Vaughn's hand, making sure to show off the three-carat diamond engagement ring on her finger, with this one larger than the one I saw at the hospital. Her phone buzzed on the table, stealing her attention.

"Oh, this is the caterer. I need to check and made sure he has the taco bar he promised me for the reception," Drea said as she scrambled from her seat and answered the call on her way out the door.

I waited for her to hit the corner before looking over at Vaughn, who was still refusing to look in my direction. After a minute of digging into the side of his face with my eyes, I decided to shoot him a text.

Me: *Oh so we marrying bitches now? Bet.*

Vaughn: *Did you really think this was going anywhere? Eventually I had to make a choice and that choice was going to have to be Drea.*

I slammed my phone on the table and rounded on Vaughn. "You're a fucking liar. You know that, right? At least have the decency to look me in my face when you lie to me! You can't because both you and I know what we had going on was real."

"Yo, calm down before my girl come back in," Vaughn said, his eyes still glued to his phone.

"It's too late; I'm already back." Drea's narrowed eyes cut from Vaughn to me. "Lemme guess: you decided to shoot your shot while I was gone and got curved. I tried to be nice by showing you who got the ring but I guess I gotta get nasty with it. Whatever you had with Vaughn is over: that was nothing more than a phase. We're getting married and there ain't a damn thing you can do about it unless you kill me, bitch, and even then Vaughn will never want a busted, money hungry, thirst bucket like you."

I guess after such a passionate speech Drea was looking for me to cry like her desperate ass did. No, that's not how I planned to handle this bitch. I leaned in and said, "You're mad at me because being mad at your man means accepting the fact that you accept anything from him. So you're lashing out while deep down you're wondering if what you said was enough to keep me away. I'mma let you win today because I'm in a good mood. That, and now you'll spend the rest of your marriage wondering when I'll pop up to reclaim the piece of Vaughn's heart that I have. I don't blame you, bitch, I would be scared too."

The cashier came and interrupted the confrontation by calling out for Vaughn to pick up their order. He rushed to grab the food and ushered a stunned Drea from the shop. Homegirl must've heard the conversation because she was standing there with a *you told her* look on her face.

"I'm scared of you," she said as she handed me my food. "Don't let her get you down; before you walked in she was getting into his ass about not being as into this wedding as her because his mother was picking up his slack."

I placed a twenty in her tip jar. "I figured as much. She's gonna spend the rest of her life mad as fuck at me because she doesn't have the balls to be mad at him. You have a blessed day, boo."

I had a little pep in my step as I walked back to the car. Today was quite a day; I had been read and paid it forward, but unlike Shahani, that wasn't good enough.

"Wassup," Lonzo said from the couch of the Crown Heights apartment we had been sharing for the better part of the year. "Oh shit, you went to Donna's. I was in the mood for that, too."

"Shut up and take your clothes off," I said, kicking off my shoes and shimmying out of my pants.

Lonzo pushed himself back into the couch. "What?"

"You heard what I said, nigga. If you don't wanna take them off then pull your pants down."

Yes, I couldn't stand Lonzo for nothing, but after seeing Vaughn and Drea together, I needed to get my mind right if I was gonna switch into savage mode. That involved getting some of what Alonzo's packing in those grey sweatpants he's always walking around wearing. Staring at it while he went off on one of his tangents was one of the only reasons I was still here. Now I needed a piece to keep me sane.

"What the fuck are you doing?" Lonzo said, fighting me as I tried to take his dick out of his sweatpants. "I'm trying to work out my situation with your cousin."

"Are you really? With her carrying another mans seed in her

body?" I questioned, causing his grip on my wrists to slacken.

"I got a plan for that," Lonzo countered.

I raised an eyebrow. "Well as of right now you're single as fuck and I want dick so you're gonna give it to me. I can give less than a fuck about your little happily ever after you're looking for with my cousin. All I want is a nut. Can I get that?"

"Nia, you're like a little sister to—"

I cut off that little sister with a kiss on the lips. Lonzo must've been thinking little stepsister because after the initial shock wore off he let go of my hands and tugged me into his lap. I began grinding my now soaking wet panties against his already throbbing dick that threatened to bust from his Champion sweats. He unbuttoned my shirt with shaking fingers, like it had been a while for him as well. I grew impatient and ripped the cheap ass H&M shirt wide open, revealing the lacy Victoria's Secret bra I wore.

"You sure you wanna do this?" Lonzo asked uneasily.

I rolled my eyes. "If I throw it any harder at you you'll get a concussion. Just shut up and take this pussy I'm tryna give you."

I whipped out Lonzo's dick and began stroking it. Oh, it's been so long since I had some dick and his was so pretty; the tip was perfect and the veins running through it throbbed under my fingertips from the sudden change of direction. Saliva dripped from my mouth in anticipation and I found myself devouring Lonzo's dick, swirling my tongue around it like a long lost piece of candy. Other than being broke and homeless, the worst part of this year was losing consistent dick. It was the reason for my sullen attitude, breakouts, and depression.

However, once I slid all ten inches of Lonzo inside of me, all the frustration I was feeling was replaced by ecstasy.

"Fuck," Lonzo and I exhaled at the same time.

Any sexual tension we had dissolved as I bounced on top of Lonzo's dick, riding him until my legs went weak. When they did, he flipped me onto my stomach and proceeded to fuck me with no abandon. This was what I had been dreaming of ever since I was a teenage girl, and it was the only part of Lonzo that didn't let me down. I arched my back and tossed it back at him, laughing when he nearly fell off the couch trying to control all this ass. Those laughs quickly became cries as he stroked my G-spot, which was enough to have me cumming all over my hand as I played with my clit. I sucked on my fingers, enjoying the taste of my pussy as Lonzo continued to beat it up. He was picking up the pace and I could tell he was ready to cum so I squeezed my pussy muscles tight.

"Shit!" he screamed as he busted his load inside of me and collapsed on top of me.

We lay in a satisfied silence, with his dick still throbbing inside of me. I knew now was my time to get what I wanted, because it was only a matter of time that this nigga came back for seconds.

"Remember how you said you would help me get Vaughn back?"

Lonzo stroked my cheek. "You still want that cornball ass nigga back?"

"I mean I don't really want him, but I don't want him to be with his current bitch—I mean fiancée," I replied, biting my lip to keep from smiling; I had Lonzo right where I wanted him. "She likes to embarrass me in public by throwing their relationship up in my face."

"Well we gotta do something about that. How you want her handled?"

I turned around and looked him in the eye. "I want that bitch dead."

Lonzo pecked me on the lips. "Say no more."

Maine

For the third time this week the sun had beat me home. I was at the house in Jersey putting together both of the cribs for the babies with the help of Nubia. Somewhere between the delivery of the cribs and the examination of the parts, we lost both sets of instructions. I was ready to have a professional come and put the whole thing together when Nubia gave me the puppy dog pout and started talking about how this would be the perfect way to build memories. We built some memories all right; today was day one of me losing my mind. It took finding the instructions online in German and Nubia reading them out for me to complete both cribs in twelve hours. When we were done, she found the instructions inside of her sweatpants pocket. I felt played until I realized it was her cute way of trying to spend more time with me. I told her she could repay me by giving me some of that pregnant pussy I had heard about, and all of a sudden it was past her bedtime. I was still chuckling about it as I entered the penthouse.

"*Buenos días*," Estalita greeted from the kitchen. "I'm making *chilaquiles. Quieres*?"

The smell was enough to wake me up. "*Sí*."

Estalita whipped up two plates and five minutes later, we were sitting at the table enjoying a nice breakfast. From the moment she returned from México, Estalita came back as less of a princess and more of a wife. She still suffered from the occasional tantrum if I spent too much time away from home, but she questioned my whereabouts less and was more willing to discuss other topics no matter how shallow they were.

“What have you been up to, Jermaine? How are things going at the club?” Estalita asked with genuine concern. “Are those girls still giving you trouble?”

My story for never being home was that aside from handling the family business, I also had to tend to some out of control strippers. Of course there was no way in hell any of my employees would dare disrespect me, but it was the only way I could see Nubia on a consistent basis without my wife noticing. So I played my part.

“Yup. I’m working on setting up a talent night so I can get some fresh faces in and these disrespectful hoes out. It should take”—I looked up and recalled Nubia's due date—“maybe two more months, three tops.”

“Why so long?”

“They’re both top billed girls. Before I toss them out I gotta make sure whatever new girls I get can bring in just as much money.”

Estalita pouted. “You sure you don’t want me to show up and handle the situation? If there's one thing I know how to do, it’s get a bitch together.”

“Who you been hanging around?” I asked, choking back a laugh. “I ain't ever heard you talk like that.”

“I've been watching this really good show called *Black Ink Chicago*. I also watch these shows about love and hip-hop. Since you’ve taken the time out to embrace my culture I thought I should at least try to understand yours better."

I figured right now would be a good time to tell Estalita that I was African, but if she thought part of black culture was ratchet television, then I could only imagine what she might think being African dictated. All she would have to do is mention me hunting animals in the wild and I would have to divorce her ass with the quickness. She looked real happy like she accomplished something so I decided to let her rock.

"What are your plans for today?" I asked as I polished off my plate of food.

Estalita placed a tortilla chip in her mouth and played coy. "I don't know, maybe going shopping for some shoes, a purse…a gift for Shahani's surprise baby shower tomorrow. Why didn't you tell me that Sampson was throwing her a shower? I had to find the invitation in your pants pocket while I was doing the laundry."

"Since when do you do laundry?"

"Since my *abuelita* told me that I should cook, clean, and do laundry for my husband. Haven't you noticed that you haven't ran out of clean underwear?"

"I thought someone else was washing it."

Estalita shook her head in disappointment. "No, I've been handling everything around here. It's only right since you're out taking care of the family. *Papí* is very satisfied with the way you've been running everything. Business is booming and those new accounts you brought in are doing very well."

"He told you that?"

"*Sí*," Estalita replied, rising from her seat and collecting our plates. "Now how about you tell me why you didn't tell me about this baby shower."

"It slipped my mind. Plus, I ain't think you would wanna go anyway," I replied, pulling her into my lap and resting my chin on her shoulder.

It was nothing but the truth; from the moment I proposed to her, Estalita acted like she never wanted to be bothered with anyone from my life. She meshed well with Shahani, but I thought that if it didn't involve one of her *chicas* that she wouldn't care whether she attended or not. That, and the fact that Nubia would be in attendance. I would have my wife and the mother of my child in one room, and unfortunately, they weren't the same person. Fortunately, both knew their roles and if they kept to them this could go off without a hitch.

******

Estalita was bouncing up and down in her seat as we approached Sampson's Long Island mansion. She had been in a good mood all day; she even wrapped our present herself, which was entertaining to see because I had to cut her out of the ribbon before she strangled herself. I was still laughing to myself as I carried the haphazardly wrapped bottle maker machine and deluxe baby bouncer up the stairs. My heart skipped a beat as I stepped over the threshold and heard a familiar voice say, "Welcome!"

"Thank you," Estalita purred. "Aww, *que linda*. You're having a baby as well?"

"Yes, I am," Nubia said politely. "Are you a friend of Sampson's?"

"My husband and Sampson are close, right, Jermaine?" Estalita asked as she removed the top box so Nubia could get a look at my face. I felt an uncomfortable pang in my chest as our eyes locked. "Don't be rude, Jermaine. Say *hola.*"

"Hey. You know where I can put these?" I asked politely, turning my attention from Nubia to the decorated home in front of me.

I saw her point towards the backyard from the corner of my eye. "Everyone's outside. There's a huge table; it's hard to miss."

"Thanks."

Estalita bounced along without a second thought at the awkward introduction. I had warned Nubia that Estalita would be coming with me to the party tomorrow so we had to keep everything on the low, but I knew it had to hurt for her to see us together like this. It hurt me too, and that hurt kept me from looking back at her because I knew if I saw her crying I might fuck around and do something stupid for me and dangerous for her.

"Shahani," Estalita shouted as she pranced over to the alcove where Shahani was sitting, dressed in a hand-embroidered gown with a train to compete with some wedding dresses. Pillows and platters of fruit surrounded her while two women fanned her with large palm leaves. "Congratulations! Do you know what you're having?"

Shahani rubbed her belly. "I have no idea. I want it to be a surprise. Me and my best friend, Nubia, are both waiting for the birth to find out," she said, smiling at Estalita. She turned her attention towards me. "Maine, can you get us something to drink from the kitchen? And a few of those little chicken sandwiches that the caterers are heating up?

I know they said it would be like five or so minutes."

I was getting ready to ask Shahani why she ain't have one of the waiters walking around to do it, but realized that would buy me at least ten minutes to check in with Nubia. "Aight, I got you."

On my way back into the house, I took a good look at the setup. Nubia did an amazing job on choosing decorations and a theme: gold tables dotted the yard, filled with flowers and tiers of cupcakes being held by mermaid statues; the large Olympic-sized swimming pool was filled with women dressed as mermaids swimming around, their smiles wide as partygoers took pictures of them; the waiters were dressed in turquoise and gold as they handed out fruity cocktails that resembled cerulean ocean water. Sampson had spared no expense and Nubia had the time of her life planning this event. I could see it as she gave orders to the wait staff. She looked beautiful in the purple floral dress she wore. Her hair was in wild, kinky curls and her skin glowed.

"You sure you don't want one?" I asked, motioning to the party in the back. "You did an amazing job."

Nubia shook her head. "Nah, I don't like the attention, and between the two of us do we really have enough people to fill a huge backyard? A dinner would be nice though."

"A dinner is what you'll get. I'll make the plans and all you have to do is show up as your beautiful self," I said, holding her chin. "I know it hurt seeing her today. I tried to keep her from showing up but if I would've—"

"You don't have to explain anything to me, Maine. It hurt at first, but at the end of the day, what can I really do? She's got the ring," Nubia replied as she gently moved her chin from between my fingers.

I bristled at her remark. “That’s all she's got: a ring. She doesn’t have my child, my heart, or my time. Don’t let what you see out there have you thinking I love you any less. Trust me; I don’t like this shit either, but I do what I have to in order to keep you safe.”

“I know, Maine.” Nubia smiled at me but it didn’t reach her eyes until she looked over my shoulder. “Hey, bitch. You made it!”

“Of course I did,” Cheyenne exclaimed as she came rushing over to Nubia with two little girls in tow. “We would’ve been here sooner but Sullivan was playing games. He brought her back to me an hour late and I still had to do her hair and put her on something cute because that hoe ass girlfriend of his loves to keep Marlee bummy while her little crumb snatchers are fresh. Ugh, she got my blood boiling. All I need you to do is point me in the direction of my boo, Shahani, and the alcohol.”

“There's an open bar. You know what? I’ll show you where it is. See you, Maine,” Nubia said politely as she ushered the group from the kitchen.

“I promise to give your girl back as soon as I’m done,” Cheyenne called over her shoulder.

A lone waitress stood there bobbing on her heels, unsure of what to do next. I’m sure she saw me walk in with Estalita, and comforting Nubia seconds after looked messy as fuck. I figured I would help her out by giving her something to do. I made my requests and checked my messages as I waited for everything to heat up.

“Look who showed up: the prodigal son.”

Sampson stood in the doorway watching me with a grin on his face. We hadn't spoken since the night he discovered Nubia was his daughter, and I thought it was for good reason; I had fulfilled my obligations to him and moved on to greener pastures. However, when I received the invitation in the mail at my Jersey residence, I took it as an olive branch I was willing to accept. If Nubia could tolerate her father after nearly kissing death on the lips, then I could be cordial with Sampson despite his betrayal.

"Wassup, Sampson," I said, dapping him casually.

Sampson punched me lightly on the arm. "Nothing much, just getting ready for the next Emerson kid to come along. It's been so long, nearly twenty years. My baby girl would've been twenty-three last month."

"How you even sure that's she's gone?"

Sampson tapped his chest lightly. "You'll come to find that as a parent you feel your kids in here. I stopped feeling her a long time ago."

"If you can feel them then why didn't you feel Nubia? You looked her in the eye and still made the decision to move the way you did. What if Jodeci didn't have a heart and you sent in one of these wild ass niggas to do what you ordered?"

"Then I would have lost another daughter, and it would've torn me up inside. Almost as much as one of my most loyal soldiers lying to my face." Sampson's words were spoken like a disappointed father. "I brought you here, gave you my last name, and treated you like damn near one of my own kids, only for you to lie to me."

"I lied to protect her from you because if I didn't then—"

"Then what?" Sampson barked.

"Then I would've ruined my life." I said, pounding my chest. "This wasn't some nameless, faceless mark that you needed me to handle; this was a woman I had known for a year, that I fell in love with. Yes, I lied to you because I had no idea how to fix the situation, but you can't tell me you haven't done anything crazier over love."

"I had a kid go in and kill her, her husband, and almost my child," Sampson said, running a hand over his hair. "I think it's safe to say that we both owe each other an apology. I had Jodeci handle business behind your back and you kept up your relationship with Nubia behind mine."

"I'm sorry for the way I handled things, man."

"I'm sorry too."

We dapped and shared a familial hug. While I knew we wouldn't be able to just jump back to being as close as we once were, it felt good to be back on positive terms with Sampson again. The waitress beckoned us to follow her with the tray of food. I noticed she had a stiff gait, and knew it might've had something to do with the conversations she had been privy too. She delivered the platter to Shahani and had barely cleared the table when Sampson grabbed her by the arm.

"You remember that confidentiality agreement you signed before starting work, don't you?"

"Y-y-yes, sir," she replied, nodding her head so fast it was a blur. "If you need anything else I'll be in the kitchen helping."

Sampson let go of her arm and watched as she scampered into the house, her golden jacket flapping in the wind like a cape. He chuckled at the sight until he turned around and found Shahani staring at him. "What?"

"What did you do to that girl?"

"Nothing, I was just reminding her of her position at this event. Don't you worry about any of that; today's your day and all I want you to do is sit back and allow yourself to be worshipped like the queen you are."

Shahani took a sip of the ginger ale in her champagne glass, observing Sampson over the rim. I thought she was going to drag it, but she surprised everyone by replying, "You know what? You're absolutely right. You and Nubia did such a good job that I won't even let any type of negativity get in the way of me enjoying myself. Speaking of Nubia, where is she?"

Everyone searched the packed party and found Nubia on the other side of the room with Cheyenne. They were setting up a table of activities as they talked amongst themselves. I could tell Shahani wanted to spend some time with Nubia, but knew it would be near impossible with Estalita over here. This was turning into a larger mess than I expected, and I knew the only way to make everything better was to get Estalita out of here ASAP.

"Sampson, where's the powder room?" Estalita asked politely.

"There's a private one on the second level. It's the third door on the left. Can't miss it," Sampson replied.

"*Gracias.* I'll be right back, *mi amor,*" she purred as she stood on her tiptoes and gave me a peck on the lips.

I watched as Estalita flounced through the party, catching the eye of every man in her path. She had also caught the attention of Nubia, who covertly checked her out from the corner of her eye, and Cheyenne, who wasn't so subtle. Estalita had barely cleared the exit when Cheyenne came storming towards me, her face contorting with rage every step she took. Nubia waddled behind her with a panicked expression on her face; she didn't want a scene and Cheyenne was looking to start one.

"You pick a mighty fine time to choose to bring your wife with you," Cheyenne hissed. "Do you know how much stress you're putting Nubia under? She's already saying that she's having pains."

"What?" Shahani moved to the edge of her seat. She motioned to the vacant cushion to her left her since Sampson sat to the right of her. "Nubia, please get off of your feet for a few. Come, take a seat next to me and explain how you managed to pull this off without telling me…"

Nubia took a seat next to Shahani, followed by Cheyenne, who I could tell wanted to argue, but dropped it for Nubia's sake. I took a seat on the adjacent sofa and made sure to leave some space for Estalita to the left of me. She did nothing to deserve being placed in direct contact of Cheyenne's venom, and no matter how one-sided our marriage might've been, I would never allow someone to disrespect her in public. I told Cheyenne as much with my eyes as Estalita returned. She sat down in the space next to me and leaned her head on my shoulder.

"Sampson, you have a beautiful home," Estalita said, motioning to the house. "The longer I stay here the more ready I become to leave the city behind and have a house of my own."

"Thank you, Estalita. It is a beautiful place, but it only became a home when Shahani moved in with me," Sampson said, earning a small smile from Shahani.

Estalita gushed at the show of affection. "Aww, that is so romantic. I can see it in your eyes how much you love her because tough men like you only melt for the women they love. When is the wedding?"

"There isn't going to be a wedding any time soon," Shahani said, holding her hands up for Estalita to slow down, and laughing at the way she raised her brows in confusion. "We've got a long way to go before we get there. If we ever get there."

"Really?" Estalita looked crushed. "But you love him and he loves you. In any relationship all you need is love."

"And trust," Cheyenne piped up. "You can have all the love in the world, but if you have to worry about where your spouse is once they leave home, then your relationship is doomed."

Estalita nuzzled into my neck. "I am happy I don't have that problem. I have been fortunate enough to find a man that loves me, treats me right, and who I can trust. Where's your man?"

"Estalita!" I exclaimed as Nubia said to Cheyenne, "Girl, please leave her alone."

Estalita's head snapped to Nubia. "Have we met before?"

"At the door an hour ago," Nubia said with forced politeness.

"No...before that. There's something really familiar about you."

No. This could not be happening right now.

Nubia shook her head. "I'm sorry, but you and I don't run in the same circles. I've never met you a day in my life."

Estalita was getting ready to press on when Shahani interrupted the conversation by announcing the arrival of Jodeci. Everyone's attention turned to him, his girl, and the baby girl she was holding in her arms. Shorty was all smiles until her eyes rested on Nubia. The animosity was the same on Nubia's end; the conversation she had with Estalita was long forgotten at the sight of her cousin.

“You know what? I can deal with her, but what I can't deal with right now is this bitch,” Nubia muttered as she rose from her seat. “I’m going to grab something to drink from the kitchen.”

“You want me to come with you?” Cheyenne offered.

“No, girl. I need a minute to myself.”

Nubia walked around one side of the table as the couple came around the other to greet Sampson and Shahani. I watched as she trudged into the house with a heavy heart. As much as she preached on trusting me, Estalita had a viselike grip on my arm and I could feel it losing circulation the long she held on.

“Wassup,” Jodeci said, dapping me and hugging Estalita. “We just came through to show some love and get our little princess out for some fresh air.”

Estalita and Ashanti kissed cheeks and started playing catch up. Soon all the women were talking with each other save for Cheyenne. I used their conversation as my cover to duck off with Jodeci so I could find Nubia. Estalita didn’t blink twice at my departure; she patted the spot next to her and Ashanti sat down.

“I told Ashanti on the ride here not to bother your girl,” Jodeci said. “She said she wouldn’t but you already know how that shit goes;

she's looking for someone to blame and it don't matter who so long as it ain't her parents. No worries though, I'll get her in line if I have to. Go handle your business. I gotta take a call so I'll come back to grab you."

"Good looks, bro," I said, and started on my search for Nubia.

I found her in the second living room at the end of the hall. She stood in the doorway watching the children of invited guests play. One of the caretakers brought Rhea over long enough for her to kiss baby girl and bounce her up and down. Rhea saw me over her shoulder and gave me a toothless grin.

"What are you smiling at behind…oh," Nubia said as our eyes met. She kissed Rhea on the forehead and handed her back to the caretaker. "I'll be back for her in a few once I'm done with my activities."

"Nubia—"

"Maine, please leave me alone. Today has been nothing but a complete slap in the face. I don't know what possessed me to think this could ever work between us," Nubia said, shaking her head in disappointment. "It's one thing to know she's out there somewhere, but to see both of you together breaks my heart."

I reached out to touch her, only to have her shrink away from me. "Oh, so it's like that now? I have done nothing but be good to you, my child, and Rhea over the past seven months and this is how you treat me? Anything you've needed I've been there, day or night, completely neglecting *her*, and you're really sitting here acting like—"

"Like what? Like you're married? I know I am," Nubia shot back as she pushed past me and stormed down the hall. She reappeared seconds later, her face contorted in rage. "Let me grab my child because

I don't have time for this shit today."

"Well you need to make time for it today," I heard Ashanti counter as she gained on Nubia. "Don't hide now, bitch."

I stepped in front of Ashanti before she could catch Nubia. "Jodeci already told you about showing up here to start some shit."

"Last I checked Jodeci ain't my father. My father is dead because of that bitch right there and I swore on my mother's grave that when I laid eyes on her ass I would put her in one next."

"Well I can promise you right now that ain't happening. If you really think I'mma move out the way for you to put a hand on Nubia you don' lost your fucking mind," I said, catching her each time she tried to duck around me to catch Nubia.

"You know what, Ashanti? I'm sick and fucking tired of you sitting here trying to be some victim that you aren't. You wanna fight me? Step into this room and let's get it popping, bitch."

Ashanti fought even harder to grab Nubia, who stood in the doorway of the office, but I held on to her tight. Jodeci came rushing down the hallway and grabbed Ashanti up, hissing in her ear for her to calm the fuck down before people came looking. Against my better judgment I told him to follow me into the room Nubia had disappeared into.

"Listen," I said, closing the door and locking it behind me. "Today's not the day for this bullshit. Ashanti and Nubia, whatever you feel like you need to say to each other, now is the time to get it out."

"I'm not the one trying to fight a pregnant woman in the middle of a baby shower. She is!" Nubia shot back.

Ashanti stopped fighting with Jodeci and straightened herself up. “Don’t act like I don’t have every right to be angry. My parents were murdered! My last image of my parents is finding them decaying in their bedroom, twisted in a position no one would ever want to see their parents in! What if it were your parents?”

Nubia pinched the bridge of her nose. “Are you forgetting that I watched my parents die? You had to see it as a grown woman, but imagine what it must've been like for me to have to witness it right in front of my face. I wish my parents would’ve died in a car crash or some other indirect way. What I don’t wish is to hold my father’s hand and feel the life drain out of it.”

“There you go again, making everything about you! Why can't it be about me for once?!”

“When has it ever been about me?” Nubia asked, her tone laced with exasperation. “When has anything ever been about me. Your father raped me and your mother destroyed my self-esteem while they placed you on this pedestal that made you untouchable. They stole the money my parents left for me and sent you to college with it while telling me I was too stupid to do anything other than work a dead end job. The home you grew up in was owned by my parents and I was raised in the attic of it while you had two rooms. I have starved while you ate, so spare me the ‘it’s all about Nubia’ mess because we both know it’s a lie.”

Ashanti shook her head. “You're the one that’s lying. My father didn’t rape you; the two of you were having an affair and you got pregnant in order to one up my mother. The rest of it is a lie too. My parents were good people and I know you had something to do with them dying."

"They were good people, Ashanti? You're going to sit there and act like you don't remember what happened that summer?" Ashanti covered her mouth and bit back a sob. "Hmmm? Are you going to stand in front of me and act like you don't remember walking in on me and her?"

"She said it wasn't what I thought…"

Nubia broke down, "It was. Your father wasn't the only one that used me. Your mother made me do things to her, too. Stuff no child should ever have to do to anyone, Ashanti. You know damn well that whatever happened to your parents was nothing but karma. Karma for the way they did me. But it was karma that I had nothing to do with and you know it!"

"Fuck, Nubia! I know! I know they did you wrong, but they were still my parents. I still have the right to love them and want justice for them," Ashanti sobbed, pounding her chest.

"And I have every right to tell you that I hope they're burning in hell, and if you ever come near me again spewing this bullshit, you'll see them sooner than you think," Nubia replied coldly.

The temperature in the room had to have dropped about ten degrees. Jodeci escorted Ashanti out of the office, shaking his head along the way. He mouthed a "sorry," which I accepted because I knew if he had it his way this would've never gone down. I approached Nubia with my arms open wide.

"Maine, move away from me," she shouted as I took her into my arms. She melted against my chest. "Just leave me alone. I wanna go home."

I rocked her back and forth, smoothing her hair as I covered her with kisses on the forehead. "I know. I'll take you home."

"No the fuck you won't."

Estalita stood in the doorway with tears spilling down her cheeks. Nubia shoved away from me, her face stricken at us being caught together. "It's not what it looks—"

"It's exactly what the fuck it looks like!" Estalita barked at Nubia. "I knew I knew you from somewhere. You were the one that called Jermaine. You're the *puta* that tried to steal my husband from me!"

"Don't call her out of her name!" I barked back, advancing on Estalita.

Estalita came out of character and shoved me. "I'll call her whatever I want! You're standing here with a pregnant mistress and I'm supposed to be quiet! No! I will not! I gave you my heart and you stomped all over it! Does everyone else know? I bet they know and I've been sitting here looking stupid! You have to make a choice right now: her or me!"

Here was the moment I spent the past year trying to avoid: the one where I had to choose Nubia and endanger her life or choose Estalita and ruin mine. It only took a split second for me to make my decision, and I had barely parted my lips to utter the verdict when Nubia made the choice for me.

"No, he doesn't," she said, shaking her head on her way out the door. "I'm done with this."

Estalita's narrowed eyes followed her out the room and darted back to me once she was gone. "How could you? How could you stand on an altar and promise me that you will spend the rest of your life with me and…and…I can't even say it! I left home for you because I thought you loved me! It was a lie, wasn't it? It was all a lie!"

"And this was a marriage of convenience," I hissed, leaning in so close that our noses touched. "You can sit here and pretend that you love me all you want to, Estalita, but you know damn well all you saw in me was an opportunity to get out of your father's house. If you want to end it then go ahead, but I'm not getting ready to sit here and beg for your forgiveness when I can give less than a fuck."

"The Cartel is going to kill you, and when they're done, they're going to rip that baby out of her and kill them both," Estalita declared, her eyes cold. "That is the price for playing with my heart."

"If your father or any of his soldiers lay a hand on her they will never find your body. That's the price for playing with my woman. Now get the fuck out of my way."

Estalita stepped to the side, her face red as a tomato as she pulled out her phone to dial up either her *chicas* or her father. At this point, I couldn't care less what the Ordonez Brothers did. I would stay strapped and ready for them when they came gunning for me, but that was the farthest thought on my mind right now. I had to make sure Nubia was good. I searched the entire party for her, Shahani, or even Cheyenne's dramatic ass, and came up empty.

"Where's Nubia?" I asked Sampson, who was standing in front of the house smoking a cigar.

He motioned to the car peeling rubber down the street. "She came to Shahani in tears saying that Estalita was popping shit and tried to fight her. I told her that wasn't happening and that I would have both of you leave, but she insisted on going home. You already know Shahani wasn't leaving her behind. They pulled off five minutes ago."

"I can still catch her on the way—"

"Leave her alone, Maine."

I dismissed Sampson with a wave of my hand, which he caught and yanked me towards him. He let go once he had my attention. "I'm not leaving her alone. I already told Estalita that I'm done with the marriage—"

"Look at you; playing this game with your heart instead of your brain. Estalita is the key unlocking a world of possibility. She is what's going to have you retired by the age of thirty-five. There is no turning down that kind of legacy."

"And what about Nubia?"

Sampson didn't miss a beat when he replied, "You can fuck around with Salvador's daughter all you want, but you're done playing with mine. I don't care if I've been her father for seven months or seven minutes; I won't allow you to make a fool out of her any longer. Go back into that house, make up with your wife, and let Nubia heal."

As if on cue, Estalita came trudging out of the house. She had refreshed her makeup and to the naked eye, you couldn't tell she had been crying minutes ago. I wasn't done with Nubia, but I would give her some time to heal. That would give me time to repair our relationship the best I could.

"You call your father?" I asked once we were in the privacy of the car.

Estalita started blankly out of the window. "No," she replied, her tone deadpanned. "I like my freedom. I'm willing to look the other way when it comes to you and your girlfriend under one condition."

"Name it."

"No matter how much you may love her, worship her, and want to be with her in private, I will always come first in public. Don't ever have me in the same room as her ever again and don't ever choose her in front of me again."

"Deal."

Nubia

You know your life is going to shit when your murderous father makes you feel better. Sampson was on his feet when he saw me come running blindly through the party. I couldn't see where I was going and ran straight into his arms where I found solace. He rocked me back and forth, soothing me the way only a father could. The last time I was held like this was by my father after I fell off my bike and scraped my knees. I snatched myself from Sampson's embrace at the vivid memory, cursing my pregnancy hormones for getting the best of me.

"She found out about us and jumped down my throat. I was stupid for thinking this would work. I just wanna go home," I choked out.

Shahani rose to her feet with the help of Cheyenne. "Then we're going home. Sampson..."

"Don't even worry about it," Sampson said, pulling out his phone and making a call. "I need to stay behind to lock up the house and pay everyone, but once I'm done I'm on my way to Brooklyn. I'll have one of my men take all of you home."

"I need to grab Rhea."

"You know what?" Cheyenne said as we entered the house. "How about I stay behind with Sampson and ride back with Rhea? It'll give you some time to get yourself together."

I didn't want Rhea to see me like this; she was so observant that my distraught appearance was likely to upset her. I agreed for her sake, and knew Cheyenne would take good care of her. "Okay, her clothes and baby bag are in the guest bathroom closet. I'll see you soon."

Cheyenne kissed me on the cheek and disappeared down the hall. Sampson led us outside where a Cadillac Escalade was waiting. I stole a furtive glance back at the entrance of the house, a small part of me wishing Maine would appear, telling me that he chose me over his wife and we could now be together. I rebuked the thought with a shake of my head, snapping out of it as the SUV door slammed shut. My eyes remained trained on the house until it disappeared from my view. I turned to Shahani, who was staring at me with motherly concern.

"I'm sorry I ruined your baby shower," I apologized. "You looked so beautiful, you were having so much fun, Sampson was on his best behavior…"

"Honey, I had an amazing time because of you and the beautiful shower you helped to put together. I have more pictures and positive memories than I have negative ones. Your job was to create an amazing day and you did, okay?"

"Oka—aaaahhh!"

THUMP!

The driver slammed down on his breaks and skidded to a halt. "Oh shit, I think I hit someone."

"What!" we shouted.

"It all happened so fast. One minute the road was empty and the next I saw her jump into the road."

"We gotta call the police," Shahani said at once.

The driver shook his head. "No, we need to call Sampson first. I got some heat on me and if the cops come, I'm sure they'll start searching the car. Lemme get out and look."

Shahani and I turned around in our seats the best we could. I gasped at the sight of the mangled body of the floor. The person's legs were bent at an awkward angle, their clothes were shredded, and from what I could see, they weren't breathing. Or moving.

"That's not a person," I said to Shahani. "It's a dummy."

No sooner had the words passed from my mouth a masked gunman appeared, shooting the driver twice in the head. I screamed at the sight while Shahani fumbled for her phone to call the police. No sooner than she had connected with the 911 operator did both car doors fly open. A masked gunman had Shahani held up, and seconds later I felt that familiar metal pressed against my neck.

"Hang up the phone and throw it on the floor," the person hissed.

Shahani did as she was told before being pulled from the car. The gunman holding me whispered in my ear, "You too. Toss the phone on the floor and step out."

I followed the directions to a tee. Shahani was being placed into a car hidden on the side of the road when I came around the SUV. The driver's body was gone as well, probably in the trunk. I took my time walking towards the car, doing my best to memorize the license plates in case we did make it out of this mess and needed to give the police some information. The gunman must've known what I was up to because they shoved me hard, telling me to walk up before I got left on the side of the road.

"And it won't be alive," they said louder in a clearly feminine voice.

I was forced into the front seat with the driver while Shahani was wedged between the other two gunmen. We pulled off right as another car came down the road. I wanted to ask what was going on, but my question was answered once the trio pulled off their masks.

"Nia?" I exclaimed as I locked eyes with Shahani's devious cousin in the back seat. Next to me was an unfamiliar man. "Who are you?"

The man leaned in and said with a wicked grin, "The nigga that has his life in your hands."

******

What should've been a tense ride was overshadowed by the antics of Nia, her friend, Essence, and the man driving the car. I had my eyes closed praying that I would make it to see my baby girl while the three of them were bopping along to the radio; these bitches had the nerve to be twerking and rapping to G-Eazy's "No Limit." Shahani sat in between them stone-faced, her hand protectively holding her belly as the women flapped their arms around. The stress of the situation had my stomach doing flips, and the only way I eased my nerves was by falling into a light slumber.

"Yo, wake up," a rough voice echoed throughout the car.

I stirred in my seat, rubbing my eyes as I tried to figure out where I was and what was going on. One look at the unfamiliar face had everything come barreling back. "Listen, I don't know what this is about, but all Shahani and I want is to make it out of this situation alive. What do you want from us?"

"Your help," dude said with a wide smile. "I heard from a friend of mine that Sampson is the one that killed your parents. He also happens to be your father."

"Yeah…and?"

"And you're not the only one he's screwed over. The nigga had me set up to be killed too. Him and my old business partner. When I found Blue he was broke as fuck living in his momma's house. Once the money was gone his woman and kids left him. That made it easier to kill him without the added guilt, but there was no payoff. That's where Sampson comes into play."

"This is about money? I can get you money," I told him. "I can get you all the money you need to leave town and set us free."

He shook his head. "This is bigger than money at this point. I wish all they took away from me was money—they took my legacy. Blue paid for his disloyalty, now it's Sampson's turn to pay for doing business with a shiesty nigga. He needs to give me back my drugs, money, and seat at the table, or else."

"Or else what? You still haven't explained to me how I'm supposed to help you."

"Isn't it obvious? I need 'Daddy's Girl' to get on the phone scared for her life with a list of demands, say a million dollars and all the coke he has. She tells him the location for him to drop off the ransom money and drugs, but makes him come by himself. He shows up and she gets the revenge she's been looking for."

Did I want revenge on Sampson for killing my parents? Was it worth me making a deal with the devil that could do irreparable damage to my soul? The answer ran through my mind as an image of my dead parents.

"I'll do it as long as we leave Shahani out of it," I choked out, extending my hand for the phone. "Make the call."

The phone rang twice before Sampson's voice filled the car. "Where are they and what do you want for them?"

My heart leapt into my throat, making it easier to sound like I was in distress. "A million dollars, Sampson. He wants a million dollars and all the coke you have, or else he's going to kill us."

"Nubia, I won't let that happen," Sampson promised. "Stay calm. I'm coming for the both of you. Where does he want me to meet with him?"

Dude leaned in and said, "That's not for you to worry about right now. Just get my shit together and wait for my call. You have two hours." He hung up the phone before Sampson could get another word in. "Good job. I don't have to worry about you going back on your word, do I?"

I knew I made a deal with the devil, but it couldn't be any worse than sharing DNA with another one. The desire for revenge flowed through my veins, and I replied without hesitation, "Of course not. Let's do this."

Shahani

"I should've killed you when I had the chance," I said to Nia as she led me through the deserted trap house. "I guess all that shit about finding an honest job was a lie, huh? Being a decent human being is beneath you. And you too, Essence. Being a fucking follower is gonna get you killed."

"Bitch, bye. I don't know whether or not you noticed, but I'm the one holding the gun right now." Essence poked me in the back. "There's but so much shit you can pop when you're getting ready to burst any day now. So shut up and keep walking."

We approached the last bedroom on the left. Nia opened the door and shoved me inside. "You're right, Shahani; you should have killed me that day in the hotel. Not because it was the right thing to do for you, but because you should've known there was no way in hell you could threaten me the way you did and think I wasn't coming back for that ass."

"Trust me: I won't make that mistake again."

"I know you won't. After today you won't be alive long enough to make it. Now get in here and keep that other sorry bitch company."

Other sorry bitch?

I walked deeper into the room and found Vaughn's fiancée, Drea, chained to the radiator. One of her eyes was swollen shut, her lip was busted, and I could tell from the awkward way she was sitting that she possibly had a bruised rib. She started crying at the sight of me. Between her lip and the sobbing, I had no clue what she was saying and told her as much.

"That bitch is evil," she said after a deep breath. "I was walking the puppy Vaughn bought me for my birthday and she comes out of nowhere with a baseball bat. I fought her the best I could, but her backup came through and they jumped me. Before I passed out, all I saw was her snap my dog's neck. He was only four months old."

I covered my mouth in shock. Nia had really fallen off the deep end with her madness. First me, now Drea? If I didn't think of something fast we were likely to all die at her hand. I took a seat at the rickety card table, trying to figure out how to get us all out of here. My baby gave me a small kick, reminding me it wasn't only my life on the line.

"I'm not feeling too well," Drea said, breaking the heavy silence. "My head is pounding and I'm getting sleepy."

"You have a concussion. Try not to fall asleep."

Drea's eyes drooped for a second. "I'm trying not to, but it's so hard."

"Think of how if you fall asleep, you can't beat Nia's ass."

From that point on, I had no complaints from Drea. She kept her eyes wide open even if they were crossed. While she kept herself awake, I silently prayed Nubia was safe. Lonzo was acting like a loose cannon, and I didn't want her to become a casualty in this war he had with Sampson. I was on my third prayer loop when he brought her in. She was fine if not shaken up.

"Don't look at me like that," Lonzo said as he shut the door. "I told you I wouldn't do anything to her."

Nubia took a seat in the chair across from me. "You know this nigga, Shahani?"

"This is the ex I was telling you about."

"The ex she's been in contact with this entire year, the same ex that saved her life when that nigga Donovan was getting ready to slaughter her ass, the same ex that has been more than willing to help her take care of another man's baby—"

"The same ex that shot a man in cold blood and kidnapped me," I shot back, enraged that he could list all of the positives and leave out this glaring negative. "If you loved me, Lonzo, like you claim you do, this wouldn't be happening right now. You're on a suicide mission. When they find you they're going to kill you on sight."

"There you go doubting a nigga. What happened to the Shahani that used to be my ride or die? The Shahani that told me anything was possible so long as I put my mind to it? The Shahani that was ready to come with me to handle the niggas that robbed us?"

"She had to learn how to survive without you," I said, swiping away the tears that threatened to fall. "When you 'died,' Alonzo, I was left to fend for myself. I went from stripping to pimping in the matter of a year because I had no backup plan. I started my life over and that meant leaving all of this childish shit behind."

"Oh, so now you tryna say that you're too good for me?" Lonzo asked with a hint of malice in his voice. "Hmmm? You're too good for the future I had planned for us?"

I pointed to my stomach and said, "I became too good for any of this mess the moment I found out that I was pregnant."

"Good," Lonzo said coldly as he backed out of the room. "Good to know so now I don't have to feel bad about killing you once I get my money from Sampson."

"Lonzo—" Nubia said warningly.

The door slammed shut. Drea stared at me nervously while Nubia's expression was hard to read. I knew they were both waiting to see how I handled the shift in attitude from Lonzo's volatile ass. I played it cool, but on the inside, I was frightened because if there was one thing I knew about Lonzo, it was that he was a man of his word.

It was one of the reasons I fell in love with him.

Maine

I was halfway home when my phone lit up in the console. Sampson's name was announced throughout the car. My finger smashed the ignore button, much to Estalita's annoyance. She sunk so deep into her seat that her ass had to be on the floor.

"You can take that little kid shit to the backseat where I won't get a ticket," I said, glancing down at her. "What the fuck is the problem?"

"Why did you ignore Sampson's call? You don't trust me? Or is it that you don't want me hearing the conversations you have about your girlfriend?"

"First off, I ignored the call because I'm not in the mood to talk to him, and second, I don't give a fuck what you hear, Estalita. You've heard worse out my mouth."

"If you feel that way, then call him back."

"I'll call him back when I'm not driving."

"You can't drive and talk on the phone? I find that hard to believe," she replied, drily.

My foot was poised to slam on the brakes so she could choke herself with her seatbelt, but was interrupted by Sampson calling again. With a pointed look in Estalita's direction, I answered the phone. "Yo."

"How far are you away from the city?"

"Forty-five minutes."

"When you're done dropping off your wife I need to you to meet up with Jodeci. It's an emergency. Call me when you're there."

"Bet."

The call disconnected, leaving Estalita and I right back in one of those crushing silences. She climbed back into her seat, her eyes never straying from my face as she tried to catch something, anything, that would make me guilty.

"What now, Estalita? I answered the fucking phone in front of you, so what's your next issue?"

"Why was the conversation so short? Why do you need to meet Jodeci after you drop me off? What's this emergency? Is it just another way for you to get to your girlfriend?"

"The answer to all of those questions is: none of your business. Whenever there's an emergency it's not unusual to be kept on a need-to-know basis."

Estalita cut her eyes at me. "Last I checked, you don't work for him anymore. You work for my family and they wouldn't be pleased to hear that you're running around handling emergencies for other people. Come home with me and let him handle whatever's going on within his organization."

I continued to cruise down the highway, mentally preparing myself for whatever this situation was. Estalita could sit here and act like she was ignorant to who she married, but if a reality check was what she needed then I would give her one. I waited until I pulled up to our building to let her know as much.

"I don't know what type of goofy ass simp you think you're married to, but it ain't me. No matter what goes down between us, we're all family and we look out for each other. There's no picking and choosing when to ride out. I'll be home when I get home, now get out of my car."

Estalita clamored out of the car. She leaned back in and hissed to me, "You are making one of the biggest mistakes of your life, Jermaine. When you realize how wrong you've done me it'll be too late to make it right."

She slammed the door shut with a resounding thud. I didn't have time for petty childish shenanigans. There were more important things going on in the world. Like finding out what was going on with Sampson, and hoping to solve my problems with Nubia by the end of the night.

******

Jodeci was at the trap house casually puffing on a blunt when I entered. Beside him sat a mountain of packaged coke, enough kilos to have our kids doing time for us if the cops raided the place. There were teeners, eight balls, and everything in between sitting on top of the pile.

I pointed between the paraphernalia and him. "What the fuck is this doing sitting here? It should've been delivered to everyone by now."

"Sampson told me to get it off the streets. All of it. I'm still waiting for a few more niggas to show up with their packs," Jodeci replied, picking up a brick and tossing it up and down. "Lonzo wants all of it or else he'll kill Nubia and Shahani."

My heart skipped several beats, with the only reminder I had to breathe coming from Jodeci. What the fuck was Sampson thinking for not telling me this when we spoke? Jodeci answered without me even having to ask aloud.

"He was scared if he told you immediately you might do something crazy, like kill Estalita if one more complaint passed through her lips. Fuck around and choke that hoe out and end up being placed in a taco shell in somebody's restaurant. I promised him I would let you know what was up once you got here."

"I hope he got a plan because all I can think of doing right now is strapping up and riding out. That nigga gotta have a mother, sister, cousin, someone I can get my hands on to get Nubia and Shahani back."

"I've been asking around and so far, he ain't got no people. His pops abandoned the family when he was younger, and his moms died of an overdose when he was a kid. His grandmother raised him, but she passed a few years ago. He's the true definition of a lone wolf."

I paced the office floor, thinking. "Nah, he ain't doing this alone. There's no way he would be able to take Nubia and Shahani without some fight. Plus, he knew where Sampson's house was. That nigga got a mole."

"A mole? You think so?"

"There's no other way to mix it. He knows too much about all of us for it to go any other way." I stopped pacing as the perfect person popped up in my head. "I know who the mole is."

"That quick?"

"It's too obvious. Let's pack all this up and head out. We need the element of surprise on our side. You ready to do this?"

Jodeci clapped his hands and rubbed them together. "I stay ready."

******

If Cheyenne was surprised to see me she didn't show it; instead she opened the door wider and welcomed me in. Jodeci followed right behind, casing the place like he normally did with unknown spots. His eyes rested on the cracked bedroom door before landing on the half-dressed Cheyenne. She wore a short white tee with a pair of Calvin Klein panties, resembling Ebony from *The Players Club*. It was a good way to know whether or not she was strapped or had something up her sleeve. I gave Jodeci a slight nod, and we got right down to it. I brandished my Glock, holding Cheyenne at gunpoint while Jodeci checked her bedroom for any company she might have.

"Maine, what are you doing?" Cheyenne cried, her entire body trembling with fear.

"Don't play stupid, bitch. I know you set Nubia and Shahani up."

Cheyenne's eyes widened. "What? Nubia is my girl. I would never do anything to put her life in jeopardy."

"So then explain to me how Lonzo knew where Sampson's home was and the exact time Nubia and Shahani left."

"Who the fuck is Lonzo and why am I giving him information? Like I said before, Nubia is my friend and I wouldn't do some grimy shit like that to her. I was there for her when Donovan left her with nothing. I gave her the confidence she needed to make her own money. Give me one good reason why I would fuck her over?"

"Because you know she was there when I killed Precious and Paco." Jodeci reappeared holding Rhea in his arms. "I checked the entire place from top to bottom. No sign of the kids, but I did find little Rhea sleeping in Cheyenne's bed with a bottle beside her. I was getting ready to give it to her when I noticed something on the dresser."

Jodeci reached into his pocket and pulled out a jar of honey. Cheyenne grew nervous as she stared at the jar, her eyes widening. All I could say was, "Nigga, what?"

"Honey. It's poisonous to children under the age of one because they can't digest it properly. It causes botulism. Cheyenne sold Nubia out to Lonzo, and she was getting ready to kill Rhea next."

I struck Cheyenne across the face with the butt of my gun, sending her flying into the coffee table. I dropped to my knees and grabbed her by the throat, choking her as I slammed her into the floor. Trying to kill Nubia was one thing, but feeding a baby a bottle of poison was evil and as far as I was concerned, not putting my hands on women went out the window.

"Where does he have them?" I hissed, pressing the gun into her forehead. "Tell me right now before I kill you."

I loosed my grip enough for her to reply, "I don't know, Maine. I swear."

"You planned Nubia's birthday party. You told Lonzo you were throwing a party for Nubia and you wanted her dead. He got there to kill her but Jodeci was already there, so he aimed for him instead. I asked Lucky to run the cameras back further and he picked up on you unlocking one of the club exits."

"She killed my cousin," Cheyenne hissed. "I heard she sat there and threw Precious under the bus so she could live. What kind of friend does that?"

"What kind of friend has their pregnant friend robbed at gunpoint?" Jodeci countered, leaning over my shoulder so Cheyenne could see him. "Nubia didn't get Precious killed; her greed did. That bitch stole from *me* and *I* killed her. It could've been any other courier and the outcome would've still been the same."

At the realization that everything she had done was in vain, Cheyenne began to cry. "Please don't kill me."

"This is my last time asking you: where does he have them?"

"Precious' daughter's father, Sullivan, has a friend that was able to give him access to one of his trap houses for the night in exchange for a few kilos of coke."

"Where's the trap house?"

Jodeci pulled out his phone and wrote down the directions to the trap house. I was familiar with the area, and knew exactly where we were headed. Cheyenne mentioned that Lonzo also gained access to a few soldiers for hire.

"I told you everything you needed to know. Can you please let me go?" Cheyenne begged. "I promise I'll leave town and you won't have to worry about me ever again."

I glanced at Jodeci. "Get the baby ready."

Cheyenne grew panicked at Jodeci's departure. She was beside herself when I let go of her neck and rose to my full height. "Maine, you don't have to do this. What about my daughter? She can't grow up without her mother."

"Because of you, mine almost grew up without her mother."

I squeezed off two shots, one hitting Cheyenne square in the head while the other tore right through her chest. She was dead before her body hit the floor with a thud. Jodeci appeared with a fully dressed Rhea in her carrier.

"I'll have my team come through to clean up," he said, shaking his head at Cheyenne's body. "What are we gon' do with Rhea?"

After this entire situation, I didn't trust a soul with Rhea. I tapped into the recesses of my mind and tried to think of at least one woman we could drop her off with. I settled with, "What is your moms doing tonight? You think she'll watch Rhea for me?"

"You're like a son to her. A son she be tryna fuck on the low, but still a son nonetheless."

"You know she be hitting on me?"

"She said that my choice for my step-pops was either you or one of these old heads, so I chose you, nigga," Jodeci joked. "That, and I like to see you sweat. Now let's get the fuck up out of here…pops."

"Nigga, shut up," I said, but I couldn't suppress the laugh bubbling in my stomach.

Everything was falling apart, the girls were in trouble, we had a body in the middle of the floor, and less than fifteen minutes before Lonzo called, and Jodeci was over here cracking jokes. If there was one person in the world I would want to deal with this, it was my brother, and I was glad to have him back.

****

Sampson was standing against my car smoking a cigarette when we came back downstairs from dropping Rhea off. He flicked it to the ground and stomped it out with the black combat boots he wore. As a matter of fact, Sampson was dressed like he was getting ready to go to war, from the black hoodie he wore to the loose fitting camo pants. I was still in my clothes from the baby shower, as was Jodeci, and we were looking a little underdressed next to Sampson.

“You did what I told you to?” Sampson asked Jodeci.

“It’s all off the street. I also have the soldiers heading to the location where we believe Lonzo has the girls. Let’s ride out and get there before he tries to do something crazy, like escape.”

I loaded the duffle bags of coke into Sampson's car and followed behind in mine. No sooner had I pulled off was I stopped by the police. Slapping on my dashboard, I pulled over to the side of the road. Sampson continued on as he should have considering that he was carrying the guns and drugs. I breathed a sigh of relief when I recalled that I left mine in my other car.

“Good evening, officer,” I said to the cop that stalked up to my car.

A bright light was flashed down on me. “Do you know why I pulled you over?” the officer asked, ignoring my greeting.

“No, officer, I have no idea.”

“License and registration please?”

I grabbed my license and registration from the dashboard, where I kept it whenever I was riding around at night. I wouldn't give any of these pigs any reason to accuse me of reaching for a weapon. The cop looked a little disappointed as he walked back to his car. My phone lit up with a text from Jodeci asking if everything was good. I didn't dare make a move until I was cleared. The cop returned five minutes later with his partner.

"Sir, I need you to step out of the vehicle," he said with his hand on his holster.

"For what?" I asked. "I haven't done anything."

"Sir…step out of the vehicle."

"I'm not stepping out until you tell me what the fuck you want me to step out for."

"We received a tip that this car is transporting a large amount of substances. Step out of the car with your hands up."

I stepped out begrudgingly, holding my hands up before they got any funny ideas. The second officer cuffed me and sat me on the sidewalk. *Where would they get the crazy idea that I had drugs on me*, I thought as I watched the pair tear apart my car. When they were done, I was released.

"Your taillight's out. Get it fixed," the first cop said, holding out a ticket.

I wanted to tell this nigga about himself, but I had business to handle. My phone lit up in the cup holder except this time it wasn't Jodeci.

“Who the fuck is this?” I asked with no preamble.

Lonzo chuckled. “Is that how you're gonna speak to the person that looked out for you. This isn’t your war to fight; you can still walk away unscathed with your girl. I promise.”

“You must be out of your motherfucking mind if you think I’m getting ready to cop any type of deal with you. It ain't even about it not being my war at this point. You’ve shot at me and mine one too many fucking times for me to even consider walking away from you. When I get you in my sights I’m lighting you up, so get all the niggas you got ready, you hear me?”

“Loud and clear.”

I hung up on Lonzo and gunned it up the ramp of the BQE. It was time to kill this ghost once and for all.

******

The trap house was silent as we pulled up. I gave myself a thorough pat down, making sure all of my pieces were in place. Jodeci nodded at me after doing the same, and we stepped out, followed by Sampson, who was double checking to make sure we were covered. My feet hadn’t even tapped the pavement when ten soldiers appeared, ready to take the trap house. We had to move quick because the cops could be here in minutes if anyone heard any gunfire.

“I’ll take the lead coming through the front,” I said, brandishing my gun as I crept towards the house. “Jodeci, back me up. Sampson, you lead them through the back. We meet up and go through the house until there’s no one left.”

“Agreed,” Sampson said, motioning for the soldiers to follow him around back.

Jodeci watched them all leave, his brows furrowed. "You don't think we need even two or three of them?"

"Nah, I got this," I replied, walking up to the door.

I knocked a beat that was common for most trap houses. Someone answered immediately, and had their life ended before they could even ask, "Who's there?" Shots fired from the stairs. I stepped back in time for Jodeci to pop a couple off, sending the young boy tumbling down the stairs. Footsteps followed, clomping down the stairs in haste. Jodeci slammed the door shut, cloaking us in darkness save for the hint of streetlight bouncing through the window. I slid down the wall, grabbed a piece of glass, and chucked it down the hall. These niggas came running down the stairs like rats to a piece of cheese. I felt Jodeci's arm brush against mine as we both lifted our arms and popped off on these niggas, listening to the resounding thumps as they dropped like flies.

Jodeci hit the lights, revealing the six bodies on the floor, including the failed lookout. We listened to see if anyone else was coming, and I wasn't the least bit surprised to discover that all these idiots came running at once.

Jodeci pressed a button in his pocket, connecting his Apple AirPods. "Sampson said the back was filled with niggas planning to ambush them. They're coming in right now."

My stomach turned at how easy it was for us to make it this far without anything happening. We ascended the stairs in record time, hitting the level and placing our backs against each other. Jodeci fired off shots behind me. I turned in time to see one last soldier hit the ground with a thud. After checking each room thoroughly, we finally entered the room he was guarding. Inside were Shahani and Drea, who was laid against a heater, her chest steadily growing red. A girl popped up from behind Shahani and placed a gun against her head.

"Ain't you that bitch that's always hanging around Nia?" Jodeci said, his eyes widening in recognition. "If you're here then that means she ain't too far."

Shorty laughed. "Actually, that means the exact opposite. Nia and Lonzo left like thirty minutes ago with Nubia."

"Where did they take her?" I demanded, taking a step towards the pair.

Shahani whimpered as the gun was pressed into her temple. "Did you forget who's holding the gun in this situation? Back the fuck up."

"Essence, you know damn well Lonzo told you to let us go when they got here. Now let us the fuck go and stop trying to be a badass," Shahani said, shooting Essence a scathing look.

"Shut the fuck up, Shahani. Always tryna run something. Guess what, bitch? You're my hoe now. I own you and you'll do what the fuck I say, and right now I'm saying let me talk." Essence turned her attention to us. "Now, where's the coke you were supposed to deliver?"

"You'll get the coke when I get a word on where Nubia is."

Essence shook her head. "Do I need to remind you that I have the gun, too? Where the fuck is the coke at?"

"Right here."

Sampson stood directly behind me. I stepped to the side, allowing him to come through with the duffle bags filled to the brim with coke. He dropped them in the middle of the floor and rejoined us. Essence withdrew her gun from Shahani's head and walked over to the duffle bags, unzipping each one to make sure it was all there.

"Now can you tell us where he has Nubia?" Sampson asked with forced patience.

"He's got her at your warehouse," Essence laughed up at him. "Isn't that ironic?"

Sampson smiled back, yet it didn't reach his eyes. "Very."

"Here's the thing: you have to go by yourself. If Lonzo sees anyone else he's killing Nubia, no questions asked. First, I have to make the call to let him know you came through with the drugs." Essence pulled out her phone and dialed up Lonzo. After a few seconds she said, "Lonzo? It's me: Essence. He came through with the drugs so now I'm sending him to you." She shoved her phone back into her pocket. "He's waiting. You've got an hour to get there with the money."

"You're not too bright, are you?" Sampson asked with a laugh.

Essence raised a brow at his remark. "What the fuck is that supposed to mean?"

"You mean to tell me you don't think it's strange that they left you behind with no type of incentive to keep you alive?"

"Nia wouldn't do me like that, which is why she gave me this gun," Essence said, raising her gun and pointing it at Sampson. "I've been hooking on the street since I was twelve-years-old. What makes you think I can't take your old ass out?"

“You might be able to take me out, but you can't take them out at the same time,” Sampson said, nudging his head over at Jodeci and me.

“Well I can try.”

Essence pulled the trigger. I laughed when nothing came out. Sampson did too as he raised his Smith & Wesson. “Next time, make sure you take off the safety.”

Sampson lit her ass up with three shots: one to the head and two to each side of her chest. Jodeci jumped into action and freed Drea, who was steadily losing blood from the wound in her chest.

“We gotta get her to the hospital right now,” Jodeci said, carrying her out the door.

“She's not the only one,” Shahani said, rising from her seat with the help of Sampson. Her dress was wet with water and blood. “The stress made my water break.”

Sampson carried her downstairs to the SUV where Drea and Jodeci waited inside. We exchanged keys. “Please make sure they're okay,” he said, squeezing me on the shoulder.

“Of course,” I replied with no hesitation. “Make sure you bring her home.”

Life was crazy as fuck. Months ago I was fighting to save Nubia from Sampson, and in the end, he has to be the one to save her. Or at least he better save her. With the way I feel for Nubia he must know to come home with her or don't come home at all.

Nubia

Nia glanced between Lonzo and me. "Lonzo, are you sure about this? As far as I'm concerned she can't be trusted. What if this is a trick to…to…shit, I don't know. I'm just thinking we shouldn't trust the bitch."

"Last I checked, nobody asked you for your opinion," I shot back, crossing my arms. "Also, you aren't the most trustworthy person either. You've been running through Shahani's exes like nobody's business. Isn't this the second one you've helped to kidnap her?"

After that, Nia had no problem keeping her mouth shut. She turned her attention to the live feed of the warehouse gate. I stared around the warehouse, thinking of how I had been here on two separate occasions with my life in jeopardy. The first time I was saved by fact, the second time by blood, but this time around I was the one who would make the choice on who would be saved.

"He should be getting here any minute. Essence called, like what, forty-five minutes ago?" Lonzo asked, breaking the silence.

Nia gave him and thumbs up, her eyes never straying from the television screen. "Yup, I think I can see them in the distance."

"You think they killed her?"

"Of course they did, and I'm sure her dumb ass gave them the ammo to do so. She probably was running her mouth and forgot to take the safety off the gun like I told her to. We were cool and all, but you were right to leave her ass behind for them to handle." Nia squinted at the screen. "There's a car approaching. You need to sit in that chair right now, and try to look scared."

I waddled over to the chair in the middle of the tarp and took a seat. Lonzo motioned for me to place my hands behind my back, giving the illusion that I was tied up. The pair rushed to the door in time to meet Sampson, who entered carrying a medium-sized duffle bag. Lonzo held him at gunpoint while Nia searched him, disarming him completely and placing the duffle bag next to the door.

"You got your fucking money. Now let Nubia go," Sampson barked.

Lonzo chuckled at the idea. "Nah, not yet. We need to have some fun first. Put your hands behind your head." Sampson obeyed. "Aight, now start making your way towards the tarp where Nubia is."

My heart was pumping so loud that I couldn't even hear, let alone think straight. The closer Sampson came, the realer this situation became. Lonzo shoved Sampson to his knees with little resistance. He gave his shoulder a pat before stepping back and mouthing to Nia, "Give her the gun."

Nia sauntered over to me, twirling the gun around her finger until the butt was facing me. "Here you go."

I brought my hands around and accepted the gun, much to Sampson's surprise. "You…you're in on this?"

"She wasn't in on the whole thing, if that's what you're thinking. This came about at the last minute, and I have to admit, it's pretty nice to see this poetic justice taking place."

I rose from my seat with a heavy heart, barely able to make eye contact with Sampson, who was willing me to look at him. I removed the safety from the weapon and cleared the chamber to prevent a possible blockage.

"Nubia," Sampson said, his voice filled with hurt. "I was waiting for the right time to speak with you, but I guess it's now or never. I'm sorry. From the bottom of my heart, I'm sorry for how I ruined your family. Ever since I found out you were my daughter, I've been making all of these excuses for what I did, except it's painfully obvious I was wrong for doing so. You didn't deserve what happened to you, and it's nothing but the grace of God that Maine had more of a heart than I did at the time to save you. With that being said, kill me."

"Damn," Lonzo exclaimed. "That would be noble as fuck if I didn't think it was a complete copout because she has a gun trained on you."

Sampson rolled his eyes. "It's not a copout because I planned on giving her a letter saying all of this. Why else would I come here with my money if not to save her?"

"Guilt. You figure you can show her how bad you feel and guilt her into keeping you alive."

"This isn't guilt. Guilt would be begging her not to kill me. I want her to because this might be the only way to right one of the biggest wrongs of my life." Sampson took a calming breath. "Take the shot, baby girl."

I raised my gun and squeezed off a shot, the force of the shot jerking me back a few steps. Lonzo staggered as the bullet tore through his chest. His eyes widened in surprise as he felt his chest, gasping when his hand came up bright red with blood. Nia screamed at the sight and made a break for the exit. Lonzo raised his gun and fired two shots of his own. Sampson rose from his feet like a panther, eating each one effortlessly. I used that split second advantage to steady my aim and hit Lonzo two more times. He crumpled to the floor shortly after Sampson, who hit the tarp with a thud.

"Sampson!" I shouted as he lay on the floor, chest heaving. I could see where the bullets tore into his shirt, one spot in his chest while the other grazed it. "Come on, we gotta get you out of here."

Sampson rose to his feet with the help of the chair. I slung his arm over my shoulder and helped him past Lonzo, whose eyes pointed to the heavens wide with shock. To think I was going to sell Sampson out for the devil that had done everything he could to ruin everyone's life. I shook my head in disgust, thanking the heavens that common sense set in at the last minute.

"You saved me," Sampson wheezed on the way to the car. "You didn't have to; I meant what I said."

"I know," I said, still trying to make sense of my change of heart myself. "I wanted to kill you, trust me I did, but as I stood there, I made the decision that I'm better than you. You played God with other people's lives, and because of it, you lost the woman you truly love. I don't want to take away someone's life only to lose a piece of mine. God can deal with you because I like going to sleep with a full heart and clear conscience."

Sampson nodded in understanding. "You're absolutely right,

Nubia. This wound is one of the many I'll have to take in the name of righting wrongs."

I slid into the driver's seat and him the passenger's. The ride home was easier, most likely because of the pain left behind between Sampson and I. While taking the low ground and killing him would have been satisfying, I had to ask myself if my loving parents would approve. They didn't die for me to hold hate in my heart for the rest of my days. They died so I could live, and that's what I planned on doing from here on out. Living life to the fullest with no shame, only love, the first recipient being myself.

Nia

I lay in the trunk of Maine's car laughing to myself, the duffle bag filled with a million dollars steadily pressing against me with each chuckle. I did it; I came out on top for once. From the moment Lonzo introduced his plan to me, I just knew we would all end up dead at the hands of Sampson: he had an infinite army behind him while aside from the soldiers we were lent, it was just the three of us. Well, two of us since we planned on Essence being killed prematurely. However, I was impressed with how everything came together in the end. At least for me anyway. While they were pushing daisies I would be pushing a Porsche through the country of my choice. I spent the entire bumpy ride imagining all the things I would do with my money when I escaped New York. After what felt like an eternity, the car pulled to a stop. I felt the vibration of the car doors slamming followed by what sounded like the hospital.

"Please don't let them need something from the trunk, please don't let them need something from the trunk," I whispered, squeezing my eyes shut and praying with each passing moment.

After a full minute of prayer I let out a sigh of relief. My great escape had worked and now it was time to move on to better pastures. I pulled the emergency trunk release, sighing in relief as the cool air kissed my skin. The lid continued opening of its own volition, which was odd as hell even though this was a luxury car. An audible swallow filled my ears as I realized the trunk lid lifted with some help. Hovering above me with a wicked smile on his face was—

"Vaughn, baby," I said with a nervous chuckle. "You're the last person I was expecting to see. Can you help me out of here?"

I started to sit up, only to be shoved back down by Vaughn. "You can't be fucking serious right now, Nia."

"I'm deadass serious. Vaughn, I was a victim of Lonzo's manipulative schemes because when you were in a coma, Drea took over and left me homeless with nowhere to go. My choices were the streets or Lonzo." I peered up at him with my puppy dog pout that got me whatever I wanted from him. "You have to believe me, Vaughn. I would never do anything purposely to hurt the people you care about."

"You mean like Drea, who you beat, stabbed, and left to die?"

I hung my head in pretend shame. "I shouldn't have went after your girl but the love I have for you makes me crazy. Drea out the picture was the only way I could ever see us together."

"Really?" Vaughn asked, wiping a stray tear from his cheek. "I was marrying Drea because everyone told me it was the right thing to do, when in reality, I knew it should've been you. We can still be together, Nia."

I placed a hand to my chest, both flattered and amazed by his stupidity. "Really?"

"Yeah," Vaughn promised. "When I see you in hell."

The sweet Vaughn I once knew was replaced by a cold monster.

His usually warm eyes went dead as he raised the Glock he'd been hiding all along. The silencer at the tip let me know this was his plan from the get go. I guess my escape wasn't as silent as I thought it was.

"Can I at least get a kiss goodbye?" I asked, thinking maybe I could disarm him.

Imagine my complete surprise when he placed the barrel of the gun to my lips. "You can kiss that nigga death; he's the only one able to control you."

Knowing I was caught with nowhere to run, I kissed the barrel of the Glock, thinking it was better to die proud than die begging. Who knows? The devil might be looking for his next side bitch.

Maine

Shahani and I sat staring at each other, repeatedly asking the same question without saying it aloud.

Did they make it out alive?

I spent the better part of this year trying to end Lonzo, with each attempt failing worst than the next. If I was unsuccessful, what would make me think Sampson could go in alone and come out on top? No sooner had I asked the question did Nubia appear.

"Yo, you good?" I asked, noticing the blood on the shoulder part of her dress.

She shrugged off my worries. "That's Sampson's blood. He…uh… jumped in front of two bullets to save me."

"And Lonzo?"

"I killed him."

My eyes widened at her admission. I held her cheeks in my hand and asked, "What did you say?"

"He set it up where I could kill Sampson and I killed him instead. I'm nobody's fucking pawn."

Never would I have imagined that the person to take out Lonzo would be my Nubia. My chest swelled with pride at the look of shock on that nigga's face when he got got. He spent so much time pulling power plays on us hustlers that he underestimated the power of a woman. I did the same as well, but it would be the last time I ever caught myself thinking the possible was impossible when it came to Nubia.

"I'm sorry for the way shit went down earlier with us—"

Nubia silenced me with a kiss. "I don't care, Maine. After one of the craziest nights of my life, you're here. That's all that matters to me right now."

I rested Nubia's head on my shoulders and held her close. Having her in my arms made me feel how real the possibility of losing her was only hours ago. tThere was no way that after tonight I could leave here and go home to another woman. As far as I was concerned, my relationship with Estalita was finished. I could handle being at odds with the cartel, but I couldn't accept having the woman I loved coming second.

******

It was going on six in the morning when I pulled up at my building. I took a deep breath, preparing myself for the conversation I would be having with Salvador concerning my marriage to his daughter. Once I got finished tucking Nubia and Rhea away at the house in Jersey, I called up Salvador and requested an urgent meeting. I was confident then, but as I sat in my car preparing my exit speech, I was shitting bricks. Marrying into the cartel was the equivalent of signing my life away and to backtrack was treason. I glanced at the screensaver on my phone, which Nubia must've done while I wasn't looking. It was a candid picture she took of us while I was driving. I calmed down instantly because there was no way I could ever fear doing what was right for her.

"Aight, it's time to handle this," I said to myself as I slid out of the car.

My feet barely touched the sidewalk when Salvador appeared out of thin air, his henchmen flanking him. He was dressed in an immaculate black suit as if he had a funeral right after our meeting. The thought of it possibly being my own set the tone.

"It's good to see you, Salvador," I said, greeting him with a firm handshake.

Salvador retuned my greeting with a granite smile. "*Buenos días,* Jermaine. When I got your call asking for a meeting this early in the morning, I assumed the worst. Everything is fine between you and Estalita, I hope."

The elevator doors pinged open, providing the perfect momentary distraction. I didn't want to share the demise of our marriage with everyone in the lobby. We boarded with each man on either side of us. I had been in tighter situations and knew if I had to I could take everyone out along with me. I took another deep breath and decided that it was now or never.

"Everything isn't fine between Estalita and I," I admitted.

Salvador's head snapped in my direction. He slowly turned to face me as his men stepped closer. "You looked me in the eye well over one year ago and told me that you loved my daughter and wanted to spend the rest of your life with her," Salvador said slowly, reaching into his suit jacket and extracting a Glock with a silencer attached. "You proposed, planned a wedding, took vows, and you stand here to tell me that there is a problem with you and my daughter? You better have one good reason for you to feel this way, or else I promise I'll give you a problem that's a little more *permanente.*"

The elevator doors sprung open and sounds of sex filled the air. I rarely ever experienced genuine surprise, but to see Estalita bent over our kitchen table being banged out by some random nigga was enough cause for my jaw to drop. She was throwing that ass back and speaking all kinds of nasty Spanish to that nigga as he handled her. Salvador stood next to me trembling with silent rage, his eyes bulging from their sockets.

"Estalita Rosita Maria Ordonez!" Salvador shouted after some time.

The couple jumped apart. Salvador raised his gun and hit the guy with a skillful shot to the head. Estalita screamed as he dropped to his knees and hit the floor with a thud. In her usual dramatic fashion, Estalita collapsed onto the floor, sobbing over the man's body, screaming profanities at her father. The men brushed past me to grab the body, only for her to kick and scream at them.

"Enough!" Salvador barked.

"No," Estalita screamed, staring up at him with hate in her eyes. "You killed Miguel, *Papí!* He was my soul mate! The one man I've wanted to marry since I was a little girl before you snatched me from México and brought me here! Now he's dead and I'm stuck with… him."

Estalita stared at me with revulsion. I shot her the same look so she could know the feeling was mutual.

Salvador let out a grunt of a laugh. "You think after catching you fucking another man Jermaine will want anything to do with you? OF COURSE NOT!"

"But he—"

"It does not matter what he may or may not have done. It obviously had everything to do with this affair you've been having in his home, where he lays his head, where he should find solace." Salvador motioned to her naked body with disgust. "I thought you were ready for the world, but obviously I was wrong. As far as I am concerned, this marriage is over. Now go and put on some clothes so you can come back home."

Estalita kissed the lips of her dead lover one final time, making sure it was long and sweet. With a scathing glance in my direction, she stood with the help of the henchmen and stormed down the hall. Salvador turned to me shaking his head, his expression apologetic.

"I sincerely apologize for the actions of my daughter, Jermaine," Salvador said, shaking his head in dismay. "She will realize in the long run that she has lost out on a good man because of her ways. However, I am sure you won't have any trouble finding a woman of quality for yourself."

I thought of Nubia waiting at home and replied, "I'm sure she's out there somewhere."

******

I stood in the living room doorway, watching her marvel over the finishing touches on her brand new brownstone. The contractors called her earlier this morning to let her know she could come see the place and make sure everything was to her liking. That gave me the perfect cover to make a pit stop to pick up her engagement ring. I had spent the past week working with an exclusive New York jeweler with enough pull to find a few conflict free rough diamonds. They were shaped to perfection and set into a platinum band engraved with the date of our very first date. I subconsciously patted the pocket it was nestled in at every stoplight on the way. Now, as I stood here watching her and Rhea, I knew it was now or never.

"They did a real good job with this place," I said, rising from the doorway.

"Didn't they? Wait until you see upstairs. I had them paint Rhea's room the prettiest shade of pink. I'm still not too sure what color scheme I want for the kitchen, so I'll probably wait for the baby to be—what?" Nubia asked, a smile playing on her lips.

I shook my head. "Nothing, I just can't get over how beautiful you are."

"You think so?" She glanced at Rhea, who was watching every word that came from her mouth. "Maine thinks your mama is beautiful."

Rhea laughed, and turned her attention to me. Nubia did the same, her expression going from humorous to mildly suspicious. "Maine, are you…nervous?"

I answered by getting down on one knee. Nubia clapped a hand over her mouth, shaking her head from side-to-side. Rhea's lip quivered at her mother freaking out as I pulled the ring box out of my pocket and popped it open.

"My name doesn't come with a fancy title like 'Dr.,' I can't promise you a life of normalcy because there ain't shit normal about me, and I don't think there ever will be. What I can give you is my last name, the one handed down to me from my father and in turn his father, a life filled with laughter because I love to see your smile, and the promise to do everything in my life to make you happy. Nubia Monroe, will you marry me?"

"Yes! Yes! Yes! Yes!" Nubia shrieked, scaring Rhea to tears.

I slid the ring on her finger and admired the way it sparkled without the help of light, like Nubia. She had come a long way from the woman she was the day we first met, and her evolution had brought about one inside of me. We weren't perfect, but it didn't matter because a relationship like ours was based on raw emotion. Like the love I could feel the way her lips pressed against mine, and the happiness of finding someone to complete me.

Shahani

I stared down at my handsome son, studying his features to see if he would take after his father or me. His smiles were contagious, and every one that crept across his face as he slept was enough to have one spread across mine. I was in the middle of covering him in air kisses when there was a knock at my bedroom door. With my blessing, the door opened and in stepped Sampson. He was dressed down in a pair of sweats with a white tee, which had to be the only comfortable clothing item he could wear with his freshly healing bullet would. Like me, he was fresh out the hospital and it showed with the sling keeping his arm in place. His eyes roamed the freshly decorated guest room in his home, impressed that I could pull of setting up the entire room in four days.

"I came to see little man," he said, sliding into bed right beside me. "You've been up with him the past few nights. Why don't you get some rest and let me help?"

"I've got everything under control," I assured him.

"I know you have everything under control; you've been handling everything by yourself for the past seven months. What I'm trying to ask you right now is to let me help you take care of the child we created. Is that so much to ask?"

Of course it wasn't too much to ask. I used to picture myself happily married to Sampson, and us starting a little family of our own. We had the little family, but we also had a shitload of trust issues between us. There was no way in hell we could ever move on without addressing them.

"Trust me, I do want your help. What's holding me back is that once I start getting comfortable with us co-parenting I know I'll end up wanting more, and that isn't possible."

Sampson grabbed my chin with his thumb and index finger, gently pulling it until we were face-to-face. "Why would picking up where we left off be impossible? Aside from what happened with Nubia, we were on the road to getting married. Honestly? Even after you packed all of your stuff and left I still knew we would end up right back here. I just didn't know it would involve Salim," he said, smiling down at our baby boy with pure affection. "Shahani, I want us to work on repairing our relationship as we raise our child."

"Your deception isn't the only reason why I've been hesitant to work on us. I had a secret of my own that I was keeping, but only because I was suspicious about your interest in Nubia, with good reason." I took a deep breath and blurted out, "I've known about Lonzo all along."

"What?" Sampson said coldly.

I broke down and told Sampson everything from the beginning to me being rescued from the trap house. Sampson listened intently, his expression unchanging throughout the entire story. When I finished, I exhaled, letting go of a breath I didn't even know I was holding in.

"I had no intentions of getting back with Lonzo, but I knew if

I told you the truth you would no longer trust me. Then the entire situation with Nubia happened, and I didn't feel the need to tell you because everything I suspected was true. However, with both situations in the past I knew I couldn't hold on to such information if we were to ever move forward."

Sampson leaned against the headboard, soaking in my entire confession. He reached out and held one of Salim's tiny fingers with one of his own. "The old Sampson probably would've had you killed simply off the strength of you fucking around with a nigga that sought to do harm to me and mine. But now, after seeing how much chaos and destruction I've caused, I can't in my right mind blame you for doing what you did. So far it's looking like some honesty on both our parts could've prevented a lot of this from happening."

"It sure could have," I replied, shaking my head at the irony of it all. "Does this mean we're good?"

He pecked me on the cheek. "Yes, we're good."

"With that being said, would you like to watch Salim while I take a cat nap?"

"Of course," Sampson replied using his good arm to reach for our baby boy. He cradled Salim close, kissing him on the cheek and greeting him with a, "Hey little man."

I sunk into bed, listening to the father and son talk until I fell into a deep sleep. The amount of time I spent taking care of Salim by myself finally caught up to me as I slept like the dead. I woke up dazed and confused, looking around my dark bedroom as I tried to figure out exactly what was going on.

"Sampson?" I called out, feeling the place next to me, my heart dropping at how cool it was; Sampson left out of here hours ago.

The house was silent as I entered the hallway. With no idea how much time had passed, I wasn't sure if I would find the pair sleeping or up watching TV. I reached the landing when I heard it: faint music playing from down below.

"Sampson?" I called out as I raced down the flight of stairs, the cold floors waking me up. "Sampson where are—oh my god."

Standing in the middle of the living room was Sampson holding a sleeping Salim. Both were all dressed up, with Sampson sporting a sleek Armani suit and Salim wearing a tuxedo onesie. Behind them was dinner set for two.

"Shahani, I know we only settled our differences hours ago, but I can't go another minute without being committed to you the way I should've been when I had the chance. I never told you this, but when we returned from Chicago, I had a ring made despite never wanting to be married again." Sampson placed Salim into the bassinet next to him and walked over to me. He dropped down on one knee, pulled a ring box from his pocket, and popped it open. "I don't normally buy into those corny clichés, but it was love at first sight when I laid eyes on you. When you were at the wedding with that young nigga placing a garter on you, I knew right then and there I wanted you all to myself for the rest of my life. My only problem was finding the courage to arrive at this moment. Shahani, will you marry me?"

"Yes," I cried, covering my mouth to hold back my sobs as he placed a beautiful six-carat diamond ring on my finger. I dropped to my knees and hugged him tight. "I love you, Sampson. You hurt me, but I never stopped loving you."

He kissed me tenderly on the lips, reigniting the fire in my stomach I had been missing for a long time. "Well you don't have to worry about being hurt ever again. I'll spend forever making it up to you."

EPILOGUE

Nubia

One year later...

I sat at the vanity admiring myself in my wedding dress, running my hands over the intricate beading with a bright smile. Today was my wedding day and I was fortunate to be saying "I do" to the man I loved. We had a handsome son, beautiful daughter, and all that was missing now was making it official. There was no one or nothing that could ruin my day today. Or at least I thought as much until I felt the cold barrel of a gun touching my temple.

"What possessed you to think you were worthy of such a celebration today?" Mr. Morris asked, smiling down at me looking every bit as wicked as his deceased son. I swallowed, unable to formulate the right words for how shocked I was. "That's exactly what I thought. I told you this wasn't the last you would see of me and here I am, ready to make sure you join my son in the afterlife."

I took a steadying breath and smiled wide at the bastard. "I'm not going anywhere because you aren't going to kill me. You're a coward just like your son was. You can't beat a man, like my fiancée, but you damn sure didn't have any problem bringing your ass here to taunt me. I'm not a scared little girl anymore, Mr. Morris." I rose from my seat and lined myself up with the barrel. "If you plan on killing me, you're gonna have to look me in the eye to do it."

Mr. Morris lowered his gun like I knew he would. He shoved it into the leather jacket he wore and disappeared as quickly as he had come, which was apparently through one of my open windows. Shahani entered with a wide smile and my bouquet in her hand. Something gave her pause, maybe the lingering smell of Mr. Morris's peppery cologne. She must've chalked it up to her imagination because she put on her brightest smile as she made a few finishing touches on my hair and makeup.

"Girl, sorry I took so long. I was making sure the kids were settled in. You look gorgeous. Are you ready for your walk down the aisle?"

I smiled at Shahani. "I sure am."

"Well then come on…"

I stepped into the hallway of the large church and readied myself to walk down the aisle. Shahani fixed my train as the music began to play. After one final once over, she smiled at me. "You look amazing, the future Mrs. Saidu Bantamoi. I'll see you down the aisle."

Sampson appeared, nervously fixing his tux. He held out his arm to me. "You look beautiful today."

"Thank you."

The wedding march started and I entered the church with

Sampson. Heads turned, all of which stared at me in adoration. While I didn't have a large amount of family and Maine didn't either, we still had people that cared about us. Like Donette and her husband, who became parental mentors for Maine and I once baby Obrahim, who was named after Maine's late father, was born. There was Jodeci, who moved in with us with his daughter after Ashanti ran off to be with some small time dope boy. Vaughn was here with his parents instead of Drea, who decided she was worth more than the drama that came with being with Vaughn. Byron, Sharita, and Sampson's entire family filled in the rest of the chairs, each one staring at me with pride. The loneliness I once felt when I was younger evaporated, and when the reverend pronounced Maine and I man and wife, it suddenly felt like a faraway dream. I was happy, whole, and loved, and ready to start the rest of my life.

******

"You know what's weird," Maine said as we shared our first dance as husband and wife. "We met at a club, I threw you a birthday party at a club, but we've never danced with each other."

"To be fair, you met me outside of the club with my crazy ex-husband, and we might've danced at the club if not for someone trying to kill me," I rationalized. "But we have eaten a lot together."

Maine chuckled and leaned in, "I can think of something else I'd like to eat right now."

"Maine…" I hissed, trying to keep a straight face, only to dissolve into giggles. "Stop being freaky in front of the guests."

He pecked me on the lips. "Nope, you knew what you were getting into when you married a savage nigga like me. I ain't got no manners."

"Well then I might have to teach you some."

Maine responded with another kiss, this one deeper and filled with the unpredictable passion that made me fall in love with him. I grew lightheaded and weak in the knees at the feeling, imagining what life was going to be like with kisses like these for all of eternity.

He broke the kiss with a bite on my lips, and after a second of staring up at him smiling down at me, I replied, "Maybe not."

THE END

ALSO BY TYA MARIE

A Brooklyn Love Affair: Vixen & Gino's Story

A Brooklyn Love Affair 2: Vixen & Gino's Story

A Brooklyn Love Affair 3: Vixen & Gino's Story

A Brooklyn Love Affair 4: Vixen & Gino's Story

Never Should've Loved a Thug

Never Should've Loved Another Thug

The Heart of a King: In Love with a Savage

The Heart of a King 2: In Love with a Savage

Grimey: Married to the King of Miami

Grimey 2: Married to the King of Miami

Ain't Nothing like a Real One: Faded Off an Inked God

Ain't Nothing like a Real One 2: Faded Off an Inked God

Chosen By The King of Miami: A Grimey Love Affair

Chosen By The King of Miami 2: A Grimey Love Affair

CONNECT WITH TYA MARIE

Facebook: https://www.facebook.com/AuthoressTyaMarie

For exclusive sneak peeks join my **Readers Group: Tea with Tya Marie** https://www.facebook.com/groups/318594828537945/

Instagram: Tya_Marie1028

Twitter: LaTya_Marie

Looking for a publishing home?

CPSIA information can be obtained
at www.ICGtesting.com
Printed in the USA
LVOW13s2305100818
586676LV00010B/98/P